ANYA BRETON

Evernight Publishing

www.evernightpublishing.com

Copyright© 2016

Anya Breton

Editor: Karyn White

Cover Artist: Sour Cherry Designs

Jacket Design: Jay Aheer

ISBN: 978-1-77233-823-2

ANYA BRETON

DEDICATION

To Scott—you're awesomely…awesome. Even if you won't ever forgive me for changing the sorceress's name. To my first fan—Jean, you gave me the courage to keep trying.

To my beta readers—Jean, Melissa, Joy, Cathryn and Lynsey, thanks for the feedback and sweet suggestions. I couldn't have done it without you!

ANYA BRETON

THE ONLY SORCERESS

The Only Sorceress, 1

Anya Breton

Copyright © 2013

Prologue

Seven years ago

I'd spotted the pair of rose embroidered Doc Martens in the window near the food court exactly one second before the fountain blew up. And of course they were on sale. *Half* price. Sales were important when one was a college student struggling to pay for obscenely priced textbooks.

A shriek to my right dragged my attention from the giant red tag. Too bad. Those boots would be a perfect match for my new wardrobe.

Right. There was the little issue of my mother's favor and the unruly fountain. Shoe shopping would have to wait.

I did a quick scan of the indoor shopping mall's landscape. A geyser had sprung up from what had once been a tame water feature. The unnatural stream broke through one of the skylights, showering the stone floor with broken blue-tinted glass. Few shoppers were in the vicinity, thank the gods, though plenty now stood gawking at the spray.

There was little doubt what flavor of magic was at work here. I was really starting to dislike Water witches. And to think, three years ago I'd thought no one could be more destructive than a Fire witch. Now I knew better.

I let my eyes trail over the scene, seeking the culprit. A woman stood a hundred feet northeast with arms clenched tightly by her side. Though I couldn't see her face, the cherry red hue of the neck extending from her blonde pixie cut was difficult to miss. Was this my naughty witch?

One sneaker in front of the other, I started across the corridor at a sedate pace. Four steps forward gave me a better view of the scene. A dark-haired male sporting a duckling yellow polo and relaxed jeans stood in front of the witch. His palms stretched out in the sign of surrender as his lips moved with tentative motions.

I opened my consciousness to the aether even as I continued forward. Magic that had been hidden now danced and sparked across my skin like urgent little imps begging to be used. I drew in a tiny bit of Air magic, closing myself off to all other magic for sanity's sake.

Once settled into the seed beneath my heart that was home to my magical ability, I directed the energy to enhance my sense of hearing. Sound waves sharpened and quickened until I could make out the lyrical, soothing voice over the geyser's roar.

"Know, Shannon," the male was saying, "You don't want to do this."

Clearly Shannon *did* want to do this, considering she already had.

"Please, let's discuss this." His voice was urging and just a touch too lovely to be genuine.

"Like we *discussed* your leaving?" Shannon's high-pitched retort echoed against the stone walls as she took a menacing step forward. "When were you going to tell me? When you were already there?"

"I haven't decided if I'm going," the man said, still in his soothing way. Olive-hued palms remained lifted in his defensive pose. "Please, Shannon, fix the fountain."

My jaw clenched and relaxed. I'd indeed found the individual my mother had sent me to stop. Unfortunately she wasn't alone. That would make finishing my job tricky.

Explaining the geyser to the vanilla humans would be easy enough. The mall staff would blame it on a mechanical malfunction or perhaps some sort of overload from the water company. But if I didn't stop the Water witch soon, she could do something worse—something that couldn't be covered up. My mother would be ticked if that happened.

That couldn't happen.

Shannon shrieked as if in response to a question I hadn't heard. "I love you! Why would you leave me? Is your ambition more important than me? Than *us*? I thought you cared about me!"

The male halved the distance between them in one graceful stride. "I do care about you."

"Not enough to stay!"

His volume lowered. My Air magic enhancements allowed me to hear him anyway. "Please, let's talk about this somewhere private."

Shannon took an equally long but far less graceful stride back. "You'll try to sweet talk me and make me forget with kisses! No. We're going to hash this out here. Or I swear to Neptune I'll level this entire mall."

Not on my watch she wouldn't.

I took stock of my options. My grasp of Water magic was that of a neophyte at best. I couldn't hope to fight an experienced witch at her own game. I'd have to rely on the other eight schools of magic.

Again I opened myself to the aether. This time I sent out pulse of magic sensing for verification of what I was up against. The metaphorical feelers immediately bounced back a report of *two* witches, both manipulating Water magic. I focused, visualizing their location, though I already knew what I'd find. Sure enough, the female *and* her male were Water witches.

Shannon's influence on the nearby fountain was easily sensed. Her companion's magic was trickier to pinpoint. But when the scent of a crisp mountain stream rose in the air, I soon understood. He was attempting to influence her behavior exactly as I would have done. However, he was doing a shit job.

A distant gong of a clock tower sent my heart into a skip-jump. There were less than fifteen minutes to wrap this up before my mother would fetch me. For the hundredth time I silently cursed her for dropping me in yet another unknown location with an indeterminate goal beyond stopping a witch from abusing their power or cleaning up after one if they did.

I was now on cleanup duty.

The gawking vanilla human shoppers paid little mind to the lovers' spat. Their distraction meant they wouldn't note me dealing with the female. However, the male was another story entirely. He would note.

I wasn't ready for the magical community to learn of my existence. A half human sorceress with access to every school of magic—even the supposedly extinct ones—wasn't the sort of thing they would take a shine to. So how did I reach Shannon without alerting her companion to my presence?

Dark magic would obscure me long enough to get to her. But any witch with half a brain would know something strange had happened if I shadow-walked feet in front of him in broad daylight.

I was deep in thought despite walking forward. And I shouldn't have been. Because *he* looked up.

Our gazes met—his a haunting color of aqua not far off from the cerulean hair I usually wore. I halted in place. The sheer force of his attention robbed me of breath. Likewise I forgot why I'd been dropped in an unknown shopping mall in an unknown American city in the first place. The only thing I knew was that he was beautiful, and he was watching me.

Full, Italian lips parted to reveal straight, white teeth and a pink tongue pushing at their edges. Above the brilliant aqua eyes sat two sculpted dark brows and a smooth forehead covered by cropped mahogany hair. His dark locks were the final detail I observed before his profile turned, breaking the brief but powerful charm.

A distraction. That was what the gorgeous male witch was. And it was also what I needed. My first thought was to release the tarantulas I'd spotted in the pet store. Shrieking women ought to do the trick. The problem with that plan was the distance. The shop was on the other side of the mall.

I scanned the area again, looking for a spark of creativity. The majority of the food court workers were as distracted as the shoppers. A slack-jawed fried chicken employee stood practically drooling on himself while soda spilled over the edges of the plastic cup he'd left on a soft drink fountain. That small flood gave me an idea.

Out of the aether I called on Water. I directed several threads of magic toward key marks along the food court's edges. I was fast running out of time. This distraction had better work.

The male witch's head whipped toward me. My lungs stilled when his eyes narrowed on my face. Had he *sensed* me?

Fear of being caught had me scrambling to finish my diversion tactic. The sinks, soda fountains, and drinking fountains burbled and exploded into their own miniature geysers. Every head in the place snapped toward the food court employees' yelps of surprise.

I acted the moment the male witch's attention switched to another area. Dropping my connection to Air magic, I tugged on Dark in its place. Few shadows naturally existed beneath the bright skylight. I concentrated on fixing that. Soon a murky cloud of black formed around me, obscuring my figure from all but other Dark witches. Once coated, I headed for the woman responsible for the entire scene.

While the male witch's eyes flitted from soda fountain to soda fountain, I snatched his companion. I pushed the heel of my palm against the hard portion of her breastbone directly above her heart. Her lips opened, forming a protest that never came. The temporary paralysis power I'd read of in an ancient Healer tome did the trick every time.

With the witch in my grasp, and motionless, I whispered a powerful invocation phrase. "Katargeō."

My body went into a spasm. The influx of power channeled into the seed beneath my heart was too much to handle. I desperately tried to funnel it somewhere, anywhere but in me. But it wasn't Water energy to be sent back to the aether or nearby fountain. What I was taking from her was the essence of her magical ability— the building blocks that enabled her to manipulate her element. She would have been shrieking if I hadn't paralyzed her first. Nevertheless, her agony twisted my consciousness like a car caught in a freeway pile-up.

This was what happened to a witch who abused their power.

The drain abruptly ceased with a mental pinging that grated on us both. Her struggle to understand what had happened pulsed against my consciousness. She'd never truly understand. There was nothing I could do to fix that.

The fountain's spray slowed to a burbling stop— proof that though she had the physiology of a witch, the female could no longer manipulate her element.

"Shannon?"

My insides tightened at the sound of the male's voice over the rapid drip of the remaining water. The distraction hadn't been enough. I needed an escape. Dark magic would jump me from my current shadow to a new one if I had the guts to engage it.

Crisp mountain stream scent rose on the air, heralding *he* was working magic. Fear of his reaction to what I'd done was enough to get me over my distaste for shadow-walking. I focused on the gloom clinging to the floor in the darkened corridor a few hundred feet to my left. And then I called on Dark magic.

The eerie feeling of swooshing through the air at an unnatural speed scrambled my thoughts for a few seconds. When reason returned, I stood five feet from the men's bathroom and a utility closet. I shot forward, bashing through the closet door to find a woman with long, flowing burgundy hair awaiting me.

No, not a woman, but rather a *goddess*.

"Mother!" I slumped in relief because Hecate's appearance meant my two hours in the unknown location were at a close.

"You've completed the favor, Kora." The goddess of magic's inexpressive tone meant I'd partially failed her. "Next time, instead of browsing for denim shorts, perhaps discover the witch *before* they blow up half the food court."

My cheeks warmed in embarrassment. "Yes, Mother."

She offered her palm—the invitation to return to my cramped dorm room. I drew in another steadying breath, readying myself for a power far worse than shadow-walking.

We stepped into the Void, leaving the naughty former Water witch and her companion behind forever.

Chapter One

Present day—roughly above Sedona, Arizona

At least one box was missing out of the back of the moving trailer. I was sure of it. Not good. I hadn't been in possession of the keys to my new big girl apartment for longer than three hours and already I'd been robbed.

Please, let it not be labeled kitchen. I couldn't afford to replace the titanium dishes my foster mother had given me when I'd been accepted to graduate school.

"Fuck me," I said under my breath after counting up the remaining items and noting one of the kitchen boxes was, in fact, missing. I hadn't seen a thing stirring outside the apartment window during the spare seconds I'd spent indoors in between trips. Whoever it was had been fast *and* quiet.

A soft snicker from the shadows to my right instantly snagged my attention. I swiveled, catching two glimmering eyes blinking away then reappearing like some sort of Cheshire cat.

"That's an interesting invocation phrase," a raspy male voice said from the darkness. "What kind of spell does it cast?"

I stiffened at the mention of magic. Instinct made me glance around the flagstone courtyard for prying vanilla human ears. One of us would be in trouble if he'd been overheard.

"You're new to Wipuk," the guy said.

Yes, this *was* Wipuk. And in Wipuk it was safe to discuss magic. I forced my spine to ease.

I sent a look into the trailer, and then back at the eyes seemingly floating in the shadows. Had *he* stolen my things?

"What happened to my boxes?" My snapped question wasn't the most courteous of greetings, but his manners hadn't been terribly impressive either.

"Vulpes youths," the male said without altering his steady tone.

A moment passed before the implication of his words made its way fully through the gray mass of my brain. "What would a werefox want with my box?"

There was a contemplative hum from the shadows. "Probably trying to figure out which faction claims you."

And so it began.

The round-about-question wasn't surprising. What was unexpected was the speed at which it had come up. True, every supernatural creature within the Underground was required to belong to a faction. Accountability purposes was the claim. When a vampire lost control and bled the governor's son dry in a fit of blood lust, someone had to step in and take control of the situation. It was a good system. For everyone but me.

A quiet grunt was the only response I gave the stranger before I twisted on my heel. This was a conversation I'd hoped to avoid until I'd at least unpacked the dishes. Besides, these boxes needed to be hauled inside before the "vulpes youths" could swipe the rest. Especially the last two labeled "kitchen".

I hoisted them both. They teetered unsteadily— together a little heavier than I could handle. But I was unwilling to let anyone snatch more of my things.

"Need a hand?" the male asked without coming forward.

It was obvious I could. He'd probably watched me heft heavy objects since I'd pulled up with the trailer two hours ago. How chivalrous of him to wait until six boxes remained and all of the furniture had been moved before volunteering.

Saying nothing was safer than accepting the favor. I didn't know what manner of creature he was. Some factions had a tendency to call in favors, and it usually wasn't a cup of sugar they wanted in return.

Two successful steps forward were all I could claim before the bottom box caved in on the right side and the top one slid for the cobblestone.

"Whoa!" The male caught it in mid-air with the help of supernatural speed and wide palms.

The soft clink of metal against metal halted as he steadied the load. The titanium! He'd saved me a bundle by rescuing the box. I lifted my eyes to his with a smile of appreciation already curving my lips.

Then I saw him. My mouth contorted into a deep frown as my heart skipped two fearful beats.

Please let him be a visitor, not a tenant!

I jerked past the guy toward the open apartment door.

"I'm Ryan," he said on my heels, "your neighbor to the west."

Hades's hair. Now I'd have to make nice.

I carefully set my box atop the stack in the middle of the bare travertine floor so I'd have an excuse to take a quiet breath for courage. Only when my heartbeat had resumed a semi-normal patter did I face where Ryan had come to rest inside the door. His cherry eyes darted around the space until he noted my hands were extended for the box he held.

He didn't move to give me my things. Instead, Ryan tossed a head of damp shoulder-length light brown hair out of his eyes as he settled them on my face. My heart skipped another beat. If I squinted he'd be the spitting image of my lifelong nemesis—Trip.

No squinting allowed.

Things like this didn't happen by coincidence. Trip was messing with me. As usual.

I catalogued their differences. Ryan's nose wasn't sharply defined with its soft lines and circular tip. A chin coated with a day's worth of light brown hair was rounded rather than rectangular. Cheeks that were blocky rather than angular were barely visible beneath his peach-brown skin. But the thick neck extending out of a white V-neck T-shirt—a neck that seemed at odds with his comparatively narrow head—was exactly like Trip's. The marked difference between the two males—apart from this one's mortality—was the deep cherry color of his irises.

Ryan made a soft sound, perhaps a snort. His raspy voice began anew. "And you would be…?"

What name should I give? At UC Berkeley I'd been Becca Walsh. Come to think of it, I'd been Becca since I'd been tossed onto the Mortal Realm fifteen years ago.

But I'd been Kora in the Underworld during the first ten years of my life. It was my middle name and a variation of one of my godmother Persephone's nicknames. Was there something in between? After all I *was* in between the Mortal and Divine Realms now in a magical pocket of space centered roughly over Sedona, Arizona. I'd need an in-between kind of name.

Reba would be in-between, but it would remind me of the country musician. Hmm. I could try my full name: Rebecca. But that would be inviting people to create nicknames I wouldn't like.

The guy's bushy eyebrows rose higher on his smooth forehead the longer it took me to answer him. It was a simple question. Why couldn't I give a simple answer?

Oh, the Styx with it!

"Kora," I said at long last.

His eyebrows righted to their usual hover, a centimeter above his eyes. "Cara?"

I stared at him dumbly for three full seconds, realizing I'd picked a name that would give me no end of trouble on the Mortal Realm.

"Kora," I said in a sharper tone as if that alone would clear up everything. "Just one 'A'."

"That's a weird name. I guess it figures."

He was insulting me, wasn't he? "Why does it figure?"

His thin lips shifted into a jaunty half grin that made my heart stumble. Hades's hair! He looked too like Trip for my own good.

"A girl with blue hair ought to have a weird name."

"Cerulean," I said frostily of the color of my straight, chin length asymmetrical bob. Usually I was patient when explaining the color of my hair. Usually I didn't have to explain it to men who looked like Trip.

The jaunty grin faded into a perplexed look of crinkled brows and squinty eyes. "Sir what?"

"Cerulean. A deep sky-blue color." I gestured to my hair. "Cerulean."

"Can you use it in a sentence for me?"

Oh, look at that grin. He thought he was funny. I wasn't laughing.

I snapped my palms closed twice. "Can I have my box back now before the rest of the stuff in the trailer gets stolen?"

"They're fine," he said despite stepping forward and putting the box on my stack in the center of the empty room. "I've been listening."

"If you've been listening then how come you didn't stop them from taking the other boxes?"

His shoulders lifted an extra inch as he stood to his full height of six feet or so. I'd clearly offended him. Good.

"I was in the can the first time," he said with a gruffer delivery. "Wasn't sure anyone had taken anything. The second time, you came out yourself before I could stop them."

He wasn't undead because the sun was still in the process of setting. I doubted he was a shapeshifter because the whole place would have to be filled with them. His keen hearing meant he was probably some flavor of Were.

I ventured a guess. "Are you a werefox, too?"

"No." His cherry eyes twinkled. "I'll tell you mine if you tell me yours."

"Sorceress," I said because it would be common knowledge soon enough even if it were a fib.

His head snapped back a good inch. "No shit? I thought those were a myth."

I gave a flippant shrug. Growing up amongst the gods, demigods and daimons of the Greek Underworld had quickly taught me how to be vague, cryptic, and downright evasive. If I didn't verbalize anything, I couldn't be held to it. And he wouldn't be able to sense the lie if he were one of the lucky factions capable of that trick.

Ryan's left eye squinted while the other widened in what looked to be a bemused expression. "What kind of magic can you wield?"

I pushed the topic back on him, wagging a finger for emphasis. "Nuh, I told you mine."

"Shapeshifter."

"Shifter?" The lifting of my pitch did little to hide my surprise. He *was* part of a faction that could sense lies. I glanced toward the door expecting to see others who looked like him hovering in the courtyard. "Does your clan live here, too?"

Ryan's eyebrows drew together in a deep wrinkle above his nose. The dark look immediately proved he wasn't, in fact, Trip. When Trip looked angry, things shook.

"No." Ryan abruptly turned and stalked to the door.

I dumbly watched him disappear. And remained in that pose when he returned with two of my boxes. His attention was on the stone-tiled floor rather than me as he set them atop my growing stack.

"I'll get the boxes from the werefox if you want," he said without lifting his gaze.

"Okay." The shifter faction wasn't one that called in their favors. Agreeing would be safe. And he was male. He'd probably offered because he wanted to impress me. It didn't matter that he could conceivably be old enough to be my great-great-great-grandfather.

Ryan's gaze touched on mine. "Give me a half hour."

I gave another flippant shrug because I had plenty of boxes to unpack as it was.

He hesitated near the boxes, brows lifting expectantly. Was I supposed to say something else? Though I'd lived among humans for the past decade and a half, I was still boning up on how to behave in the Underground. Was there a specific shapeshifter farewell custom I'd missed?

In any case Ryan loped to the door, calling back, "A beer for my trouble would be nice."

Beer. Ours was a love that could never be.

****

I whipped my hair from the left to the right in time with the hip-hop song my iPod blared across the room. With the hope the upstairs apartment was empty of tenants, I belted out the words while putting away the pots and plates that hadn't been swiped.

I was cautiously happy. I'd have been fully happy if moving to Wipuk—the magical community's private colony—had been my idea. It hadn't. That was a rant for another day. Today was all about moving into my very first apartment.

With a titanium plate held perpendicularly in front of me in both hands, I whipped my hair to the left, kicking my 8-eye Doc Marten out like a regular old Rockette. I shook my hips provocatively during the song's bridge, singing louder in a cracking voice. I'd never have done this on campus. Those places were hives of peeping toms.

"Practicing for goth girls on ice?"

The baritone voice startled half the divine out of me. I damn near tossed my plate to the stone floor before I managed to calm the slice of fear.

"Kore's knees!" I shouted once I'd figured out what and *who* had happened. I whirled on the ball of my boot and glared at him.

Trip stood slouched against the front door in all his irritating glory. My lifelong nemesis had the unfortunate trait of being a honey-skinned hottie. I shouldn't have found him attractive, not when he'd made it his hobby to torment me for as long as I could remember.

The surfer boy cut of his shoulder-length dark ash blond hair softly waved around his long, oval face. Hazel green hooded eyes peeped lazily from around a gentle curl. The left corner of his mauve lips drew up in his usual smirk. I suspected the expression was because he lived to catch me in embarrassing situations. The only safe feature I could look at was the bright highlight on his Roman nose, so sharply delineated that it could have cut butter. Though the blunt, uneven tip saved the feature from appearing ugly.

"My weekly check-in isn't until Wednesday, Trip," I said between teeth clenched like a penny pincher's butt cheeks on Black Friday. "Let me guess, you're just here to annoy me?"

He lifted a hand of long fingers, scratching his rectangular jaw as if he were deep in contemplation. The haze of light fog that clung to him floated out in a gentle wave. Fog meant he was in the Spirit Realm, as always. He couldn't cause too much trouble from over there.

My attention caught on his chin. He must have shaved recently because the ash brown beard and goatee he stroked were light today.

"It's not Wednesday?" he asked with an exaggerated raise of his sculpted brows. "My bad." An irreverent half shrug was his next feigned motion. "You know how it is in the Underworld."

He hadn't been confused about the day. We both knew it. I merely stared until he gave me a better explanation for his visit.

Trip settled his back against the door as if he could actually touch it, tossing one leg over the other. The new pose looked supremely indolent. It was his "I-have-all-eternity, Kora" pose. When all was said and done Trip lacked patience.

"I'm here to verify your living quarters are Underworld-approved," he said.

I snorted. "That's not even a thing."

"How do you know? You've been gone for a decade and a half. Hades and my father could have enacted any number of regulations since you've been on the Mortal Realm. Time *does* move differently there."

"Could have," I said, ignoring the importance he'd placed on his father. "But Hades didn't. Mom would have given me a checklist."

The iPod changed tracks to something slow and sensual—a tune I enjoyed listening to when I wanted to chill out.

Trip turned his head toward the speaker. His dark blond brows lifted faintly. "Music to screw by, Kora?"

He wanted another fight? He could watch me set my new plate atop the stack in the center cabinet above my dishwasher instead.

Glee sparked within me. *I had a dishwasher*! The warm sensation soothed part of my ire over Trip's untimely visit. So a partial smile was affixed to my lips when I retrieved another load of plates.

Trip's arm dropped noisily to his side. "What are you smiling about?"

"If I tell you, you'll only mess it up."

There was an irritated snuffle as I put the next set of plates away. "It's the dishwasher," Trip said with quick exultation. "You've never had a dishwasher before."

I stiffened from my mandible on down to my Achilles tendon.

"Isn't it, Kora?"

"Yes, Trip. It's the dishwasher," I said in a sour voice that could be construed as sarcasm. Let him figure out if it was the truth.

"How 'bout that new neighbor of yours?"

I inhaled a sharp breath, hating that he'd already seen Ryan.

"Handsome guy," Trip said.

Now I was definitely leaning toward a setup. Wouldn't it figure dear old Mum had stationed some goon in the apartment to my west to make sure I was doing my familial duty? And if she'd asked for help from Trip—which she often did no matter how many times I argued—this was the outcome: a guy who looked disturbingly like my lifelong nemesis stationed feet away, twenty-four seven.

Trip adopted his own variation of the sour-could-be-construed-as-sarcasm tone. "Did you accept his favor so you could settle up at lovers' point with this song on the radio?"

I shot a glance over my shoulder. Unlike virtually every other immortal, Trip's face was an open book. By the darkening of his eyes I was pretty sure this book didn't have a happy ending. No, he was legitimately ticked off. Maybe the shapeshifter next door who looked too much like Trip wasn't a setup.

I made him wait a few seconds while I sauntered to my box for a stack of glasses. He was made to wait longer still so I could move back to the cabinet.

"I've never heard of a shapeshifter calling in favors," I said once I was spared the view of him.

Trip let out a harsh snort. "I just sent one to Tartarus for cashing in favors at the Cat Box."

I snorted without turning. "Hades's hair, you're such a buzz kill."

"Buzz kill." The slow, disgusted speed in which he repeated the phrase implied Trip had taken the bait. "The loser babysat the owner's house during a week-long vacation, then cashed the favor in for a half hour with the Box's tiger twins! And that's just one instance, Kora. He did this repeatedly over the course of fifty-two years! You know cheapening the act of lovemaking with payment tarnishes the soul."

25

I pivoted on my heel, settling my tush against the counter in a pose I hoped was half as indolent as his. "Would you have tossed him into Tartarus if he'd babysat the tiger twins' house in exchange for sex?"

His jaw set tightly. A muscle in his cheek twitched in time with his heartbeat. Trip despised when I made him think about the gray areas of existence. After nine years serving as backup for the North American judge of souls in the afterlife, Trip really should be past all this.

"Yes," he said.

A fib. I tilted my head to the left while simultaneously lifting my right eyebrow into the incredulous zone atop my forehead. "Trip."

"Kora."

He was clearly spoiling for another fight. "There's no difference between babysitting hookers' houses for sex and buying a girl dinner and a movie for it."

"It only takes you three dances and two drinks," he said.

My already squinty eyes narrowed to slivers. I loathed that he was a supernatural voyeur. My mother had promised he'd be punished if he were caught doing it again. Apparently no one was trying all that hard to catch him.

I gave Trip a feigned beatific smile. "I'll have to do it in two dances and one drink next time."

The muscle in his jaw twitched faster. "With Mr. let-me-touch-your-box?"

"I wonder if his hair is as soft as it looks." A dreamy sigh slipped through my slightly parted lips. "I doubt I'll even need my mood music for him."

"You won't." Baritone voice going steely, Trip said, "You'll be thinking of me when he touches you."

I met his gaze. "Why is that?"

"Because the only way he'll ever have sex with you is if you pay him for it."

That hadn't been the answer I'd expected at all.

Trip pushed off the wall, stalking two broad steps closer. His hazel-green eyes glittered dangerously beneath the kitchen's overhead light. I held my breath for the punch line I now knew was coming.

"And then your soul will belong to me," he said.

A nanosecond later I was alone in the apartment.

My breath expelled in a rush.

No, Ryan Steele definitely wasn't a setup. It was just one of Fate's sick coincidences. Clotho's sense of humor was as warm and fluffy as a Komodo dragon. But like every other male who had ever expressed even a minutia of interest in me or I him, Trip was going to scare him off.

Oh, how I hated that creature.

Chapter Two

There were only two reasons why I'd opened my front door a half hour later. The first was that Trip never deigned to knock. And the other was that I was pretty sure whoever was on the other side could hear me breathing.

Ryan Steele held the forearm of a sullen teenager on my porch. The scowling kid held two boxes labeled "bedroom" and one labeled "kitchen". Was this the werefox youth who had pilfered my stuff?

Was it common for Arizona werefoxes to have black hair tipped with red, orange, and yellow? If it was, did they all grow it out to five inches so they could style it straight up off their head? It looked like he was trying to give the impression of his head being on fire.

I could help him get closer to reality with a mere snap of my fingers. I restrained a wicked smile.

"This is Miss Kora." Ryan spoke in a condescendingly slow pace as though the kid wasn't right in the brain.

The teenager pinned a narrow gaze at Ryan in disgust before pointing it at me. His attention quickly dropped, glaring at the black shirt three sizes too large for his narrow frame.

I glanced between the two of them, scenting their differences. The kid smelled like a human with only the hint of wildness. There was a good reason for that if he were truly a human infected with the werefox virus.

"This is little Kenny Tykal," Ryan said.

"I ain't little." Kenny's lower lip became more pronounced as he puffed up his puny chest. "And it's Kenneth."

Ryan lifted his volume, effectively drowning out the softly cursing kid. "Like I said, this is little Kenny

Tykal. He's Keith Tykal's kid. Keith isn't a bad guy." Ryan gestured behind him at the building on the opposite side of the courtyard. "Lives over in one twenty-six. He's trying to raise this little guy all on his own."

"I *ain't* little," Kenny said a second, louder time. "And don't be tellin' her no shit 'bout me and my dad, y'hear?"

Ryan's lips quivered from restrained mirth. He hid it long enough to say, "Kenny thinks he's a cholo."

"Old guy." Kenny tried to shake off the older male's hand. "Does this hair look cholo to you?"

I shook my head. "Nah, that's emo all the way."

"Shit yeah," Kenny said, shooting a triumphant look over at Ryan. A moment later he peered over my shoulder into the apartment. "Where should I put these boxes?"

Though he was being civil now, the little shit had stolen my things. I wasn't sure inviting him inside was a good idea. He could be casing the place.

Then again he'd seen everything I'd lugged inside. And what were the odds these apartments had vastly different floor plans anyway?

I stepped away from the door so Kenny could bring the boxes inside. He set them on the stone floor beside the leaning tower of the other boxes, his eyes scanning everything as he moved. He was definitely Were.

"Now what do you say to Miss Kora, Kenny?"

The sullen expression turned into one of malevolence only a teenager could pull off. More than likely he was silently telling us both to piss off and die. Aloud he feigned a saccharine voice. "I'm sorry I took your boxes, Miss Kora. If you need any help takin' out the trash for the next six months, sign me up."

The smug expression on Ryan's face explained the strange offer. They'd worked out a deal. I bet Kenny's dad wouldn't hear of the incident provided Kenny helped me out.

I wasn't about to let the kid back into my place so he could steal something else. At least not until I'd properly tagged all of my expensive things for their new locale.

"I'm okay," I said.

Kenny's malevolent look deepened.

I ignored him in favor of Ryan. "Thanks for the help."

No doubt this was the last time I'd see the guy. Trip would do his thing and then the shifter would take pains to avoid me here on out. It was just as well. I wouldn't have been able to handle being friendly with someone who looked like my nemesis.

"It's no problem." Ryan inclined his head, a nod of some sort. "We'll see you 'round."

They both turned. Kenny flailed his scrawny limbs against Ryan's grip rather like a fox trying to escape a dog. I closed the door to stop to any other foxhunt metaphors that thought to slip into my head. And then I went back to the tiring but surprisingly rewarding task of setting up my very first apartment.

Chapter Three

Every mutt in Sedona was baying, and half of them were outside my bedroom window.

"Mother." I let out a low grunt of irritation.

Another round of baying persuaded me to whip back the sheets so I could stomp into the next room. She was snuggled into the beanbag chair the size of a small elephant with her delicate legs kicked up into the air and her head of flowing burgundy hair fanned out across the floor. The gauzy skirt of her ceremonial robes pooled at her narrow hips. Any red-blooded male—and several green- and blue-blooded, too—would have gotten naughty ideas

"Mother," I said louder so I could hear myself over the canine howls out the windows. "I really wish you'd visit me in the Spirit Realm."

She kicked a single narrow ankle toward the window. Her pale eyes focused on the wall rather than on me. "I did. You didn't hear me."

I got my natural hair color (raven) and height (five foot nine) from my dad, a full-blooded Irish human. But I got my pale gray eyes from her, along with just about everything else.

I'd never met Jack Walsh. He'd died two months after my conception. It was the only reason my mother had allowed me to remain in the Underworld. Had he not died before my birth, I'd have been shipped up to the Mortal Realm to live life as a normal kid with a single parent. Or at least as normal as a half-divine, half-human girl could be.

While I wouldn't have called my mother beautiful, she certainly wasn't ugly. She had a smooth forehead cut by two finely sculpted burgundy eyebrows I'd envied as a small child. Her cool gray irises were barely visible beneath the dark fringe of her eyelashes. It lent her a dramatic look she hadn't needed. Perhaps the cute button nose was to blame for pushing her into the doll-like category rather than the supermodel category. But the full Cupid's bow lips perched above a gently curved chin all set atop a swan-like neck were closer to a Barbie doll than a baby doll.

I didn't doubt she was right. Hecate, or Catey as she preferred to be called these days, had probably stood whispering, calling, and shouting at me for a good five minutes from the safety of the Spirit Realm. I wouldn't have heard it. Once I fell asleep, I slept like the dead.

Her image shuddered like a television screen flicker. A haze of water-like particles formed over her when it cleared. She was in the Spirit Realm again. Unlike Trip, my mother could hop between every realm at will. Her status as one of the big guns granted her the ability.

Four dogs whimpered outside, or one dog whimpered four times. Whatever the case, they scattered back to wherever they'd come. Maybe my neighbors wouldn't work out whom they'd been visiting.

"Trip was here yesterday," I said once I could hear myself think. "I haven't got any new news. I need a few days."

My mother extended a hand into the shaft of light the lamp in the courtyard cast into my living room. Her eyes fanatically tracked the shadows' movements like a cat stalking a laser pointer. I didn't dare get in the way of her fun. She had a mean streak in her like no other, and the quickest way to engage it was to mess with her fun. She'd stop playing shadow puppets when the light faded with the rising sun. In the meantime, I could get some shuteye. I headed back into the bedroom.

"This is bigger than your last place," she said from just behind me. Apparently she'd stopped her playtime early.

"Yeah," I said rather than explain that I'd graduated from grad school and was now in a big-girl apartment.

"Did I buy the whole building?"

I shook my head as I pulled the sheet taut, smoothing it with my hand before pulling it back so I could slide beneath. "No."

She'd given me a lump sum of money when I'd turned twenty in celebration of reaching my majority and not being eaten by Cerberus. At least that's what the card had read. I'd known better than to use that money to buy a house, a car, or a vacation to Iceland. It had been the only support she'd given me on the Mortal Realm in fifteen years. I was fairly certain I'd not be getting any more.

If I had any chance of making a go of owning my own business, it would require that chunk of change to finance. So I was renting. The business would have to become solvent before my student loan payments kicked in or I'd be screwed.

"You should buy cotton," my mother said without so much as touching the sheets I pulled up to my chin. "It's natural and breathes better."

"Cotton also soaks up the memories of nearby objects like a sponge," I said sourly. "Poly blends dampen it. I wouldn't be able to sleep if I had to relive every dust mote, insect, or breeze that hit each object in a five foot radius around the bed."

Her blank stare hinted she had no idea what I was going on about. It was unsurprising. My mother lived the majority of her time in a section of the Divine Realm that was her creation. Every item within it, right down to the dirt smears on the tiles, came from her imagination. And since it was all a big fat illusion, none of the objects retained history.

She began twisting the thin silk of her outer robe between her index finger and thumb. The precursor to a mood swing. Quickly I murmured an apology for arguing with her.

Satisfied, she dropped the robe. "I came to give you your graduation gifts."

My lips parted in surprise. I'd not expected gifts because she'd been irritated I'd wanted to go to college in the first place. I'd experienced one of her famed tantrums when I'd asked to go to graduate school. My conscience was still smarting from that one and the "natural disaster" it had sparked.

"The first is already on your left middle finger," she said.

I popped upright, drawing my hand into my lap so I could look. The room was too dark to make out much more than the shape and feel of the narrow band around my finger. I fumbled to find the new location of my bedside lamp. Only luck saved me from knocking it off the table.

My mother waited patiently while I held my fingers up for a proper look. The narrow band was made of a heavy metal, perhaps tungsten, featuring an etched wave pattern that gave it visual interest without being gaudy.

"A ring," I said dumbly.

"Not just any ring." She carefully pronounced each word in her proudest tone. I imagined her chest puffed out much like the werefox who had visited earlier. "That ring enables the wearer to access all schools of magic upon uttering the invocation word 'apotropaios'."

My eyebrows drew together in confusion, and then deepened into a suspicious V when I worked through what she'd said. "But I can access all schools of magic without a ring."

She tossed her long hair over her shoulder. "It's all too easy for a half-blooded mortal to be hindered. Consuming copious amounts of alcohol or drugs as well as a lack of sleep or vitamins can trigger a failure of your power." My mother pointed a narrow finger at the ring. "That will give you access when all else fails."

I held in a grunt. She wouldn't be able to tell me if there was a sixty-foot sea monster knocking on my door let alone what incident might happen in my future that would trigger a failure in my power. The gods had few rules they were required to keep. Staying out of Fate's business was one they all observed.

My mother's bosom buddy status with the fate spinner meant I was often given top-secret information that would have gotten any other deity sent to Tartarus— the Greeks' answer to hell. This ring was just another in a long line of freebies I got because Catey and Clotho liked to play the slots in Reno once a month.

Next she held up a two-inch arm cuff made of hammered silver. "This bracelet will enhance your divine half's endurance. You won't have to sleep nearly as long while wearing it."

What in Hades was her game? Her gifts were a useless ring and a bracelet I could have used six years ago when I'd been cramming for my first round of final exams. Why did I need to be awake longer now? Witches slept during the night just as humans did!

In the motherly tone she rarely utilized, she said, "Do remember to drink plenty of water while you're awake." She let a charm on a gold chain drop from her fingers. "And this is for when you find that certain someone special."

I was barren. I'd finally stopped wishing for my period when I'd gotten my driver's license. My female friends all envied me for not having to deal with the monthly curse while they simultaneously looked on me in pity knowing I'd never have kids. Could that necklace be what I thought it was?

"Is that some sort of wedding charm?" I asked in the hope of getting a firm answer from her before she got distracted by one of her shadow puppet shows.

She loudly scoffed. She'd never married. Few in the Greek pantheon had. "No. Wear this necklace during intercourse on a full moon and you will conceive."

My breath left me in a mighty gust. I could have a child! Or … children? "Is it a one time casting?"

She set the miraculous piece of jewelry on the scuffed wood surface of my dresser. "It will only work with one lover. As many times as you like."

I could have children!

I could hardly breathe.

Out of a hidden pocket she drew a small rectangular golden gift box. It looked like a package of truffles I'd once received for a holiday gift swap—three truffles that had probably cost as much as a whole steak dinner. Had my mother bought me fancy chocolate?

"These are for when you are in dire straits," she said with a bounce of her palm. "Eating one will solve a financial problem."

A financial problem. I'd just bet it would pay a fifteen-dollar parking ticket for me when I was in the red by a few thousand dollars. But I wouldn't look a gift horse in the mouth, not after that miraculous necklace.

I'd opened my mouth to thank her for the gifts when she pulled out yet another item to add to the cache.

Curiously, it was a blue metallic penlight. My mother flicked the switch and then waved the miniature flashlight around the room. I gasped at the collection of amorphous blobs skulking about my new bedroom. Clearly her penlight allowed me to see into the Spirit Realm without invoking magic.

"This is for checking to make sure Trip isn't spying on you," she said. "But beware, it will show any eye, mortal and faction alike, the images you see."

While I'd been known to call on necromancy to check if Trip were hiding when I'd felt an overwhelming sense of being watched, I very rarely ever caught him in the act. The power involved an invocation word he recognized. He'd always disappeared into the Underworld before I'd finished speaking it … or so I thought. Provided he didn't work out what the flashlight was for, I could use this to catch him.

"And it will feed the findings back to me," my mother said.

Finally, there'd be some proof Trip had been tormenting me for years.

She added one more piece of information. "Store them in a safe place, my daughter, for these objects do not require attunement. Any may wield them and reap their benefits. I entrust their safety to you."

I nodded my understanding and then found myself shaking my head in awe. "These gifts … they are truly amazing, Mother. Thank you."

"Thank me with deeds not words." She turned her back on me so she could set the rest of the gifts on the dresser beside the others. "I expect an update on Wednesday."

I nodded for her because there was no other option.

"The necklace," she said in a grave tone as she ran a finger across the tiny chain links. "Do not use it with a god or another Diakonos."

I was a Diakonos—the half-blood child of a god. And I was the only one I'd met. That urge wouldn't be terribly difficult to avoid.

"It will be an automatic trip to Tartarus for you if you do." She let that sit before facing me. "And your torturer will most likely be Trip."

"Okay." I extended the syllables out, illustrating my unease. "No gods or kids of gods, got it."

Her mouth widened into a lovely smile that reminded me of many Sunday mornings spent together stretched out on the grasses of Elysian Fields. "Happy housewarming, Kora."

Happy housewarming indeed! My new trinkets were almost worth the torment by Trip. Almost.

"Try on your new bracelet," she said while holding the silver toward me. "Because I have a favor to ask of you."

My mother's "favors" were never favors. They were always tasks in which I risked my mortal life. And they couldn't be refused.

I grabbed shorts and the bracelet. It was going to be a long night.

Chapter Four

My entire body shuddered with revulsion the moment Catey released my hand within the Spirit Realm. Though I was accustomed to traveling in the Void—the space of literal nothing that filled in the crevices within the universe—it never ceased to throw me for a serious loop. If it weren't so damn speedy, I'd insist on using another method of transportation.

It didn't help that my mother always ended in the Spirit Realm. The spirits of the recently deceased crowded us. I hadn't opened my eyes yet, but I didn't have to. I could smell them. The stench was horrific.

The sounds of a busy street drew my eyelids open despite the concern of what I'd see. We stood on the edge of a mud coated square surrounded by a low aqua metal fence in front of a higher cement wall. African women dressed in colorful dresses huddled in clumps on the edge of the street with stuffed sacks in hand. Muslim women if the scarfs over their heads meant anything. The spirits hovering were similarly clad. We must have Voidwalked to the north of Africa.

Though morning here, the sun was already beating down on us with an uncomfortable intensity. I certainly hoped whatever she meant me to do would be quick before it got any worse.

I strained to hear the voices of the living mingling within the square. Some spoke in French, some in Arabic, and yet others in a language I didn't recognize.

"You will need two more gifts to handle this favor."

The first additional gift she produced was a blue scarf and dress set, most likely so I'd fit in with the locals. My mother stopped me from pulling on the dress with a hand on my chest just above my tank top's bodice. Ancient words she'd never taught me spilled from her lips as golden light shot down her arm and into my chest. I now had a new language at my disposal courtesy of magical brute force. It was the one I hadn't recognized moments ago—Somali.

I pulled on the dress and scarf before she grew impatient.

My mother adjusted the headscarf, covering my cerulean hair and most of my face. "You have two hours."

In a heartbeat she was gone, and I was plunged into the thick heat. More than likely my mother had dropped me at the scene of a major event shortly before it would happen. This wasn't the first time. I'd stopped massacres, robberies of national treasures, and even the assassination of a political figure, all by witches who should have known better than to use their magic for evil. As always, I had my work cut out for me with just two hours to ferret out the witch and stop the event in Zeus knew what country I'd been left.

I pulled in a deep breath, scenting for magic and hints as to where I was. The smell of brine was strong— *true* brine, not simply the hint of it. I was on the coast. French, Arabic, and Somali languages mingled must mean I was near Somalia. I didn't think they spoke French in Somalia, and the number of people speaking it here was far fewer than the speakers of the other languages. I was most likely in one of the neighboring countries. A former French colony perhaps? None of this was terribly helpful.

A gnarled and hunched man stood in the shade of a nearby building. His gaze was already on me. Had he noted my sudden appearance? Time to move on in any case.

Experience told me Mother had dropped me within two miles of the incident. She'd never brought me to the same city block as the event I was meant to stop. I doubted she'd start any time soon. Walking for the water was probably the best idea. Perhaps I'd find something along the way that would tell me where I was.

I trudged through the battered streets for a quarter of a mile until I emerged into a crowded bazaar filled with large umbrellas and sheets haphazardly tacked across leaning wooden frames over displays of wares. Toyota minibuses congested the roads leading in and out of the shopping area. Their license plates told me nothing of use.

A young man in a red shirt several sizes too large for him stopped a couple in European clothing. He offered tourist trinkets emblazoned with the word "Djibouti". In French, the male half of the couple suggested they buy something to remember their trip to Djibouti Town. The female muttered she'd rather use the money to get a faster boat out of the hole of a country.

I sent out a pulse of awareness, seeking out magic and quickly found this was the least magical city I'd ever visited. Sedona hummed with an almost painful intensity that required I shut down my magic awareness, but Djibouti Town was barren. Even the lifeforce of the gathered people was dimmer than those within other cities. This was definitely a hole of a country.

The pulse hit upon something in the distance in the direction of the heavy brine scent. The signature I received back had enough latent energy to be a place of power to rival Stonehenge. Places of energy didn't move from side to side like this signature did. This was a *person*.

I walked faster, ignoring the cab that crept along beside me honking its horn. I didn't have any of their currency to pay the driver, and I wasn't going to use magic to make him think I had. It would tarnish my soul and please Trip far too much.

A woman shrieked to my left. I slowed my pace. The sound abruptly ceased, almost too quickly for me to work out where it had come from. A young woman wildly thrashed against a rotund man's grip across the square. His hand clamped over her mouth, stifling her loud protests. A bawling white-haired woman stood with her arms stretched out toward the retreating pair. Her whimpering sounded an awful lot like, "Not my granddaughter! Allah, keep her safe!"

I hurried to the old woman's side, calling out in her native tongue. "Why are they taking her?"

"To sell her for guns and heroin," the old woman shouted in a roughened voice. "They took my daughter last week! Don't let them take my baby girl!"

While I couldn't do anything about the daughter, I could help the granddaughter. I eased into the shadows between the buildings where the fat man had disappeared. I tugged a thread of Air magic from the aether, sending it whirling between the structures in the form of breeze. The whistling covered my trailing footsteps.

The thick man burst into an empty street, rushing the girl toward a white Toyota pick-up truck that looked as if it had been made in the eighties and run ragged ever since. I silently focused my breeze into a short burst. I directed it at the front of his legs with a press of my palms emulating the motion I wanted it to take.

An invisible gust lifted the fat man two feet off the ground. He lost his hold on the girl before crashing into the hard, dirty surface with a dull thud. Now free to move, the young woman broke into a run toward the alley he'd dragged her through seconds earlier.

He hollered an Arabic curse before threatening to kill her entire family if she didn't come back. The young woman slowed, turning. The fat man had no idea who her family was. It was an empty threat. I used a small gust of wind to nudge her away. She tore off in the opposite direction, taking the silent suggestion to heart. Meanwhile, I faced the kidnapper.

Hiding my magic meant generating an intricate set of cause and effect points rather like a Rube Goldberg machine. I directed wind against a fence. The rattling metal knocked a tree stump loose. That rounded bit of wood rolled to an empty crate that then clattered into the center of the muddy road where it dispatched a bright red bucket across the street. I guided the bucket toward a metal trashcan that teetered atop uneven rocks. And then using wind, I made sure the trashcan hit the fat man square in the head with a little extra force than was natural. Only when his slumped body remained still, but breathing, did I start down the road in the direction of the heavy brine scent.

That was not the event I'd been placed here to stop. Like a side mission in a video game, I'd been tested. I hoped I'd passed the test.
****

I reclined against a golden building with azure doors. All paint, of course, but it was better than the grey and ick color the industrial buildings in the States generally claimed. A freighter named the *Aliman Wonsan* was in the process of docking two hundred feet to my right. I kept an eye on it in my peripheral vision while watching the dockworkers hustling around the space between us.

Men in colorful fishing dories competed for dock space alongside the large ship. It was a far different port from any I'd seen in other cities. This one specialized in livestock where others pushed oil, cars and manufactured items.

Though there was a shout in the distance to my left, my attention switched to the freighter. The pulse of energy I'd felt had come from there, I was sure of it. What I'd sensed had moved with a small side to side motion similar to pacing. The energy had also traveled toward the east at a slow speed—perhaps the speed of a freighter being brought in with a tugboat. Now that the larger ship had come to a standstill, the pulse only moved side to side.

My witch was on that boat. I just had to hope the pulse I felt was the reason my mother had brought me here.

Someone hooked up the gangplank. A man in ragged, stained clothing charged down onto the dock, knocking aside everyone in his path. The pulse went with him. He spoke rapid words to the man holding the boat's heavy rope. I engaged a handy little Air ability to filter his conversation back to me.

My person of interest shook a piece of crinkled paper in front of the rope holder. "Have you seen her?" He gave the man a half second to respond before rephrasing it in broken French.

The rope guy brushed him off with little more than a wave of his hand. The pulse of energy I'd followed spiked angrily. The newcomer stomped across the planks toward a cluster of dockworkers congregated in the middle of the wooden structure. I dropped into place behind him. He repeated his question in both languages to the group, earning a similarly dismissive response. The anger spike was twice as powerful now that a larger group had ignored him.

Did he have a clue the power he funneled into himself each time his ire was tested? This had to be why my mother had brought me. An unpredictable witch was a dangerous witch.

The newcomer shoved through the group of dockworkers. One muttered an insult about the stinking Somali. He whirled around, eyes livid and body shaking. The hair on the back of my neck prickled from the force of his rage.

He would hurt someone if he didn't calm down. But I didn't think Mother had gotten me involved merely to stop one Somali from attacking a group of dockworkers. Still, I couldn't stand idly by while he unloaded his rage, and more importantly his power, onto unsuspecting vanilla humans.

I drew in energy from the nearby ocean, noting someone in the vicinity did the same. The direction of the magical vessel was ahead of me. I'd bet cash the Somali was a Water witch draining directly from the source. I hoped he wouldn't notice my subtle calming influence— a Water witch power. Though I supposed it was better that he target me than them.

Visualizing a peaceful, glass-like pond, I sent the emotion toward him, willing it to slip softly within his consciousness. I varied the intensity of the calm while watching his face. The ocean served as a battery for my steady soothing. Finally he tossed his arms up in disgust and stalked toward the town center.

So far so good.

I kept pace with him, maintaining the calming influence as he moved. He was looking for someone—a woman. Had they had a falling out and he needed to apologize? Or was it something more sinister?

From the level of fury he exhibited, it had to be the latter. That made me go cold inside after what I'd seen nearly happen on this street minutes earlier.

The Somali tramped up the littered mud surface, stopping each person who passed. With sharp words but pleading eyes, he requested they look at his photograph. Each new individual who dismissed him or gave him a negative answer lifted his bad emotions higher.

I continued my soothing influence. He was a powder keg merely waiting to blow. Time to be proactive rather than reactive. I quietly syphoned his store of magical energy back to the ocean, using myself as a conductor. His magic felt red hot as it passed through me as though it were emotionally charged.

My stomach grew uneasy with the realization I couldn't do this indefinitely. At some point I was going to have to go home. And though I wished there was a happy ending to his story, the chances of him finding his lady friend in this hole of a country simply by showing the locals her photograph weren't good.

We made it to the bazaar after an aching half hour. The Somali stopped each person he spotted. And each brushed him off or downright ignored him. Only the women gave him sympathetic yet pitying looks.

"You!"

My attention snapped toward the male shout from across the busy square. The rotund man who had kidnapped the poor granddaughter shoved his way through the crowd with a finger outstretched in my direction. I darted glances between the Somali and the fat man. This couldn't be good. I backed up into an open space where we'd do less damage.

The Somali screamed an obscenity and launched himself at the fat man. There was recognition on his anger-pinched face. He *knew* the fat man! A tidal wave of rage drowned my calming magic.

The Somali bellowed a chest-busting question as his livid eyes went as black as the bottom of the ocean. "Where did you take her?"

The rotund man's oh-so-intelligent response was to laugh derisively and ask, "Which her? I have taken many of your women!"

Fury overwhelmed my soothing effort. The Somali charged his quarry with murder in his eyes. Rather than drown the fat man in his own saliva, the witch swung a fist at him. One of the most powerful Water witches I'd come across in recent history ended up on the ground, knocked out cold by a fleshy vanilla human who even now chortled in victory.

And then the fleshy kidnapper started for me.

My lingering shock made me slow. I barely scrambled back in time to avoid him. Unfortunately, I scrambled right into one of his buddies.

The thick man hurried as fast as his chubby legs would allow. In one surprisingly smooth move, he pulled his arm back, and then punched me exactly as he had the Somali.

I blacked out. Cold.

****

Years of brawling with Trip in the Underworld had conditioned me to automatically Heal myself when I awoke with minor aches and pains. Particularly with a throbbing head like I'd experienced today. A small sigh escaped me once the pain eased. The brine, excrement, and livestock scent surrounding became obvious.

I snapped my eyes open, discovering someone had trapped me within a broad cage atop a ship. Perhaps the same ship that had docked earlier. Screaming rose up from the dock—a hoarse male voice that accompanied dull, fleshy thuds. I lumbered to my cramped knees and then scooted to the metal bars keeping me hostage. I needed to find a door, and probably the explanation for the screaming.

I squinted through the bars. The Somali straddled the rotund man in between stacks of thick rope on the dock. He'd clawed fingers into the fat man's blue tunic and repeatedly smashed the large male's torso against the wood.

The fat asshole deserved a beating. Why should I help him?

I noted two things. The first was the fat man choked and spit up water. And the second was the worrying roar in the distance.

A full second passed before I found the exit to the animal pen, another two seconds before I was able to melt the metal padlock using a high intensity blast of Fire magic. These delays combined meant I didn't make it to the dock in time to save the fat man's life. Though it wasn't my place to judge, I didn't think it was a particular loss for humanity.

However if I didn't get control of the Somali in the next thirty seconds, there *would* be a considerable loss. The entire dock stood gaping at the wall of water roaring in off the coast.

"Run!" I screamed in French.

I grabbed hold of the Somali, temporarily paralyzing him with an ancient Healer power. He'd done a bad, bad thing, and he would be dealt with as soon as I resolved the first crisis. Funneling his energy into me, I built a contrary water current a few hundred feet behind the tidal wave. The unnatural occurrence took all of the power he had in him as well as our combined bodies to draw more energy from the source. Bit by bit I brought the height of the wave down until it was too late to do anything but hold my breath.

The tidal wave crested over the ship, crashing down atop us and against the building with brutal force only nature could provide. Everything that had been unsecured atop the dock was hauled into the water when the wave receded. Everything except the Somali and me, thanks to a last minute casting of Earth magic to fix us to the spot using an overabundance of gravity. As soon as it was safe, I ran to the edge of the dock, looking for any humans who had gone over the side. It appeared everyone had run to safety when I'd screamed.

A ragged gasp left my lungs. I'd barely diffused a tsunami that would have washed away the entire city. Now I knew what my mother had brought me here to do.

I retraced my steps to the Somali. He'd lost someone close to him to the human trafficker. I sympathized with his horror. But he'd abused his power. He'd killed a man using magic, and he'd nearly caused the deaths of thousands of others. I only had one choice. He had to be neutralized.

Setting a hand atop his damp forehead, I whispered the invocation word that would render him powerless. For good. "Katargeō."

My body went into a spasm from the influx of power. His agony squeezed me in a hot grip that was every bit as painful now as it had been the first time I'd utilized the ability.

Though he'd earned this, guilt plagued me. I doubted he was a bad person under normal circumstances. But this hadn't been normal circumstances. Perhaps I could soothe my conscience a tiny bit by trying to help.

I retrieved the Somali's photograph from his death grip. The rotund man was laid out like a lump of useless meat on the planks. If he'd not been dead prior to the wave, he surely would have been later. I crouched until his clammy skin was in reach. Silently I called his spirit back from the Spirit Realm before any of the bystanders could return. The dead man's eyes flipped open as he drew in a mighty choke.

"Dead man," I said in French. "I have called you back from the beyond. You are bound in my service while you are here. Answer me truly, and I will release you painlessly." I didn't admit I would release him painlessly either way. I shook the photograph at him. "Tell me what you did with this woman."

The dead fat man spoke with the raspy voice of the recently asphyxiated. "She's with the other women I caught. They're being held in a house in Yemen."

I set the photograph down and touched the Somali without releasing my grip on the fat man.

My gaze locked on the former witch's frozen pupils. "Remain calm, and I will get you the names and locations you need to find her. If you attack anyone, including me, I won't help you." I gave him a few seconds to mull that over, and then I released him from the paralysis power.

The Somali shrieked helplessly, collapsing to the moist dock in a clump of shivering flesh. To have an integral part of your being stripped away would be akin to dying a partial death. He might get his female back, but he would never get himself back.

I hoped it was worth it. I truly did. But I really doubted it. No one was worth nearly destroying an entire city.

Were they?

Chapter Five

I might have considered the hotness factor of the guy in the tailored suit standing on my porch if I hadn't been operating on three hours of sleep. Instead, I repeatedly rubbed the crust out of my eyes and contemplated what kind of insurance he could possibly be selling.

Was there a company that insured members of the Underground against accidents? Whatever it was, it would cost me an arm and a leg because the outfit covering his sinewy body couldn't have had a price tag for less than a thousand dollars.

"Yeah?" I asked over a particularly aggressive yawn. It came out as "Eeeaaa?" I took the opportunity to pull my polyester robe around myself while he peered over my shoulder into my empty living room.

"I'm Desmond Marino," the guy on my front stoop said.

The matter-of-fact tone of his smooth, masculine voice suggested he expected I'd heard of him. Likewise he didn't extend the arm hanging beside his black silk-blend jacket to offer me a shake—the implication being he didn't feel I deserved the courtesy. Nor did he lift his eyes from their hooded position. That gaze combined with his flat, dark eyebrows and the full lips of a Michelangelo statue gave off the impression of sensual menace. Then again, maybe it was that he was hot in an international male model sort of way with his short blue-black hair, chiseled nose, and posh wardrobe.

He scrutinized me up and down. This guy could give my nemesis a run for his money in the menace department.

What in the world had made me think of Trip *now?*

The smoky tang of incense floated on the air. I hadn't burnt any, and the breeze was too brisk for it to have come from a neighbor. But no, that wasn't incense. It was the marker of a witch.

I took a stealthy sniff while blinking slowly. The crisp note of a fresh mountain stream overtook the smoky tang. *Water witch.* My stomach twisted into a tight knot. Water witches' empathic ability often caused the most trouble of the magical community.

"You are not welcome here," he said in a voice loud enough to wake the neighbors.

Despite the volume I wasn't sure I'd heard him correctly during my twentieth yawn of the morning. "Pardon?"

His eyes—a disturbing aqua blue not far off from my cerulean hair—somehow managed to hood more without completely closing. He was familiar. Strange, considering I'd never officially met a Water witch.

"This is a colony for witches," he said haughtily. "You aren't a witch. How did you get in here?"

"I signed a year lease just like everyone else," I said, deliberately misunderstanding him.

"This is Wipuk," he said as if he thought I'd gotten lost on my way to Phoenix. "If you aren't a witch then you aren't welcome. You shouldn't have even been able to *cross* without magical ability."

I made damn sure he saw my eyebrows shoot up to the middle of my forehead. Desmond Marino was a dick. But if he felt like he could knock on my door at whatever time it was and tell me I wasn't welcome, then I figured he fancied himself important. I couldn't simply tell him to stick his head in Cerberus's maw if I had any chance of completing the task my mother had set forth for me. Infiltrating the magical community's leadership would be a difficult task *without* ticking off anyone who might have their ear.

So I emulated an airhead. Guys were always nicer to stupid girls.

"Really?" I blinked vacuously blank eyes twice. "I have a shapeshifter neighbor. And over there in apartment one twenty-six are a werefox dad and son." I pointed past Desmond the dick's shoulder toward the building across the courtyard. I let my head tilt to the right so my hair would fall away from my cheek in a girlish way. "I didn't know witches could be infected by Were-viruses."

They couldn't. Nor could a shapeshifter be born a witch. The analogy would be like a dog being born a cat.

Desmond the dick's full lips puckered, giving him a Muppet-like appearance. "They have been given dispensation to live in Wipuk and keys to cross. You haven't."

"Oh gosh," I said ruefully with noticeably slow blinks I'd always imagined equated to idiocy. "I have this letter from the Centralized Coven Coalition that says… Hang on." I held up my index finger in the "one moment" sign. "Let me go get it. I don't want to misquote anyone."

I scampered to the breakfast bar where I'd dropped my laptop bag. In the stack of papers that included my business plan for my intended shop, my bank statements, and market research into the Sedona economy, was a letter from the coalition. I returned to the door as I flipped through the pages.

"Here it is," I said in an appropriately vacant tone. "It's addressed to Rebecca Kora Walsh." I glanced at him. "That's me." At his darkened look, I continued. "It says, I quote, 'Thank you for your recent interest in relocating to the Wipuk colony. Any faction capable of finding Wipuk is welcome to join us.'" I gave Desmond the dick my beatific smile along with a playful little bounce that sent my cerulean hair sliding away from my face. "I found it!"

His chin was flush with his collar now. The whites of his eyes were no longer visible. Clearly he didn't enjoy my airhead act.

"Someone helped you," he said with careful enunciation. "You didn't simply *walk* into Wipuk on our own."

I shook my head slowly, allowing my eyes to widen in my Golly-Gee-Mr. Wilson expression. "I don't know anyone here except for the shapeshifter I met last night and the teenage werefox who stole my boxes but brought them back. No one helped me find Wipuk. I just found it." I gestured to the paper in my hand. "Like I said in my original letter to the coalition, I'm a sorceress. I think that's why I was able to find the colony."

Desmond the dick stared at my eyes furiously for three seconds as if he'd expected me to change my tune merely to please him. His next words came out in the same careful tone as his previous statement. "There is no such thing as a sorceress. You had to have help."

There wasn't. But he didn't need to know that. He *did* need to know I could wield magic. I'd have to give him a show of it.

I considered using the water in the small fountain behind him to prove my ability but didn't want him to claim any sort of dominion over me because of utilizing Water magic. Likewise, I'd had bad experiences with Fire witches. I'd stay away from that flavor as well. However, Earth witches rarely gave me trouble. I'd try a little something with that school of magic.

"May I?" I asked while holding my hand toward him. The surest way to drown in your own saliva was to startle a powerful Water witch.

The guy gave me a dubious look of lowered eyebrows and grimly still lips. I waited, silent, while he worked through the pros and cons of letting an airhead touch him. He must have decided he could hold his own against one dumb human because he eventually nodded his assent.

I cautiously extended my hand until I sensed the cool temperature of his suit beneath my fingers. He must have had the air conditioning cranked in his car on the drive over here because it was already warm outside. I let my thoughts fade into the periphery to make room for the data I was about to receive. Then I dropped my fingers the remaining half-inch.

Flashes of the pricey interior of a car popped into my head. They were followed by images of Desmond the dick stopping at a small coffee shop where the barista fingered his cuff as she'd handed him his drink—a double espresso he'd held against his left thigh until it was empty. The history of the fabric brought me back in time to an office that smelled of a mountain stream.

An assistant coated in rosewater had brushed his left arm while she'd told him about my arrival in town. There was a long interval in which he'd sat in a mesh task chair working at a computer. The sleeves had repeatedly hit the track pad. I sneered at the knowledge he was a PC user. Soon I was in a bedroom where he'd meticulously drawn the jacket off its hanger and over his shoulders, presumably this morning.

The jacket's history got tedious. The garment had endured hours of resting on its hanger within the man's dark closet. I learned nothing more before he lifted my hand from his sleeve.

"You have a BMW with leather interiors," I said, certain to keep my tone neutral so he'd not catch my opinions of these factoids. "You got a double espresso on your way over here. The barista slipped you her phone number. It's in the breast pocket. Your assistant goes heavy on the rosewater perfume."

Desmond the dick's expression remained unchanged as I recounted my findings. I didn't know if he was truly unbothered by the information I revealed or if he was merely good at hiding it. In either case, I continued with my show of Earth magic.

"You use a black laptop, I believe seventeen inches wide. The left shift button sticks. You had a boring morning of work, but you spent most of it on the phone while tapping your thigh with your knuckles. You pulled the jacket off its satin padded hanger this morning."

He inhaled a sharp breath upon hearing the description of his hanger. "Psychometry doesn't make you a sorceress."

So he was going to be like that.

Another show of magic was in order. This time I'd hint how I'd like him to leave. The tall weed butting against the front of the porch would be perfect for this. Its roots were fairly entrenched. And it had plenty of reach.

I called on more Earth magic. Abundant energy drawn directly from the soil quickly rushed up my feet. I drew out a small tendril of power from my cache and willed it to join with the weed beside me. Then I visualized the greenery unfurling forward, entwining around Desmond the dick's ankle, and finally giving a good tug toward the courtyard.

The weed took a second and a half to complete the order. When it was finished, the Water witch scrambled for balance on my porch while he clawed at the weed. I leaned against the doorframe, noting the torso he'd hid beneath his crossed arms and closed jacket was trim.

Soon the weed was in shreds on the cement. I said a silent apology to it.

Desmond pulled the bright white pocket square from his breast pocket, wiping away the remnants of the weed from his pale left hand with meticulous care. When he was finished, he folded it into his right palm, and then leaned forward with a menacing glare. "Report to the Earth witch delegation to request dispensation to live here. But I wouldn't suggest you unpack."

"Oh?" I let my eyebrows drift up again. "Why not?"

His head lifted fully for the first time. Aqua eyes widened in exasperation. "Because you're not a witch. You don't belong here."

"I just demonstrated psychometry and the ability to manipulate plants," I said in a droll tone I'd forgotten to hide. "Way I see it, I have more of a right to be here than the werefoxes across the way because I at least have magical abilities."

"Report to the Earth witch delegation," he said through tightly clenched, perfectly aligned teeth.

I tilted my head to the right while I blinked my vacant eyes. "But I'm not an Earth witch."

"You just said that you used psychometry and have the ability to manipulate plants!"

His lifting pitch and volume told me he was growing angry. Good. I was unhappy I hadn't gotten my eight hours of sleep.

Calling on Air magic next, I made a little circular gesture with my right index finger while visualizing a small funnel behind him. The thing soon picked up fine particles of dust to become a dust devil. Desmond's profile turned at the hissing sound coming from behind him. His aqua eyes narrowed into tiny slivers.

"You're using a weave," he said.

Oh, what a dick.

Not only had he woken me from a sound sleep, but he'd also accused me of utilizing a weave. I'd never support spellweavers' magical rape, even if the talisman had come from a willing witch.

"I just got out of bed." My voice soured rather than continuing with the stupid girl act. "Because *someone* rudely pounded on my door. I didn't have time to put on a bra let alone grab a weave."

Desmond the dick's gaze dropped to my chest. My cheeks warmed. That had been the first truly air-headed thing I'd said to him. With his attention firmly on my breasts, I'd try for a reasonable response.

"Can you give me a month's probation or something?" I waved the letter at him. "Someone authorized me to be here. I packed up everything I owned, moved it hundreds of miles east, and plunked down money on a deposit for this place. At least give me a month."

His eyes tracked the paper's movement. A thick wrinkle formed above his nose.

"A year." He grunted the words. "You're on probation for a *year*. If you cause *any* problems in the next year, I will personally escort you out of Wipuk."

I resisted the urge to slump. A *year*! That wasn't fair.

However, the witches of Wipuk could probably oust me and anyone else any time they liked. My only hope of making a go of my mother's plan was to play nice with them.

I nodded—a large gesture so the dick was sure to see it. "Thank you."

"In the meantime," Desmond the dick said, "you need to appear before the Centralized Coven Coalition so they can decide which faction claims you. Do *not* use your weaves until someone takes responsibility for you and gives you authorization."

A knot the size of a fist formed in my stomach. This was going to be bad if they realized I could wield the power of every school of magic without a weave. I'd just have to keep a tight wrap on that bit of information.

I bobbed my head in an appropriately ditzy fashion without verbalizing an agreement.

Desmond pinned a last dark look on me before he turned on the heel of his leather loafer. I caught glimpses of his nice tush as he stalked through the courtyard.

He was a complete dick. But then the hot ones always were.

Chapter Six

"Don't answer it."

I damn near screamed when Trip's voice spoke just outside the closet where I'd been hanging up my nicer clothes. I hadn't heard the knocking at the door until he'd spoken up.

How the Hades long had he been watching me? And why? A second visit from him in less than a week probably meant he was plotting.

Whoever was at the door was someone Trip didn't like. Curiosity overwhelmed me. I called on the aether for a little magical help.

"It's a vampire," Trip said. The shift of misty particles moved as he gestured to the door. Only I would be able to hear him since he was in the Spirit Realm. Well, only me and any lingering spirits in that beyond realm.

So a vampire was outside. I'd successfully avoided their notice for fifteen years by being as unassuming and useless a sorceress as I could be. In my defense, I'd been concentrating on school. I hadn't had time to play vigilante, and my mother hadn't insisted I do more than her occasional "favors" since I'd been slated for bigger things.

The vampire on the porch would hear more than a muscle moving even with the walls and heavy door between us. But I couldn't stand in the closet all night. And I couldn't avoid the undead of Wipuk forever if I was going to enact my mother's plan. I pushed off my left foot in a sprint to the door.

"Kora!" Trip appeared in front of the door before I could reach it. "They're nasty creatures. They don't have souls. They'll kill you as soon as greet you."

I stared at him in bewilderment. Trip had never been protective before. His game had always been to tarnish my soul so he could have it when I kicked the bucket. Was he finally maturing?

The truth sparked into a full-fledged flame of realization. He wasn't trying to protect me. He was making sure my soul didn't become trapped in a dead body, forever out of his reach. Oh, that stinking Minotaur's balls!

I took a deep breath, steeling my nerves before I shoved my arm through him, seeking the doorknob. The eerie sensation of ice crackling over my skin shot up my arm where it pierced the mist coating him. He stared down gape-mouthed, shocked I'd put my hand through him. It was a good sight, a damn good sight. I'd solve half my problems if I could do that for real.

He disappeared, and then reappeared to my left. I seized the knob now that it was in sight and opened the door before Trip could protest.

The whole "vampires needing an invitation to enter a residence thing" was a myth. But apart from that and their subsistence on blood plus extreme sun allergy, those were the only things I really knew of their kind. I'd been researching the witches, not the undead.

Still, I was shocked when the ginger-haired male vampire merely reached an arm inside … and then grabbed me. And when I screamed, he had the audacity to punch me in the head. Hard.

****

"She screamed."

The statement spoken in a tenor pitch hadn't woken me. No, the bone-jarring slam against a hard surface had that honor. My head pounded. Instinctively I called on Healing, asking it to fix whatever was wrong with me.

"You didn't think to mesmerize her?" a sharp feminine voice said.

"I'm no good at that," the original speaker said.

"I supposed if I'd wanted her unhurt, I shouldn't have sent a brute like you. I'd hoped to have the pleasure all to myself. Go on. I can handle it from here." Her voice went sharp as she faced me. "I know you're awake. Open your eyes, blue-hair."

Oh, like I'd never heard that one before. Nonetheless, I opened my eyes. A sultry woman with pouty pink lips, long wavy black hair, and bedroom eyes scrutinized me. She wore a crimson cocktail dress with a bold gold vegetative pattern over her statuesque body. The color made her sun-kissed skin glow.

The female—another vampire I assumed—stood within a room awash with color and floral patterns that clashed with her dress. Scattered around the space were two red sofas that didn't look particularly comfortable, two bold patterned chairs similarly forbidding, and a handful of tables in what was probably locations for optimal feng shui. Each table held a knick-knack, statuette, or basket of dried flowers that may have been chosen simply for their complementary colors rather than any sentimental value. My attention returned to focal point—an imposing hearth made out of a porous gray rock. I could probably fit inside the thing standing up.

Who needed a fireplace that large in Arizona?

The interior had a curious hodgepodge of styles, as if someone had taken a dim drafty castle and attempted to modernize it. Were there castles in Arizona? I hadn't seen any in my travels around Wipuk and Sedona in the past day, but I hadn't poked in every corner. Maybe I wasn't even *in* Arizona. Who knew how long I'd been unconscious.

I stiffened, calling on Earth magic for a hint of my location.

The female vampire called out to someone hidden in another room. "Darling, dinner just woke up!"

How painfully cliché. Still, I had to admit my pulse jumped. Vampires were faster and stronger than just about everything apart from demons and gods. Would my magic help me if she decided she wanted to snap my neck?

But the knowledge the undead and magical communities were rarely in accord gave me the courage to adopt a bad attitude. Though I suspected my throbbing temple had something to do with that decision.

"If you so much as touch a fang to my skin," I said in the warning tone I usually saved for aggressive witches, "I'll annihilate you before you can draw a single sip."

"Lovely." The beautiful brunette's drawl lowered mockingly. She twisted for a view of both me and an open door behind her. Soft incandescent light filtered from the space, casting warm tones across her skin. "Dinner is threatening me. Max, darling, will you put down that blasted toy and come eat?"

Was there such a thing as vampire children? How embarrassing would it be if a kid vamp killed me before I'd had a chance to begin my mother's plan? Wouldn't happen. I was too powerful to be stopped by a mere child, even if the mere child had the strength of six strongman competition entrants.

Earth reported my general location—Arizona. At least that much was good.

"It isn't a toy," a resonant, deep voice said from the open door.

Two fully-grown vampires. Could I handle that many?

The female inhaled a martyred breath. Her delivery became tight and stilted. "Fine. I'll start without you until you can pry yourself from your gadgets."

Her ice cold hands gripped my shoulders without warning. I let out a surprised yelp. The female's frosty breath whooshed over my neck, drawing an involuntary shudder up my back. Stupidly I stood frozen in place.

Too long had passed since I'd experienced supernatural speed. I should have been ready. But after the warning I'd given, I hadn't expected her to attack. Since I *had* warned her, I felt completely justified in taking my next action.

I called up Fire from deep within the Earth's crust, feeling the energy slide into my feet in that freaky way that I'd never adjusted to. With intent to maim, I shot a small flame sphere from my back-turned fingertips while simultaneously hitting the leech with a gust of Air meant to dislodge her grip.

Years of practice had gone into my ability to pull on multiple elements at the same time. I had Trip to thank for it. Not because he'd helped me, but because his taunting me as a small child had prompted me to learn how to fight back against a larger, stronger foe any way I could.

The female shrieked and flailed as her costly cocktail dress went up in flame like the overpriced polyester it probably was. She danced around the room screeching like a harpy. The concept of stop, drop, and roll must have been invented after her time.

Two men entered the room following her initial shout. The first had seemingly appeared out of thin air, I assumed because he'd used supernatural speed to arrive. I recognized him as being the ginger-haired jerkwad who had punched me in the head. His arms stretched in front of his torso while he gaped at the flaming figure—palms opening and closing helplessly. Horror crinkled his freckled features in an unattractive fashion.

The second male simply stood within the doorway to the golden-lit room, watching the scene with a nearly impassive expression. Only his dark, flat eyebrows had lifted in surprise. This must be Max.

The female's shrieking continued with no help from the first asshole. The second male gestured a set of fine fingers at the woman as though directing someone to do something. Exasperation was clear in his voice when he finally spoke. "Don't just stand there numbly. Put her out."

The other guy made a strangled sound while the temperature rose several degrees. "But it's fire!"

"Oh, for crying out loud," I said in disgust at their poor showing.

Though it was an exceedingly bad idea to get involved after Ms. Thang's homicidal attitude, I willed the Air out of the fire coating her. Orange flame immediately faded to red embers that soon went dark. Smoke billowed around the once beautiful woman who continued flailing like a crazed lunatic beneath the pull of the moon.

I examined the damage from the comparative safety of feet away. Her dress was nonexistent. The front half of Ms. Thang's hair was reduced to a few charred clumps sticking up from her skull, and her once beautiful tan skin was sickly red. At least it wasn't black.

Her shrieks continued despite the lack of fire. She windmilled around the room, knocking over knick-knacks every four feet. Then she froze in place and dropped to the floor like a paper cutout of a person.

"Take her to bed."

Max's resonant voice held an unflustered tone—strange considering his woman had recently been on fire.

I cast a glance his way, discovering a pair of deep-set milk chocolate colored eyes fixed on me. My cheeks flushed with warmth.

"I did warn her," I said in defense of the accusation he would soon hurl.

He inhaled a quick breath. I didn't know what that meant, and I didn't want to find out.

"The warning goes for any vampire," I said. "Get your fangs near me, and I won't go as easy on you as I did on her."

"I'm not going to eat you for dinner," the vampire said in his same steady tone. "Like many of my contemporaries, I prefer willing donors."

Looking like a menswear catalogue model in the flesh, I didn't doubt he'd easily find willing donors. Menswear catalogue? No, he was probably the inspiration for an entire line of sportswear.

I couldn't seem to look away from the firm, classical body clothed in a button-up charcoal dress shirt. The garment had been unbuttoned halfway down revealing smooth olive sienna skin with only a thin coating of the dark hair he sported elsewhere.

His sable mane was short, kept in a tousled and slightly spiked style. A lock hung down over the narrow forehead crowning his diamond-shaped face giving him a rather regal, Augustus Caesar look. Dusky pink lips, both wide and full, held no hint of mirth or misery with the situation.

"I'm not willing," I said for the record even though I'd have given it up after one drink and one dance if he'd been a human I'd met at a bar. "Are you going to try to kill me for hurting your wife?"

"Lover," he said, correcting me. "No. You did warn her."

My lips threatened to quirk. I hadn't expected that answer.

"I am Maximo de Sole." His hand stretched out though he hadn't moved closer.

He expected me to shake? I'd have to close the eight feet to him to set my palm in his. No way was I getting that close.

"Pardon me if I don't shake your hand," I said without explaining why I didn't want to touch him. By way of an introduction, I said, "Kora Walsh."

"The human?" His eyebrows lifted again. I wasn't sure my name receiving the same reaction his flaming "lover" had gained was a good thing.

I nodded rather than lie. I was technically only *half* human.

Max's eyes dropped to my hand for no apparent reason. I followed his gaze, flushing when I noted the ring my mother had given me still hugging my finger.

"Desmond Marino believes you're using weaves."

Though his tone was neutral, there was a definite accusation implied. The sight of the ring must have triggered it. Desmond Marino was apparently "in" with the vampires as well as the coalition. That probably wasn't a good sign.

The vampire let the silence stretch on for a pregnant pause. "Are you?"

I slowly shook my head—a motion meant to illustrate my disgust. "I just graduated from graduate school. I can't afford one weave, let alone the two I would have needed just now."

"Two?"

I lifted my fingers to count them as I spoke. "One for the fire and another to put it out."

Max's head tilted to the right while the beginnings of a real expression formed on his face. Those milk chocolate eyes rounded slightly, and his lips parted. "You put it out?"

"Uh, yeah." I barely resisted the urge to snort. "Fire doesn't miraculously go out that quickly without help. Especially not when it's being given air by flapping arms."

"She threatened to eat you for dinner," Max said as if I'd forgotten that part. "She'd have made good on her threat. Why would you voluntarily help her?"

I lifted my shoulders in a flippant shrug. "I don't know. It seemed like the right thing to do."

A wrinkle between his eyes grew more pronounced the deeper his stare got. "Why didn't you go harder on her?"

A nervous laugh escaped me. "Did you want me to kill her?"

Rather than answer my question, he pressed with another of his own. "You warned her. Ascencion dismissed you as a threat. You were well within your right to enact the punishment you'd promised. Why didn't you?"

I held up my palms in a sign of surrender. "Look, I don't want to get tangled up in whatever screwed up relationship the two of you have, so how about you point me in the direction of the door out of here instead?"

"Answer my question, and I'll have someone drive you home."

I drew in a ticked off sigh. Then I gave him his answer. "I don't kill people, Mr. de Sole."

He inhaled another quick breath. His lips lifted at the corners in what looked like a disturbingly indulgent smile. After staring at me silently for a pair of seconds, he called out, "Jacob, take Miss Walsh home." Once the asshole red-haired vampire appeared, Max said, "And apologize for knocking her unconscious."

The glower the demand earned him from the ginger jerkwad almost made admitting I wasn't a killer to the ultimate of predators worth it. Almost.

Chapter Seven

The prickling of the hair on the back of my neck went ignored as I scooped at the caramel pudding hiding in the crevice of the snack cup. Nearly one in the morning was far too late for me to be eating sweets, but I was wired. I'd be awake for half the night without sugar, and it had everything to do with narrowly escaping death by vampire.

Again the fine hairs at the nape of my neck tingled. I hopped up from my futon and headed into the kitchen. The empty pudding cup—a left-over from my store of snacks for the moving trip—was an excuse to get near my purse on the breakfast bar. After tossing the cup in the plastic shopping bag that served as my trash bin, I rummaged in my black vinyl purse until my fingers circled the penlight I'd hidden in the inner pocket.

This would have to be done carefully. I only had one chance to catch Trip before he'd discover the existence of my new toy.

I quickly lifted my hand out of the purse with a grunt—the implication that I'd been unable to find what I'd rummaged for. Then I dropped my arm to my side where he wouldn't see the narrow metal tube behind the counter as I faced the living room.

Now, if I were a creepy peeping Tom watching me, where would I be?

I'd been sitting on the futon seconds ago. He would have been somewhere in front of me. But had he moved now that I was in the kitchen? How disturbing would it be if I flashed the light to find him inches from my face? I restrained a shudder.

I'd go back to the futon because there were only so many places he could stand in front of me if I were there. In an effort to keep it hidden, I pushed the penlight firmly between my jean skirt and my palm, ignoring the sweat breaking out within it.

The prickle of my hair repeated when my back was turned to the front door. I hoped to Hades the tingling wasn't an indicator he'd tried to touch me. This time I wasn't able to restrain my shudder at that thought.

Once settled back on the futon, I lifted my business plan back into my lap with my left hand while the right remained smashed to my thigh atop the penlight. I curled my legs beneath me in one of my usual poses. He'd know something was up if I sat stiff and alert.

Mentally I worked out the optimal location for him to stand while pretending to read the words on the page. He'd be near the front door, most likely between it and the window to the right. That spot was the best vantage point.

I took a stealthy breath, steeling myself for the visuals I was about to see with or without Trip's presence, and then I clicked the button on the penlight. Quicker than I thought possible with purely human reflexes, I shone the light on the wall between the front door and the window.

There he stood, watching me with an intensely focused gaze and thinned, almost brooding lips. He was clad in what looked like relaxed jeans and a black turtleneck. A lock of his surfer boy hair curled within the collar coiled around his tan neck like a pet boa constrictor. Fleetingly I wondered if it were as soft now as it had been fifteen years ago. Then I realized he was *here,* spying on me like a first class creep.

"Trip!" I jumped to my knees atop the futon. "Bacchus's balls! I *knew* it!"

Trip stood stunned beneath the narrow beam of light. His frozen state gave me long enough to wave my hand in a broad gesture in front of me and whisper,

"Psukhē aisthesthai." Everything in the Spirit Realm became visible for the entire room.

There weren't any recently deceased spirits in sight, probably because the building was a few years old. Plenty of amorphous blobs of energy hovered over the futon. No doubt they were drawn to me because I could wield Death magic. Nevertheless, I disliked having the visual of the shapeless, insentient beings crowding me.

I glared at Trip. "I knew you've been spying on me in the Spirit Realm, you creepy kerkopes!"

Trip's shock quickly faded into ire. He despised it when I compared him to the monkey-men thieves. His frame drew up to his full height of what looked to be at least six feet two. I didn't know how tall he was anymore. He'd been fourteen when I'd left the Underworld. And the Spirit Realm distorted images.

"I was checking up to see if you were working on Catey's task," he said with a feigned indignant tone and the expression to match. But even Trip's indignant expression looked wicked. It had something to do with the glint in his eye.

"Your check-ups are Wednesday nights. Get the Hades out of my place!"

My shout went ignored so he could adopt his smuggest of tones. "You weren't working on Catey's task. You were working on building your new business."

"Humans have bills. I'll need a wage if I plan to stay in Wipuk for any length of time. No one in this colony will hire a human. That means I have to fund myself. And I only have six months to do it before my bills— Why the Styx am I defending myself? Get out!"

His face contorted into a twist of dark features. "You're lucky I can't touch you!" A split second later he was gone.

I flicked the penlight off and whispered the reverse words so I wouldn't have to see the hovering blobs. But my mind wasn't on them. It was on his parting words.

Yes, I was supremely lucky Trip couldn't touch me because I had absolutely no idea what he'd do if he could. He'd broken, bruised, slashed, and generally wounded me plenty using brute strength when we were kids. Now that he had a few of his divine powers, he'd be truly dangerous. But would Trip still punch and claw me now that he was twenty-nine?

I truly hoped his father didn't intend to retire during my lifetime because I never wanted to find out the answer to that question.

****

"Six hundred square feet." The woman's tight blonde curls shook slightly during her perusal of the space. Her lisp drew a cringe from me each time she opened her mouth. The habit was more pronounced when she was excited like now. "Utilities, rent tax of three percent, and common area expense are included in the monthly rent figure of eight hundred and ninety dollars a month. It's a prime location for tourists."

She was lying. The location was abysmal. The property wasn't off the main drag through Sedona, or even the roads leading to the vortices. Surrounded by cacti and overgrown weeds, it was in the middle of nowhere. And not even the picturesque nowhere. But what lisping Anne Hardwick didn't know was the shop straddled the line between Sedona and Wipuk. That made it the ideal spot for *my* venture.

I'd run across the curiously abandoned two-story adobe building while out mapping Wipuk's edges. The trip had been a joint effort to improve my research of the witches' colony and look for a retail spot. I'd struck gold because the sign out front claimed the "single-story building" had been zoned for commercial use. That meant the second story was in Wipuk—hidden from humans.

"Does the rent go up if the utility bills spike in the winter or summer?" I asked so I wouldn't seem as eager as I was.

I'd called the phone number listed on the sign outside and asked them to show me their available retail space, but this was the only one I had any interest renting. Lisping Anne had already brought me by two storefronts located in strip malls within the populated areas, not that Sedona was particularly populated. Still, there were places businesses could survive. This wasn't one of them. I hoped she'd make me a better offer than the nearly nine hundred a month they were asking.

"No," Anne said. "Spikes have been taken into account when figuring the monthly rate."

"The structure looks questionable. The interior needs work. It smells of mold." I drew in a hissing breath, gesturing up toward the black dots lining one side of the ceiling seam. "There's some right there."

Anne followed my gaze. Her brow knit, and her lips wobbled queasily upon spotting the mold. "We can knock a hundred dollars off the monthly rate if you'll take care of cleaning the interior. I'll have someone come out to make sure the structure is sound and the mold isn't indicative of a larger problem."

Seven hundred and ninety dollars was still too much. I stared out the bank of dust-coated windows toward the two-lane road that passed out front. "I do think it's charming, and there's a good energy here," I said for good measure. The whole vortexes and good energy thing was just a bunch of new age nonsense. She did need to know I had a passing interest in the space before I hit her with the kicker. "But I haven't seen a single car pass by since we pulled into the lot." I started toward the door, shaking my head in dismay.

"You'd get more traffic during the morning and evening commutes," she called after me. Footsteps padded along the dull carpet in her hurry to catch up.

"That would be locals," I said, turning and slowing so she'd see the disappointment creasing my features. "Are locals going to want to visit yet another crystal shop?"

"They might…"

I fixed my cool grey eyes on hers. "They didn't visit the last four that tried to set up shop here in the past three years."

The woman's skin faded to a sick green pallor. Apparently she hadn't expected a twenty-five-year-old girl with cerulean hair to have done her homework.

"Two hundred off if you clean the interior yourself," the woman said.

"The locals also failed to visit the dress shop, computer repair store, or even the Goodwill that tried to make a go of this location." I tilted my head up and to the left, eyeing the moldy spot on the ceiling while giving the impression I was deep in thought. "Didn't we pass the Goodwill's new location on the way here? It was busy for ten in the morning."

I caught Anne's souring expression when she realized I'd been playing with her since I called. Her voice hardened and lost its lisp. "Four hundred is the lowest we can go on this property and still pay our bills."

"Deal." I extended my hand toward her.

She didn't take it. Instead, she brushed past me on the way to the door. "We can do the paperwork at the office *after* I do a credit check."

I grinned at her back. She thought I'd fail the check. Apart from the student loans, my credit was exceptional. No doubt my unconventional look colored her opinion.

Today I'd worn black fishnet tights beneath my faded short jean skirt and Doc Martens. The orange blouse covering my narrow torso was stain-free thanks to the plain piece of bread I'd had for breakfast. There'd have been a spot of purple if I'd slathered it in grape jelly like I'd craved. But I'd yet to get out to buy groceries. The end result was a nicer outfit than usual—perfect for shopping for retail space. Clearly it wasn't perfect in lisping Anne's eyes.

Anne's pantsuit reminded me of the early morning visitor I'd received at the apartment. A brunette in a beige asymmetrical cut pantsuit, smelling of a rare Arizona wetland beneath a coating of rosewater, had knocked on my door. I'd deduced she was Desmond the dick's assistant long before she'd handed me an envelope with his name and address printed in the upper left hand corner. She'd said nothing before turning her model-thin body and hurrying back to her car.

The envelope's history had been boring—from the assistant's pushing the letter inside the pebbled paper to the trip over on her passenger seat. The letter inside, however, wasn't boring at all.

According to the neatly printed serif font, the Centralized Coven Coalition had granted me dispensation to live in Wipuk indefinitely. There'd been no mention of a probationary period of a year. A single line toward the bottom of the letter had explained the change. Listed in the space labeled "responsible faction" had been the name "Maximo de Sole".

I hadn't considered it too deeply. If the vampire wanted to claim me as his responsibility as an apology for his girlfriend kidnapping and trying to eat me, then who was I to argue?

Rather than wait until dusk to march over to his place—a stately Spanish Colonial styled villa—I'd decided to begin work on the details for my business in earnest. The vampire would eventually call in his favor. I'd find a way around owing him something when the time came.

Until then, I'd work on bringing in regular income before my loan payments kicked in. That would definitely keep me busy for the foreseeable future.

Chapter Eight

I hummed my way through the Flagstaff Target's aisles, picking up mops, brooms, and the occasional lamp as dancing partners. Shoppers steered clear of my gleeful twirls, hiding their children from who they assumed was a crazy person escaped from the loony bin. I didn't care. I was far too happy to worry about the opinions of vanilla humans.

I had the keys to the new shop.

I was one step closer to being a business owner. Now I only had to clean up the interior, come up with shelving, and order a sign. I already knew what the store name would be, had known since I was thirteen: *Rarities*. Short. Sweet. And mysterious.

Hopefully the name was mysterious enough to lure people in the door. Then I'd interest them in the collection of rare books, charms, and divine items I'd amassed over the past fifteen years. What I couldn't sell in the store, I'd sell on-line through a website I'd pay someone to develop. The combination would be enough to cover my bills.

My shopping cart quickly filled with cleaning supplies for both the shop and my apartment. I winced with each new addition. This would hurt my savings account.

The furniture aisles snagged my focus for several minutes. There was a beautiful glass and black metal television stand that would have looked nice in my apartment … provided I'd had a television to set on it. Perhaps in a few months the shop would make enough for me to pull a wage. Then I'd get a television. In the meantime I'd have to continue watching DVDs on my laptop.

I ran my fingers over the interior of a set of oak veneer bookshelves, receiving only a small murmur of memories. A knock of my knuckles against the back portion gave off a small, barely perceptible thud against the material. Cardboard backing. This craftsmanship left much to be desired. Some of my items had sharp edges. I needed something sturdier all around or no backing at all.

I did the math in my head for parts and labor to have shelving created by hand. Had I been back in California where I had access to the artists in the university's woodworking department it would have been far cheaper. But this was home now.

Sighing, I moved the two feet to knock the interior of the next set of shelves.

"There is an unfinished wood store not far from here." A deep male voice interrupted my movement to a third set of shelves. "Their workmanship is superior to this pressboard. Your wallet might not thank you, but your books certainly will."

The wording caught my attention. Few contractions, an easy pace that made each syllable intelligible despite his slight European accent, and he'd used the word "superior". That was a sexy word when used properly.

I turned, prepared to find a skinny, college-aged nerd with coke bottle glasses eyeing me. What I found instead was the complete opposite. With his straight mahogany hair hanging carelessly around his handsome face and rich olive-hued skin, he looked an awful lot like the Israeli guy who had starred in one of the zombie films I'd seen in high school—the Israeli guy I'd drooled over for months. I even liked the scruff of a few days' worth of unshaved hair coating his face.

That facial hair combined with the shoulder-length mane should have brought Trip to mind. It didn't.

This guy was far too foreign in appearance for me to even compare the two. It helped that the stranger had an earnest expression on his face that would have been alien on Trip's.

He cleared his throat, tugging at the hem of his white ribbed T-shirt almost nervously. My perusal took all of a second, perhaps too long, because he felt the need to speak again.

"Unless you were looking for inexpensive?"

While he spoke I lifted my eyes to his face, noting his brilliantly white teeth. The color just wasn't normal for a human unless some sort of cosmetic whitener had been involved. The only people who paid for those treatments were actors and models. Maybe he *was* an actor.

"I'm sorry." His shoulders dropped slightly as his cheeks grew rosy. The motion sent a breeze of heady cologne into my nose. "You probably think I'm some sort of creep."

A creep who looked like a movie star but behaved like a bashful schoolboy? Not likely. Had Mr. Movie Star been deposited on the Mortal Realm days ago? That was the only explanation I could come up with for how someone as gorgeous as he was would suffer from nervousness.

The combination of good looks and possessing a shy attitude, yet having the balls to strike up a conversation with a complete stranger in a store, made this man the sexiest guy on Earth. So could I get Mr. Movie Star into my car and back to his place before Trip intervened? More importantly, did I want to? I had a fresh start in Arizona. Was this how I wanted to begin?

My lips softened into a smile meant to put him at ease. "I don't think you're a creep. I was just thinking about trying to find someone to build me shelves. Your suggestion is an intelligent compromise."

His handsome face burst into a smile that would probably be visible in a lightless room. Despite its blinding appearance, he looked wonderful when he was happy. I definitely wanted to get him in bed. Or on top of a counter.

He stretched out a hand of strong, tan fingers toward me. "Eamonn Cary."

A handshake seemed terribly formal given we were in the middle of a big box store. Nonetheless, I reached out and took his hand. A shot of energy spiked up my arm, over my shoulder, and down into the seed beneath my heart where I kept latent energy for emergencies. My gaze shot up in time to see the widening of his eyes.

I drew in a breath, taking in the hint of a moonlit glen and belladonna. Dark witch? It was hard to tell with all that cologne covering it. And I'd only met one Dark witch. She'd smelled of belladonna and a musty cellar. This flavor of witch was rare, at least in the United States.

He ducked his head close to mine, features pinching in confusion. No doubt he wanted to ask me what had happened when our hands touched. Accidental discharges of latent energy weren't uncommon when a witch brushed my skin. If I'd known he was a witch, I wouldn't have touched him, or I'd have prepared myself for it.

Eamonn's attention darted around the aisle before he lowered his head closer. We were now a mere half a foot apart. Wintergreen mingled with the other scents. I found the scent nice, just like the rest of him.

"I don't want to be rude," he said quietly, "But I have to ask. What are you?"

I glanced around just as he had, making sure no one could eavesdrop on my whispered answer. "Sorceress."

The Dark witch's heels snapped against the linoleum floor. His head jerked, and then he spoke at a cautious pace. "Rebecca Kora Walsh?"

There were only two explanations for why he'd know my full name. Either he was a member of the Centralized Coven Coalition that had received my application for admittance, or Desmond Marino had a larger mouth than I thought. I was betting on the latter.

"I go by Kora."

"But it *is* you?"

I nodded for him. "Yeah."

Eamonn's profile tilted to the left as if he'd see a different part of me from that angle, perhaps a part more magical. "I thought you'd be…"

I lifted an eyebrow, truly interested in what he'd thought I'd be.

"Older," he said.

A ripple of laughter escaped me. "Older? I didn't expect that answer."

The Dark witch glanced around before speaking in a soft volume again. "Desmond did say you had blue hair. I assumed he meant you were a little old lady."

Talk of Desmond made me give an unladylike grunt. "I should have guessed."

"But that isn't blue at all." And then Eamonn made me fall head over heels in love with him when he added, "It's cerulean."

I must have looked frightening with stars in my eyes because he took a step back, and then adopted an uneasy tone. "Did I say something wrong?"

"*No*." I waved my fingers in emphasis of how much I meant the word. "My hair *is* cerulean. No one ever gets that."

His lips spread into a larger smile. "I know colors."

I was willing to bet hard cash the guy's closet was organized like the spectrum of light. A fleeting urge to ask him to show it to me passed through my head. And then the equally fleeting wish that I could ask him to dinner so I could make a legitimate attempt at a relationship popped in before I immediately squashed it.

Trip had ruined every relationship I'd ever tried with a male. And the one time I'd gotten drunk, indignant, and curious enough to try a female, Trip had scared the girl so badly she'd withdrawn from Berkeley and gone back to Oklahoma within forty-eight hours. He wanted me to be miserable and tormented even when he wasn't around to taunt me.

But oh, how much I wanted this gorgeous man who knew the exact hue of my hair without being told. The only way I could have him was to cling to him until the act was over. And the only way I could do that without him thinking I was crazy was to behave like a nymphomaniac. There had to be middle ground.

"This is going to sound forward," I said softly, not because I didn't want the people in the nearby aisles to overhear but because it bothered me to say it. "But would you like to take me to that furniture place?"

Eamonn's deep-set dark eyes rounded until flecks of amber and black were visible within their mahogany depths. His mauve lips parted in surprise, revealing a slack jaw of lovely teeth. He said nothing for an uncomfortable interval. My cheeks flushed crimson.

"I'm sorry," I whispered while turning back to my cart so I wouldn't have to see the disgust grow in his eyes.

He was probably engaged, in a committed relationship, or gay, and here I was practically throwing myself at him. I'd at least checked his finger for a wedding ring, but the lack of one didn't mean much these days.

"I'd love to take you up on that offer, but I'm in town for a dinner meeting in a half hour," Eamonn said with a soft manner that hinted at genuine regret. "Perhaps you'll give me a rain check?"

"Rain check," I said woodenly without looking at him. I'd basically propositioned him in the middle of Target for nothing. "Sure."

It was a brush off. Even if he hadn't meant it as one, Trip would ensure it was. I reacted accordingly, pushing my cart down the aisle toward the linens across the main aisle. Anything to avoid the mortifying reminder of what I'd been reduced to.

"Uh," Eamonn said close on my heels. "Can I get your phone number?"

With as much false enthusiasm as I could muster, I rattled off the digits, avoiding his eyes in the process. Fast fingers moved in my peripheral vision. He was entering me into his phone? How many entries filled his address book? It had to be hundreds if he added everyone who ever asked him out.

He pocketed the phone, drawing a card from the other pocket. And then he scribbled atop the gray card stock.

"Here—the name of the unfinished furniture store if you decide not to wait for me." After a beat he said, "And my numbers are on the other side."

Like I'd ever call him.

"Thanks," I muttered. "Good luck with your business meeting."

Eamonn took it as the invitation to leave that it was, calling out on his way past me, "Thank you. Good luck with your shelving."

I released a small, dismayed sigh at the sight of his trim tush walking out of my life.

Chapter Nine

I was sweaty, stinky, and coated in tiny droplets of macchiato colored paint that would probably take days to scrub off my skin. The mess was worth my effort because the shop's first floor interior now looked warm and inviting with a hint of sugar. My stomach had been growling for the past four hours, but I'd wanted to get the last coat of paint on the walls before I called it a night.

I'd had no idea what time it was until Trip appeared in the room. I'd leaned down to bang the top of the paint clan closed and caught his jean and white T-shirt clad figure out of the corner of my eye.

It must be eleven thirty. Where had the time gone? If I hadn't been bone tired, I might have considered using the bracelet my mother had given me so I could get a few more things accomplished.

Standing to my full height, I leveled an impatient eye on Trip. I wasn't going to give him the information he'd come for until he asked.

"What have you to report to your mother?" He slouched against a slick wall and examined his cuticles, looking for all the world bored with the task given him.

"I've met two witches. Desmond Marino—a Water witch who acts like he has access to the inner circle. And Eamonn Cary—a Dark witch who at least knows Desmond." I squelched a small sigh for my failed one-night stand. "I've also met a vampire who claimed me under his faction, enabling me to stay in Wipuk despite Desmond's complaints. I'm not sure what that means, but I'm not going to call over there to find out."

"You're not working on your mother's plan." His voice went acidic. "You're too busy flirting and getting your precious shop off the ground." Trip's derisive gaze scanned over the newly coated walls.

He was trying to get a rise out of me, and while it had worked to some degree, I could do him one better. I formed my lips into my best sneer. "You're serving as my mother's messenger, not her warrior."

"You really *are* your mother's daughter." He mimed the shoving gesture that was an insult in the Underworld. Its meaning was clear: "*to Tartarus with you*". After a darker glower, he disappeared back to his little hole in Hades.

I'd have been insulted if I didn't admire my mother despite all of her quirks, demanding nature, and unpredictable mood swings. She was a feared goddess, yes, with good reason. But I'd spent the first ten years of my life living in her home, eating only the food she gave me like a mama bird providing for her chicks.

Now I understood her refusal to let me partake in any of the feasts hadn't been a parent's miserly attitude but instead her protection. I'd have been stuck in the Underworld if I'd eaten anything but what she'd given me, exactly as my godmother had been.

My decade in the Underworld, as horrific as it sometimes had been, had created an unbreakable bond between us that I would cherish forever. Rather like my fifteen years topside had prepared me for what I was about to do.

So Trip be damned. I didn't mind being my mother's daughter.

I would infiltrate the coalition of covens. And then I would make the magical community accountable for their actions. Someone had to take them to task for their many offenses against nature and mankind.

Who better than the daughter of the goddess of magic?

****

I didn't recognize the number displayed on my mobile phone's screen. The digits were an Arizona number, that much I knew. Was it lisping Anne calling to tell me to bring the keys to the shop back?

No, I had a lease. They couldn't do that.

Or was the Wipuk leasing agent—the guy who had told me the shop was solely owned by the humans despite having an upper floor in Wipuk—calling to tell me he'd been wrong?

I took in a deep breath to soothe the knotting in my stomach, and then pressed the button to accept the call. "Hi?"

"Kora?"

It was a deep, slightly accented male voice, possibly European. I'd only met one person who fit that description. Eamonn Cary—drool-worthy man-meat. Was he in need of a set of buns? I winced at my own stupid innuendo, immensely glad he couldn't see my expression. I wouldn't have wanted to explain it.

I'd play it cool, pretend I hadn't recognized the sound of his voice after only one meeting. "Yes?"

"This is Eamonn Cary."

I liked how he spoke his own name. The specific syllables he formed made him sound smooth and warm like a Rastafarian, but the slight accent gave him European sophistication. The image of him standing in front of me in the aisle at Target flashed in my head. Saliva glands kicked into overdrive.

Desperately I maintained my cool. "Yes?"

"We met at Target on Tuesday?"

It was Thursday evening. When I hadn't heard from him on Wednesday, I'd assumed Trip had worked him over, and my phone number had been burnt in fear that simply having the digits would enable me to target him. It was what had happened with every other male who had taken my phone number. So why was this male different?

"Oh, the creep," I said playfully. Sometimes I really *was* my mother's daughter.

There was no noise on the other end of the line for a full three seconds.

What was I doing trying to play it cool? I'd practically *propositioned* the guy. He already knew I was desperate for human contact. Who was I to insult him?

Eamonn cleared his throat—an almost nervous sound. "You gave me your phone number."

I had, knowing full well he'd never use it. But here we were, two days later, and he'd called me.

Two days later. What was Trip's game this time? Was he going to let me fall in love with the guy before he pulled the rug out from under me?

"I did," I said despite my thoughts being mixed up elsewhere.

"I know that it is last minute…"

Was he going to ask me to use my psychometry power to give him the complete history on a family heirloom, in writing, by midnight? Why else would he be calling me if not to ask a favor?

His deep voice continued. "But I'd like to take you up on that rain check for tomorrow evening if you are free."

Rain check? What rain check?

Oh, dear Zeus! He couldn't possibly … no, Eamonn wasn't asking me out on a date. That sort of thing simply didn't happen to me.

I held my breath, fearful of interrupting him. I needed to know if he intended to take me to the unfinished furniture store sans complications, or if he'd invited me on an honest to Hera date. And I wouldn't find out if I prodded him.

"I'm free," I said in as neutral a tone as I could muster, and then waited to see what else he'd say.

"Six?"

The drive to Flagstaff from Sedona would take a half hour. If the store closed at nine, we'd have plenty of time to shop.

"That works," I said.

"Do you eat seafood? There is a nice restaurant in Flagstaff."

He wanted to take me to a nice restaurant. It *was* a date! I reined in my pleasure, so the only thing that came out of my mouth was a calm, "I eat seafood."

"Then I will see you tomorrow at your apartment at six. Have a good evening, Kora."

The mention of my apartment threw me so much that I didn't respond to his parting words before the phone clicked off. He knew I lived in an apartment *and* where it was without asking. Desmond was blabbing way more of my business than he had any right sharing. Maybe it was time I paid him a visit so I could find out exactly who in Hades he thought he was.

Monday. I'd do it Monday after my date so he wouldn't have a chance to ruin it.

My shoulders slumped. It was pointless to get my hopes up. Avoiding Desmond until Monday wasn't going to help. Trip would get involved now that an actual date had been set. But it had been a nice few minutes' dream.

Chapter Ten

The open office door was mere feet away. All I had to do was get past the glaring assistant. Her palms were already flat against her desk's cherry surface as though she'd stand.

"I'm sure he'll want to see me," I said as I darted toward the opening.

. She beat me there, blocking my progress with her rosewater-scented figure. Desmond Marino's smooth cadence rose and fell behind her as he spoke about the moon cycle. His frame faced away, and his hands were clasped at the small of his back.

There was a barely perceptible stiffening of his body. He was aware of what was happening behind him despite the Bluetooth headset curled around his left ear.

The scent of brine rose in the room. A faint tickle brushed my consciousness. My eyes narrowed into angry lines. The dick's assistant was trying to manipulate me.

I lowered my volume so her boss wouldn't hear my warning. "I wouldn't suggest trying that on me."

She tossed her perfectly plaited hair over one narrow shoulder. "Trying what?" The water scent faded, and the tickling ceased despite her bewildered act.

I could play perplexed as well as the next girl. And it would keep the questions of why I was able to sense Water magic to a minimum. Desmond the dick appeared behind his assistant a split second before I launched into my stupid-girl-act. My jaw clamped down on the words I'd intended to say.

His fleshy lips were pressed together in neither a smile nor a frown while his gaze tracked something on her neck. The pose they had—his thighs so close they might have been touching her tush—spoke volumes about their relationship. As did his feather soft words in her ear. "Thank you, Allison. I will take it from here."

The pink flushing of her skin to match her linen suit and the fluttering of her eyelids told me the rest. There was definite sexual attraction between these two and probably a sordid history to boot.

The pretty woman nodded briefly before returning to her desk—a smooth cherry surface covered with neat piles of papers, envelopes and sticky notes. When I brought my attention forward it was to find Desmond watching me through a pair of bright aqua irises. His blank expression told me nothing but that he'd caught me eyeing his assistant's orderly desk.

"I am very busy, Ms. Walsh," he said brusquely before I could open my mouth. He reached down, brushing imaginary lint off his tan seersucker sports coat—a garment that was expertly cut to hang cleanly from his fit body. "What do you want?"

I didn't like him about as much as he didn't like me. Nonetheless I forced myself to adopt a soft smile. It wasn't a stretch considering he was really quite a beautiful man.

"A few short minutes of your time," I said.

"A minute is a finite amount of time that can neither be long nor short."

I allowed myself a light laugh. I could keep up the act that I was an airhead, but debating with him would be far more fun.

"Indeed," I said. "But it is the perception of those sixty seconds that makes all the difference."

The dick's eyes widened slightly, a marker, perhaps, that he was surprised my vocabulary contained a word like "perception".

Thoroughly invested in destroying my dumb act forever, I went on. "Take, for example, the sixty seconds spent in a lover's arms. It will feel as fleeting as the blink of the eye. While sixty seconds spent debating with a nemesis can seem to stretch on for an age."

I couldn't be sure, because I'd timed my blink incorrectly, but his gaze might have darted to my orange T-shirt's bust line when I'd mentioned a lover's arms. Men's ability to separate their feelings from their urges was astonishing.

His dark eyebrows lifted mockingly. "You have many nemeses that you know this from experience?"

Maybe he'd see the twinkle in my eye—the indication he would quickly join the ranks of Trip if he continued as he had. "Everyone has someone who really presses their buttons."

Desmond's full lips curved ever so slightly upward. "You said you wanted a few short minutes. Did you plan to take me in your arms to alter my perception, Ms. Walsh?"

A sharp noise from Allison's desk threatened to draw my attention. I couldn't look, not with a threat like Desmond standing within a few feet.

"We've wasted a few minutes debating my few short minutes," I said.

The dick's flat eyebrows pinched slightly. "Would you like something to drink? Coffee, tea?" Desmond gestured for Allison to get up.

I'd had a tall latte with extra cream a half hour ago, but getting another drink here might help me in the long run. It would certainly give me an excuse to linger longer than a few minutes. I might need the delay.

I gave him my beatific smile. "Coffee would be great. Thanks."

Desmond gestured for me to precede him. I cocked my head to the right as if in confusion despite knowing exactly what he was doing. He was trying to keep me out of his office. But that was exactly where I wanted to go.

"We'll be more comfortable in the lounge," he said while walking the few steps forward until he was flush with my shoulder.

"Oh!" I set my hand to my chest, feigning breathlessness. Then I used my angular figure to slip past him into his office before he could stop me. "Look at this view! You can see all of Wipuk from here. It's so beautiful."

Because Wipuk looked exactly like Sedona but with a gentle shimmer on the far edges, the view was indeed beautiful with its stratified rock formations and desert flora. I slumped into the first leather chair in front of Desmond's desk before he could come up with an excuse to drag me away. He puffed out an irritated breath at the door, and then moved toward the desk. It took a mere second for him to cross to the mesh task chair, body stiff with irritation. I shot him another of my beatific smiles to make up for his effort.

He carefully settled himself onto his chair with his back flush against the black nylon. At a maddeningly sedate pace, he fixed the cuffs on his coat, and then set steepled hands atop the desk. Desmond's gaze lowered into the hooded expression he'd used on me the very first day. Was the look meant to intimidate me? He had nothing on Hades.

"Posh office." I gestured a single finger around the room as if he'd needed the reminder of which office I referenced. He didn't, of course, but maybe the dismissive motion would tick him off. "Beautiful natural woods, hand-made carpets, and real leather."

Real leather that had held onto the history of everyone who had ever sat in it. I filtered through the initial images the chair shared of a spastic, frizzy-haired man jabbering on about monthly dues from earlier this morning and the witch who had been called on the carpet about a domestic dispute before that. None of this was what I was looking for.

"Much of Wipuk's inhabitants prefer natural materials," he said tightly, eyes darting toward the door probably in search of his assistant and my coffee.

I spoke at a slow pace because my chair's night had been cold, quiet, and tediously long. "I wanted to thank you for the letter you sent. You did send the letter on behalf of the coalition, didn't you?"

"Yes," Desmond said.

"Do you do all of their clerical work?"

He lifted his chin. "I'm not their secretary. They look to me for guidance."

I loved it when pride made people tell me things they would have otherwise kept quiet. "The Water witches?"

"You are fishing for information in dangerous waters, Ms. Walsh," he said warningly. His aqua eyes hooded yet further without fully closing.

Oh, marine puns from a Water witch. Despite how cliché it was, I found myself stifling a smile.

If he'd resorted to blunt declarations, I'd return the favor. "I want to know what gave you the right to knock on my door to demand I vacate Wipuk."

Desmond pulled his hands up to his mouth. The steeple obscured whatever expression those lips had held. I experienced a feather-soft brush against my consciousness, almost too subdued to note. But I *had* noted it.

Like his assistant, Desmond was trying to set up an empathic link to me. I'd allow it. This time.

"Why?" He'd switched back into his neutral tone now that he believed he had complete control over the situation.

"I like to know whose pool I'm peeing in."

His mouth might have twitched. But when he replied, it was with his same, professionally blank tone. "I am the high priest of Neptune's Fellowship."

Drown me in Cerberus's drool! The dick was the head over the entire country's Water witches? No wonder he acted like he owned the whole damn city!

My lips pressed into a thin, angry line I could no more stop than I could the stunned rounding of my eyes. How was I supposed to guess his position? He didn't look old enough to have experienced his first gray hair let alone have risen through the ranks of hundreds of priests to take the throne of power.

Our antagonistic relationship was going to cause me problems. Big, Hydra-sized problems.

Desmond leaned further into his chair, shifting his weight onto one hip while dropping his arms against the chair. He was working to hide his satisfaction, but I could see it glow on his face as surely as he could *feel* the emotions flowing through me. It was a good thing Water witches could only sense emotions but couldn't understand their origins.

"I see," I said.

There was no way in Hades I was going to kiss his ass now. Doing so would be disrespectful to us both.

Allison arrived with my coffee. The beverage came in a recycled paper cup with a ring of corrugated cardboard around it to keep my fingers from burning. They'd made sure I wouldn't be able to use the coffee as an excuse to stay.

I took a stealthy sniff of the liquid for anything suspicious. I didn't note poison—the few I'd come in contact with over the years. Allison set two containers of fake cream and two packets of sugar on the chair beside me. I ignored both despite those being the exact combination my mother preferred.

Desmond made a dismissive wave in his assistant's direction. Her smart pumps thudded on the low pile carpet in the opposite direction.

Maybe Desmond enjoyed our debate because rather than claim a tight schedule and suggest I leave with my coffee, he barely hid a smug smile. "Did I have a right to knock on your door and demand you vacate?"

"No."

Eyebrow arching, he echoed me with a lifting pitch. "No?"

"The coalition," of which he was a member, "responded to my inquiry with permission to move to Wipuk if I could find it. I found it."

We were rehashing an old argument. But he'd started it. Yes, I could be immature. I *was* a mere twenty-five years old.

"You failed to find it on your own. I don't know who helped you across or what weave you used, but I was within my right to banish you. Only your affiliation with de Sole has kept you here." He lifted two fingers toward the left portion of his office in a half-assed questioning gesture. "How did you manage that during your first week here, by the way?"

The guy was *unbelievable*. But there was no point arguing with a bigot. I lifted my shoulders flippantly. "Don't know. Don't care."

A combination of irritation and something I couldn't name pinched his lovely features. "He is a vampire. You understand this? You understand what it is to be claimed by one?"

"He didn't claim me," I said with a defiant lift of my chin.

Desmond let out an amused laugh. "You have no clue what you've gotten yourself into."

And that was *funny*? Zeus, what a dick!

The whole vampire topic was one I wanted to avoid. "I told you I didn't have help. I found Wipuk on my own. I've since mapped out its edges." I dropped into a baby voice meant to tick him off. "All by my widdle self." If the tightening around his eyes were any indication, then it had worked. "I'm a sorceress, not a human with a bunch of weaved items. I'd offer to have you search me." I paused for drama's sake. "But frankly I don't want you that close."

Plus I'd have to get naked to truly prove I wasn't using weaves. There was no chance in Hades I'd do that in front of *him*.

The chair's history stole my attention. Some time yesterday afternoon Eamonn had paid Desmond a visit. He'd sat in this very chair—strong, tan fingers holding onto the very arms I tightly gripped. I gently pushed Desmond's empathic link to the periphery so he'd get a low-level hum rather than the broadcast of my emotions.

My teeth clenched. They'd made a *bet* about me! The wager was whether or not my breasts were real or the result of a push-up bra … or worse—a weaved shirt. Should I be disgusted or pleased Eamonn had bet they were real?

Desmond leaned forward in his chair, reminding me of the present while I listened to the past. "If you ever have a falling out with de Sole," he said in an ominous tone to rival Trip's, "I'll make you prove your claims in front of the coalition. Then you'll wish you'd let me search you."

The chair replayed Eamonn writing down directions to my apartment yesterday in between a discussion of who would win the World Series. I urged it to go faster because Desmond stood from behind his desk in real time.

"Now I want you and your psychometry out of my office, Ms. Walsh." He jabbed his finger toward the door.

There was a push on the outer reaches of my consciousness. He was trying to manipulate me into going. He knew what I'd been doing in his chair.

Stubbornly I held out, waiting for Eamonn's visit to play out in the chair's past. Just as Desmond stepped around his desk with a promise of getting physical, Eamonn stood from the chair in the replay in my head. He'd stood in the middle of a comment about the weather. They'd clearly held part of their conversation outside of the room. And I couldn't stay to see if it picked up again.

Angry at my failure, I curled metaphorical fingers around Desmond's empathic link, drawing it back like a magical rubber band. And then I snapped it back at him. He flinched when the backlash hit.

I let my lips spread into a sneer to rival any Trip had shown me. "Next time you try to manipulate me with your magic, you're going to find out why the vampire claimed me."

With that threat uttered, I tossed the full cup of coffee into the copper waste bin beside his desk, and then sauntered out of the room to the tune of the steaming liquid splashing against the sides of his costly trashcan. He was a Water witch; he ought to be able to stop it from staining his carpet. And if not, all the better.

Chapter Eleven

I stared at the phone's LCD screen with a mixture of indecision and anger—anger at myself and anger at Eamonn. He'd been a different person while he was with Desmond, not shy or nervous in the least. Had his behavior in the store been an act? Or like many males, did he adopt a different persona while with "his boys"?

Did any of the answers really matter in the end?

He'd made a bet with Desmond the dick that my breasts were real. That meant if I were dumb enough to *show* him, Eamonn would report back to Desmond. I didn't want Desmond to know anything about me that I didn't tell him myself, even something as pointless as the validity of my body parts.

I drew my lower lip between my teeth, gnawing gently in frustration. The Dark witch's business card lay on the breakfast bar in front of me. My phone held the spot beside it. I couldn't decide if what I'd learned was enough to call off the date for unfinished wood furniture and seafood. The screen claimed it was nearly four thirty. I'd need to come up with an answer soon otherwise I wouldn't have time to get ready if I chose to go through with it.

My brain screeched to a halt. It was nearly four thirty. On Friday. Three days later.

Why hadn't Trip interfered?

Or had he? Perhaps I wouldn't find out until Eamonn failed to show at six.

Then again, what if Trip hadn't interfered because he knew something I didn't? Maybe my nemesis knew the Dark witch was in cahoots with the Water witch. And maybe Trip knew letting me go out with Eamonn would be more damaging than if he'd scared him away. The idea ticked me off despite it merely being a theory. I might have done something about it if I'd known who to be angry at.

The baying of a dog inches from my window startled me half out of my wits. When two more howled, I hopped up from my crouch. I hurried into the bedroom. My mother reclined on the bed playing with the penlight I'd left on the side table last night. She'd dressed in her favored outfit for non-feast days—a pair of denim overalls and a short-sleeved, bright, babydoll styled T-shirt, this one in lime green.

I stood quietly waiting for an explanation for her second visit in a week's time. Frequency was an odd occurrence when we often went months without seeing each other. She was a goddess. I understood she was busy.

"I need another favor," Catey said without lifting her eye from the beam of light she cast on her outstretched palm.

"Tonight?" My voice came out high-pitched in a partial whine.

She shot me an impatient look from beneath lowered eyelids. That peevish expression with its partial duck lips had generally preceded me being forced into some sort of manual labor, like single handedly cleaning the floor in Cerberus's chamber. I clamped my mouth shut.

"Yes, tonight," she said calmly, dark look now only a memory. "Right now. Our deal was that you would go to college for six years and then you would begin your duty."

For the rest of my unnaturally born life, was what she didn't say aloud. No one had told me what my life span would be since I'd been born of a divine mother and had grown up in the Underworld. I shuddered to think I'd be doing my duty when I was ninety.

She set the flashlight back on the side table. "I would like to talk about Trip before we go."

My stomach did an uneasy flip at her continued calm despite the topic change. We never spoke about Trip unless I complained. And nothing ever came of my complaints except her disapproval. *Please, don't let this be a worse deal that involves me taking orders from him rather than merely reporting my findings once a week.*

"The evidence of his spying on you from the Spirit Realm has been given to his father," Catey said, calming my worries. "I have also given it to Hades."

Hades had the final say on promotions in management positions. Triptolemus—the demigod who had the unfortunate distinction of being Trip's father—had the job judging the North American souls in the afterlife. Soul judging was considered a management position. I was a little surprised my mother had gone as far as to involve Hades in our squabble.

"They both are of the opinion this is a childish obsession that will pass once Trip is busy with his new position." My mother's voice softened in an approximation of sympathy. "I am sorry, Kora."

I nodded woodenly. Though she hadn't had to do anything at all, it had been too little too late. But maybe the gods were correct. Maybe Trip would be so busy judging souls full-time that he wouldn't bother me any longer. But I had to wonder if a two and a half decade old fixation would go away simply because Trip had plenty to keep him occupied.

I shoved off the doorframe before my mother could say anything else. "I have to make a phone call."

The sound of the bed's frame creaking seemed impatient. A moment later she entered the room with an annoyed expression creasing her pretty features. I ignored it to punch the digits into the phone's keyboard.

I had no idea what to expect. Had Eamonn left a business, home, or cellular phone number on the business card? Would an assistant like Desmond's Allison answer? Would I be pawned off on voice mail?

Four rings echoed in my ear, and then a deep voice answered. "Hello?"

"Hi, it's Kora," I said, not knowing who I was speaking to.

"Good afternoon, Kora." The slightly accented syllables proved Eamonn himself had answered.

"An emergency came up. I'm going to have to cancel our rain check."

The Dark witch made a sound of disappointment. "I hope everything is all right?"

"I hope so, too," I said cryptically.

"I will be available all evening. Call me if your emergency wraps up early or if you could use help." He paused before dropping his voice into a sexy register. "I'd like to see you tonight."

The bashful man I'd met in Target wouldn't have had the guts to say that, would he?

Eamonn's new sensual side made me uneasy. "I've g-got to go." I hung up before he could form a syllable of protest.

My mother awaited me with her hip jutted to the right and her palm outstretched. I'd made her wait far too long. I'd pay in the Void.

I slunk to her, already cringing in anticipation of the pain.

She shot me a half smile and then offered me a hug. I tossed my arms around her before she could change her mind. The embrace would halve the discomfort of traveling in the soul-splitting Void.

"We're not done speaking," she said before the light of the world was swallowed into a tiny pinpoint that faded into nothing.

The roaring of the empty space filled my ears more effectively than if we'd been walking beside an F-16. Here in the inky black, my body seemed virtually nonexistent. But that didn't stop me from experiencing the sensation of my soul splitting into three pieces. And somehow those pieces felt as if they were tossed about in a monstrous dryer with a dozen pebbles clattering along for the ride. And this was a *comfortable* visit to the Void.

Catey dropped us lightly onto a plot of sand on the edge of a city that could have been any number of towns in Arizona. However, the location of the sun, a soft easterly light and the temperature—somewhere in the mid fifties—told me we weren't in Arizona after all. It was morning wherever we'd appeared. One final clue helped me deduce where I was: English language signs in the distance. This was Australia.

My mother extracted her arms so she could put a few feet between us. When she adopted a stern tone, I understood the first portion of our conversation at the apartment had been the softener. Now she was going in for the kill. "Trip is concerned you are letting your personal goals interfere with the Olympians' goals."

I stiffened in irritation. Of course Trip would say that. He lived to get me in trouble.

My voice was calm because I had no choice but to present my case without hysterics, or my mother might have one of her tantrums. "I'll focus entirely on the Olympians' goals when the Olympians' finance everything of mine. Until then, I am living in the Mortal Realm. I have mortal bills and concerns that need to be addressed along with the concerns of the Olympians. I am working hard to make everyone happy. Trip would understand that if he'd ever had to live on this side of the Void."

She nodded her head, perhaps content that she'd given me a warning. My mother pushed me into the Mortal Realm. "You have two hours," she said and then disappeared into thin air.

"Charon take it." I snarled at the dust cloud she'd kicked up.
****

Though I ached all over, I couldn't seem to fall asleep. My mother's two hours had turned into ten. A jealous Air witch had spawned two dust devils in Alice Springs, Australia. I hadn't been able to locate the witch until it was too late. Five people had been injured. That smacked at my conscience. I'd stayed to help clean up the destruction in penance.

How had my mother expected me to stop a domestic dispute that had happened behind closed doors? Sometimes I wondered if I had latent abilities she was simply waiting for me to discover—abilities like foretelling the future. Clairvoyance would have been the only way to stop the douche-bag from leveling a caravan park because his girlfriend had cheated on him with a werecougar.

I lay staring up at the ceiling, wondering if I'd brought in the mail. An important package from an antiques dealer in Calcutta was due soon. Had the mailbox been empty when I'd checked it at half past three this afternoon? I could wait until the sun rose, and then go check. It would be safer.

I hadn't thought about them in days, but there *were* vampires in Wipuk, and they *did* know who I was. They'd all be snug in their coffins after the sun rose. But that would mean I'd have to stare at the ceiling for three hours until then. I wouldn't be able to sleep unless I knew if the package had arrived. It had a rare crystal in it that would make the local crystal shop owners pee their pants.

With a low groan, I popped up out of bed, reaching for my jean shorts so I'd be presentable when I stepped outside. I paused long enough to lace up my Docs so I wouldn't trip, and then I grabbed my keys off the breakfast bar.

The courtyard was quiet at four in the morning. Apparently we didn't have any vampires living in the collection of buildings around mine. That was good news.

I was cautious when I emerged from the walkway at the mouth of the parking lot. The big bank of mailboxes was across the road. Walking out there would put me in the prime position to be run over by a car or knocked out by a vampire before I saw anyone.

There wasn't a hint of a sentient creature anywhere to be seen. It seemed safe enough. Nonetheless, I quickly made my way across the street. To my dismay there was mail but no package from India. On my way back to the sidewalk, I flipped through the catalogue for meats and cheeses addressed to the previous occupant.

A sound from my right drew me to a standstill when I reached the entrance to the courtyard. The door to an apartment was open, light spilling out of the foot wide opening around the figure blocking it. Had someone spotted me earlier?

The combination of paranoia and curiosity had me squinting for a better view. I pulled back against the entrance's wall when it registered that the figure in the door was *nude*. While I doubted a nude person would attack me, I didn't want to embarrass them by walking by at this exact moment.

"Shhh," a male voice said in a harsh tone from around the corner.

"You're such a bitch," another male said—this one in the tenor range.

"You said you had to go." The original male's reply was raspy. "Are you going, or are you staying? Because I can't leave this door open all night."

"Should I stay, or should I go now?" the second male sang the punk tune.

"Henry…"

"If I go there will be trou-ble," Henry said in his singsong voice. "And if I stay there will be dou—"

A wet, smacking sound silenced the singer's punk tune. That had been suspiciously like a lip-smacking kiss. I couldn't help but smile. It was cute.

Seconds later, a quiet and breathy Henry said, "You're lucky you're fantastic in bed, or I wouldn't put up with this shit."

There was a hiss in response. Henry's footsteps and answering laugh echoed in the opposite direction.

I counted to ten after the thunk of the door closing, and then I started for my apartment. A door snapped open once I'd reached the mid-point. I jumped six inches, startled that I'd been caught.

"Fuck! You heard the whole damn thing, didn't you?"

The glare of the light from inside the apartment made it nearly impossible to focus on the male speaker. I set my hand over my brows to shield some of it. My vision slowly adjusted. Ryan Steele stood in the doorway, shirtless with a towel wrapped around his lower half.

Ryan was *gay*? I'd never heard of a homosexual shapeshifter, not that I'd heard all that much about their faction in the first place.

"Uh…" I couldn't think of a response.

The shapeshifter was in my face before I'd worked out that he'd moved. "You cannot tell *anyone*."

If he didn't want people to know he was gay then he probably shouldn't have had his lover over where people might see—people like me. But I couldn't *say* that.

The shifter snapped an angry question. "What the hell are you even doing awake at four in the morning?"

I dropped my hand from my eyes, drawing my head a few inches away from his pinched expression. "I was checking my mail." I shook the catalogue at him. "Couldn't sleep."

"You cannot tell *anyone*."

He was really worked up about this. Maybe I could use it to my advantage. I wasn't opposed to a little blackmail. I'd even resort to blackmailing a guy with killer abs like his.

I tilted my head to the right in what I hoped came off as a thoughtful expression. "How much is it worth to you?"

He let out a low growl that might have been frightening if I didn't have every school of magic at my fingertips. "I'm not paying you to keep your mouth shut."

I let my lips curve into a smile. "That was a cute little thing you did there." I wiggled my fingers toward him. "Shutting him up with a kiss."

Ryan drew in a sharp breath, realizing exactly how much I'd overheard. "How much do you want?"

"I don't want your money. I need information."

He eyed me warily. "What information?"

I formed a pair of legs with my index and middle fingers and then mimed them walking into his apartment. "How about you make some coffee and then tell me everything you know about Wipuk?"

He rolled back onto his bare heels, gazing with squinty-eyed suspicion. "You won't tell anyone what you witnessed if I tell you about Wipuk?"

I gave a firm nod for emphasis. "You scratch my back, and I'll scratch yours."

"Deal. Give me ten minutes to get dressed."

I gave him fifteen.

Chapter Twelve

Ryan had pulled on a gray T-shirt featuring blue printed birds, a collection of clouds, and a hand with the All Seeing Eye on it. I didn't put too much thought into what it all represented, glad only that he was fully dressed in jeans and a top now, so I wouldn't have to lust after him. His cherry eyes narrowed in irritation as I invited myself to sit on the green chenille sofa that had the focus in his living room. Strangely, it was easier to look at him now despite his disturbing resemblance to my nemesis.

"What do you take in your coffee?"

"Extra cream if you have it, and two spoons of sugar," I said as I scanned the carefully decorated room—a match for mine only in floor plan.

I might have had inkling about his sexuality if he'd invited me in here days ago. The place was too neat, too carefully planned, and too stylish to belong to a straight man, at least a straight man who hadn't dated an interior designer. I mean, the man had fake flowers!

He set a hand-thrown ceramic mug coated in blue and gold glazes in front of me. I stealthily sniffed the mouth-watering aromatic coffee for poison just as I had earlier at Desmond's office. Never could be too careful.

"Why do you want to know about Wipuk?" Ryan asked while dropping into the taupe Berkline recliner beside me. He held his own mug of coffee between strangely chubby hands.

I wagged a finger at him. "You don't get to ask that."

He grunted. "Fine. What do you want to know?"

"Who is Desmond Marino, and why does he act like he rules the world?"

Since I knew most of the answer already, it was the perfect opening question. I could gauge if Ryan were truly going to play ball or if I'd have to use my new damaging knowledge to get what I wanted.

"Desmond is the high priest of Neptune's Fellowship. That's the Water witch coven for the United States," he said—I assume in case I hadn't known that. "I don't know why he acts like he rules the world."

"How long has be been high priest?"

"Um." Ryan leaned back in the chair, focusing on the ceiling as if the answer could be found there. "He wasn't even a blip on the radar when I moved here ten years ago. Then one day he was running the Water witches. I'd say it's been about five years?"

"He acts like he has sway over the Centralized Coven Coalition."

The shifter lifted his shoulders. "Maybe he does."

"Any idea how he became the head of the Water witches? Did he kill his predecessor?" I really wanted a legitimate reason to despise Desmond the dick.

Ryan shook his head, tossing his shoulder-length hair into his face. "No, nothing like that." He made me wait while he took a sip from his own handmade mug of steaming coffee. "Neptune's Fellowship had been ruled over by a committee of nine high priestesses for as long as anyone could remember. But you know Water witches." He rolled his eyes. "They're emotional, overly empathic, and flighty. Put a group of nine females like that together, and you're asking for trouble. They were the least organized coven in the entire country. It was impossible to get them to make any decisions because none of them could agree on anything. Word is Desmond came along and cleaned it all up."

Or Desmond came along and became their dictator. I'd have to look into that.

I moved on to the next name on my list. "What about Eamonn Cary?"

"High priest of The Coven of Nyx," Ryan said.

My tush practically shot off the sofa before I caught myself. "High priest?"

Ryan nodded, seemingly oblivious to my vehement response. "Of the Dark witches. He's slick. You gotta watch out for that guy."

I slumped back against the chenille, letting my hand smack against my forehead. I'd avoided a catastrophe today. Had Catey done it on purpose? And Trip … That harpy's nose hair! No wonder he hadn't interfered!

Ryan ventured a guess. "You met Eamonn?"

"Yeah. At Target in Flagstaff. It seemed like a coincidence, but now I'm pretty sure it wasn't."

"Eamonn Cary was shopping at Target?" Ryan snorted roughly. "Yeah, that wasn't a coincidence. He's Pierre Cary's son. He doesn't do his own shopping."

Charon take it! I'd let the witch's good looks and bashful behavior cloud my brain! If I'd been thinking at all, I would have made the connection to Pierre. Pierre was the high priest of the European Dark witches.

Using the analogy of countries of the world, if each continental high priest or priestess had to be represented by one, Pierre would be Russia. He was a tyrannical beast who was on just about everyone's shit list, and yet they all invited him to their Christmas parties simply to stay on his good side. A large part of that had to do with the fact he was an international arms dealer … with magical power. And I'd almost gone on a date with the man's son.

"They're feeling you out," Ryan said. "You're a human in Wipuk, and they don't like that. I'm surprised they haven't kicked you out yet."

"Desmond tried."

The shapeshifter leaned further back into his recliner, hitting the footrest so it popped open noisily. He was getting comfortable. Was that a good or bad thing?

"Tried?" Ryan said. "If Desmond tried to get you kicked out, then you would have been kicked out."

So Ryan had been holding out on me. Desmond *did* have sway over the coalition.

"He tried, but someone put the kibosh on it." I pulled the mug up to my lips.

"Who? Eamonn?"

Hmm. Did that mean Eamonn had just as much sway over the coalition as Desmond?

"No." I shook my head. "Maximo de Sole."

Ryan choked on his coffee, sputtering as he rolled the chair forward again. Broad cherry eyes widened in shock. "Maximo de Sole. The vampire?"

Based on his reaction, I was beginning to get a picture of the power structure in Wipuk. It may be a witch colony, but de Sole apparently trumped them all.

"Yes," I said uneasily.

"Maximo de Sole put the kibosh on you getting kicked out of Wipuk?"

This called for an explanation. "Desmond showed up Sunday morning demanding I leave. Monday night I met Maximo. Tuesday morning Desmond's assistant delivered a letter from the coalition that said I'd been granted dispensation to live in Wipuk indefinitely. Beside 'responsible faction' Maximo de Sole was listed."

Ryan shot to his feet. "You're a fucking thrall! You're going to ruin everything for me! Get the fuck out!"

The force of his sudden anger was shocking. I lifted my palms in the sign of surrender. "Whoa! I'm not anyone's thrall."

The shapeshifter wasn't convinced "If he claimed you on the dispensation form then you're a stinking thrall."

My skin warmed from anxiety. Pitch lifting fearfully, I found myself arguing. "I don't have any missing time."

But could Ryan be correct? Had de Sole done something to me before he'd let me leave his place? Vampires had the ability to screw with people's memories. Had he screwed with mine?

"Let me smell your neck," Ryan said. His frame shook with agitation and anger. Apparently he hadn't truly been worried about his secret until now.

I kept my hands in front of me where he could see them. "Okay."

He stalked to the side of the sofa where he bent toward my hair. The slight snuffle of his deep breath made me hold mine. I was terrified he was correct.

If all it took was one exchange of blood for a vampire to enthrall a human, could Maximo have accomplished it without my knowledge? He'd have complete control over me if he had. I was far too powerful to be bound into a leech's service.

"You're clean," Ryan begrudgingly said. He came around the sofa, dropping into his chair as though the whole sniffing task had taken a lot out of him. "Why the fuck would Max claim you among his faction if you're not his thrall?"

I shrugged because his guess was as good as mine. The vampire topic still made me terribly uneasy. "Who are the other players in the coalition?"

Ryan gave me a twisted frown, perhaps the sign he didn't appreciate my avoidance. He answered me anyway. "A council of thirteen priests and priestesses rule over the Western Phoenix Coven. They take turns sitting on the coalition. It changes by quarter I think."

Good to know a committee ruled the Fire witches rather than a dictator like Desmond ... despite their violent method of succession.

"Aer Association is headed up by Curtis Hawksley and Alina Kranz. Curtis handles the weekend meetings while Alina sits in on weekdays. Curtis has a business that keeps him in Phoenix through the week."

Air witches had co-rulers? Interesting.

"The Earth Witch Monarchy is represented on the coalition by an ambassador. At the moment that's Dea Woods." He paused for a sip of coffee. "And the Cult of Osiris has a priest and priestess who are supposedly stand-ins for Osiris and Isis. Andoni Arima serves as Osiris. He's a crazy old goat. But I can't remember who is standing as Isis this year. It changed not long ago."

I hadn't met many of the cult's Death witches because necromancy had been banned in California.

"The Healers of America are supposed to appoint a new representative every quarter, but for the past three years it's been Viho Hiamovi. He's the most pure-blooded Healer left in the world."

I waited to see if Ryan would mention a Time or Light coven, the two branches of magic were supposedly extinct. Vampires had hunted Light witches to eradication for their ability to soak in and manipulate sunlight. And Time witches had been the most reviled school of all because of their destructive ability to screw with the past. Everyone had hunted them mutually. Or so it was believed. I was pretty sure there were witches somewhere, hiding. The two schools of magic hadn't simply died out.

I had to ask it even though I was afraid of the answer. "How does de Sole fit into all of this?"

"He's Wipuk's First," Ryan said. "Actually, he's Wipuk's one and only. He's been ruler here long enough that when the vampires revised the city charter, he didn't bother to change with the times. And since this is a witch colony and not technically a city, none in his community have forced the issue."

I'd done just enough research on the undead community to understand Ryan referenced the sixty-year-old city charter that had brought the semblance of democracy to the vampires instead of the liege lord system that had been in place prior. Cities of any size had three elected rulers who were given the title First, Second, or Third, depending on when they'd been voted into service. Because Wipuk boasted a mere thousand inhabitants, it wasn't particularly surprising to learn there was only one undead ruler.

"Who is Sedona's ruler?"

"Maximo," Ryan said.

That was a little more surprising but still not terribly so. Sedona wasn't large.

"What's his girlfriend's story?"

"Ascencion?" Ryan snorted. "She's like a stay-at-home wife from hell. She puts her nose into everything. I don't know if Maximo realizes it and turns a blind eye or if she's keeping it hidden, but she's trying to run Wipuk behind his back. If you ask me, I'd say she's the real power."

There was at least one thing de Sole's girlfriend hadn't been able to do behind his back—stop my dispensation. Was that because she'd been healing from first-degree burns?

My thoughts skipped ahead. If she were the real power in Wipuk's vampire scene, then why hadn't she sought vengeance for what I did to her nearly a week ago?

Maybe Ryan's opinion wasn't accurate. Ascencion would have come gunning for my blood as soon as she'd been up and around if it were. De Sole must have stopped her. While that was good for me *now*, in the long run it would suck. The woman wouldn't easily forgive and forget that I'd set her on fire, even if I *had* warned her.

"So what's *your* story?" Ryan asked during the silence my thoughts had generated.

Avoiding him on this subject would make him twice as suspicious. I shrugged. "I'm fascinated by witches. So Wipuk seemed like the natural place to move after I graduated."

"But the witches don't want you here," he said with brutal honesty I respected. "How are you going to make a living?"

"I'm opening a store on the border that caters to both humans and the factions. The downstairs is in Sedona and the upstairs in Wipuk."

"Ah, clever. The witches will boycott you, but you can earn money off the vanilla tourists."

My future depended on him being wrong.

He sipped at his mug. "I'm assuming you're going to have another crystal store?"

I followed his lead with a larger gulp of my drink. "There will be some tourist trinkets, yeah. But mostly the inventory will be hard to find items."

The shifter's eyebrows drifted upward. "Like what?"

"Like jewelry that can focus energy, clothing that can dampen it, and good luck charms."

"You mean weaves," he said with a low, disdainful delivery.

"No. Weaves are objects that have been infused with a specific witch's power to do a specific task. What

I'm talking about are more like the things right out of story books—good luck charms like rabbits' feet and four leaf clovers, magic bracelets that clear the mind to make room for cleaner casting, protective armor against specific elements, shoes that make you jump higher, and plenty of items to augment a witch's natural power."

They were *divine* objects. But to the untrained eye the items would definitely seem like weaves. I understood I'd be looked on as a menace in Wipuk because of it. I had faith that once one or two of the power players tried a few of the items, I'd be the most popular destination in town.

"The heavy stuff will only be offered to the factions," I said. "But even a vanilla human could use a good luck charm."

And if any of my rarities were used to harm someone, the buyer would be paid a visit by an avenging angel.

Me.

Ryan shook his head. "You're gonna be lynched."

I spread my lips, making sure he saw my wicked grin. "Let 'em try."

Chapter Thirteen

I felt like a slacker for arriving at the shop at three in the afternoon. My plan was to open the doors on Wednesday—four days away—and have a grand opening sale a week and a half later. I needed to get the place cleaned up, painted, and ready *yesterday* so I could begin advertising. Sleeping half the day away hadn't been part of the plan.

Today's task was ripping up the old Berber carpet and putting down bamboo flooring. The ebony tongue and groove slats would look perfect with my warm macchiato walls. It had been a splurge. But thanks to the overwhelming mold scent, the carpet had needed to come up. And Lisping Anne had knocked another fifty bucks off my monthly rate when I'd told her what I wanted to do.

I settled in to work with a radio tuned to the local station, hoping the noise would keep my mind off the pain in my lower back. After a half hour of pop songs and two broken nails, I thought I should have blackmailed Ryan into helping me tear up the carpet. But manual labor would have been pushing my luck.

He'd agreed to keep an ear open for town gossip in exchange for my keeping mum about his sexual preference. Ryan wouldn't engage in home improvement to keep me quiet. Probably.

"We're gearing up for Midsummer Madness," the male DJ said between songs. "This year's summer solstice charity ball will be held at the Poco Diablo Resort. The Q will have tickets beginning next week as part of our month of madness. Win tickets and you can rub shoulders with Northern Arizona's elite. I don't know about you, but I wanna go just to see if Maximo de Sole is a vampire like the rumors all say!"

My head came up from the carpet pad stubbornly stuck to the floor.

The vanilla humans *knew* about Maximo? I still found it unbelievable that vampires had come out on the evening news a few short months ago. The witches could be next if I didn't work on Catey's task faster.

The DJ's thick radio voice broke into my thoughts. "What will you do with your ticket if you win? Call me or post a message on our Facebook page. I want to hear from you!"

Poco Diablo was on the border between Sedona and Wipuk. I suspected this solstice charity ball happened on both sides of the line. But what charity would de Sole sponsor? Blood mobiles for vamps?

I had the last of the carpet pad torn up by the time the DJ played the first phone call—a breathless teenage girl with an ear-piercing pitch. "I would go just to check out Desmond Marino's butt in a tux!"

The Water witch wasn't solely a figure in Wipuk? Why hadn't Ryan told me *that* detail? I supposed Marino's office *was* in Sedona with a view of Wipuk.

The DJ's gave an indulgent chuckle. "Are you going to bid on the date with him?"

"I would if I had that kind of money! Oh my God, he's so hot! And he seems so nice!"

Stupid teenage girls. What in Hades did they know?

"What do you think about the rumor that he's gay?"

Apparently the DJ wanted to rile the girl up because she shrieked an indignant answer. "No *way*!"

"But no one has ever seen him on a date that wasn't for charity," the DJ said. "He's gotta be hiding something."

"Well, it's not *that*," the girl said.

The DJ laughed again. "Well, okay then. Thanks for your call. We're going to jump back into the tunes with this new one…"

I settled back onto my tush and considered what I'd learned. Marino and de Sole were public figures both in and out of the Underground. They must live in homes straddling the line. I made a mental note for future reference.

The interior of the shop began to smell usable once the remnants of the carpet pad went into the dumpster out back. I swept years of accumulated dust bunnies out the open door. The space needed airing out despite the temperature surpassing the eighty-degree. I'd sweated with the air conditioning on anyway. After checking the floor for structural and water damage, of which I found none, I let the afternoon breeze freshen it while I headed upstairs to work on the Wipuk side.

Magical interference from the hidden colony made the radio station nearly impossible to listen to until I'd stuck the stereo in the stairwell with both doors open. A nice cross breeze carried through the place once I'd unlocked the door upstairs. I found myself smiling stupidly because I was beginning to think there really *was* good energy here.

"Toss me over the boat if I turn into one of these new age freaks."

Of course the one time I chose to mutter an Underworld joke aloud, someone had to overhear it.

A deep voice spoke from the open door behind me. "You sail as well as strip floors?"

My spine stiffened. I softened my jaw when I realized it hadn't been Trip's voice that startled me. But whose slightly accented voice was that? It was just on the edge of my mind…

Eamonn Cary.

Wonderful. I had my tush stuck up in the air. My fishnets had torn on a half dozen carpet tacks. And I stank like Cerberus after chasing an interloper on a feast day. I'd feign ignorance in the hope he'd go away. I didn't want to deal with him right now. Or maybe ever.

"The shop isn't open yet," I called out.

"I came to see you, not the shop." He gave me a handful of seconds to respond. "I see you have yet to buy shelving. Were you waiting on me?"

I eased my bottom down from its spot hovering near the last scrap of carpet pad. Slowly I stood and faced him while working out the kinks in my muscles.

The Dark witch had come to rest against the doorframe, neither inside nor outside. He'd shoved his hands into the pockets of a pair of dark rinse jeans. Smooth, tan skin gleamed from in between the parted collar of his plaid shirt.

Eamonn didn't scrutinize me as I'd done him. His eyes remained on my face, seemingly waiting for my answer. I glanced around my shop in an effort to see it through his eyes. The walls were the only things that looked good in the storefront. And that wasn't saying much. They'd need to be touched up before opening as it were.

"There's no place to put shelves yet," I said. "I'll worry about it once I have the floors installed."

"Floors?" he asked, emphasizing the plural.

"I'm installing it downstairs, too."

Eamonn's brows lifted as he gave an impressed, slow nod of his head. "A shop in both Wipuk and Sedona is certainly ambitious."

I hadn't told him downstairs was in Sedona or that I was opening a shop down there rather than using it as storage. Had he guessed it, or was someone talking? Someone like Ryan Steele?

I said nothing because it seemed safest.

"You are doing it all on your own?" he asked.

I wanted to snark out, *No, I have nymphs handling the manual labor*, because it seemed obvious to me that I was going it alone. Why else would I be sweaty, snagged, and bruised on the floor of my six hundred square foot storefront?

What I actually said was, "Cheaper that way."

"Want some help?"

Pierre Cary's son was offering to help me install bamboo flooring in his Diesel jeans and Hugo Boss shirt? A choked noise was stifled before it could make its way up my throat. No way was I agreeing to that. I didn't want to be in debt to him. Witches might not be a faction that regularly called in favors, but Pierre Cary wasn't a typical witch. It stood to reason his son would behave similarly.

"I'm almost done ripping out the carpet, and then the place has to air out before I can do anything else," I said.

He didn't need to know I had on the silver cuff that would keep me alert and awake so I could begin in a few hours and work through the night.

"I'll be fine," I said. "But thanks for the offer." I turned toward my pile of stinking carpet and deposited the handful of fuzz I'd torn up.

Eamonn's voice went quiet. "Do you want to get some dinner after you finish?"

Kore's knees. He was persistent. What would he say if I told him I knew he'd made a bet with Desmond?

I'd burned my bridge with one coven leader. Adding another to the count wouldn't be smart. But it also wouldn't be smart to get involved with a Cary, even if it meant I might get inside information on Wipuk.

"I really need to concentrate on the shop," I said in all seriousness. "I may not be able to work on the floor, but I have plenty of other work with the inventory, finances, and all that to keep me busy." Maybe discussion of finances would send a guy dressed in designer jeans running.

"I am good at finance," he said, dashing my plan. "I can reduce your monthly operating budget by ten percent. Let me buy us a pizza. There is a good little place uptown that delivers."

Now I was offended. He hadn't looked at my budget, and already he assumed I had superfluous items in it. Was it because I was female?

What if he *could* reduce costs on a business that hadn't even opened its doors yet? No … He was a Cary. I needed to stay as far away from him as possible.

"Not to offend." I faced him for the remainder of the careful reply. "But this business is my baby. I kind of want to try it my way first."

Eamonn allowed a soft smile to play on his lips. "I don't plan to take over your business, Kora. I only want to give you business advice. There is nothing wrong with listening to advice from someone who has been where you are."

There was if that someone came from a long line of international arms dealers responsible for one or two of the worst atrocities in human history.

"You can discount everything I say," he said.

If I discounted it and he turned out to be correct, I'd kick myself. But was that a reason to accept or deny him?

"My treat," Eamonn said in a coaxing voice, looking incredibly sexy in his spiffed up casual clothing.

"I didn't know you were Pierre Cary's son."

Eamonn's frame stiffened like a warrior beneath Medusa's destructive gaze.

Smooth, Kora, real smooth.

It was a good five seconds before he relaxed enough to speak. "You have heard of my father?"

Despite easing his shoulders and tight jaw, it was a false relaxation. His agitation was great enough I could feel it without an empathic link. Could it be that Eamonn was ashamed of his father? Or was he worked up because a human had heard of his family?

I nodded. Time to get the gossip going about me. "I've been obsessed with witches since I was ten." It wasn't an obsession. It had been a chore. My mother had been grooming me for this task since I'd been born. But he didn't need to know that. "Of course I've heard of your father."

"The world believes he is an evil man," Eamonn said woodenly as if he'd been taught to speak the party line from an early age just as I had been. "They can't see the good he has done for our people."

Asking him to explain how putting weapons in the hands of humans so they could kill each other would benefit anyone would be foolish. I also wasn't going to ask Eamonn if he was by any chance supplying weapons to the Mexican drug cartels over the border on his father's behalf. But I wanted to know the answer to both.

"Is this why you cancelled our date last night?"

His quiet question caught me off guard. Eamonn's droopy-eyed expression looked as though I'd wounded him by bringing up his parentage. I made myself remember how he'd behaved with Desmond. I recalled that bet. And I recalled Ryan telling me they were feeling me out. I couldn't let this act of Eamonn's turn me into a love-struck dweeb.

But was he acting now? He hadn't blushed or stammered once.

"I had an emergency last night," I said. "I didn't get home until four in the morning." I lived my chin. "And I didn't realize it was a date."

Eamonn's eyebrows rose questioningly. He cleared his throat. Twin red spots appeared on his cheeks. I bit my tongue to keep from making a noise.

Why did he have to go the bashful route now when I'd been so sure he'd been manipulating me?

His tone was as cautious as mine had been. "What did you think it was?"

"I thought you were trying to make a newcomer feel welcome."

Lies. Lies. Liiiiesss. This wasn't a good position to get myself into, but I didn't feel like I had a choice.

"I see," he said tightly. His deep-set eyes had taken on a hard edge.

My stomach knotted in worry. A Cary wasn't the sort of person to tick off, especially not one who was part of the very coalition I needed to infiltrate. I was making a mess of this whole situation. Could I salvage it without accepting his offer for pizza and finances?

Emitting a self-depreciating laugh, I said, "I figured the odds of someone like you wanting to date me were nil. In any case, I have so much to do with the shop that I don't have time to sleep, let alone date. But it's really nice of you to offer to help me."

"Someone like me?"

I forced a flush to color my cheeks by recalling an embarrassing moment from my youth. He needed to think I was legitimately smitten. "You look like you could be a movie star."

My answer didn't soften his darkened eyes.

"Kora, I don't understand you one whit." His tone had hardened to match his gaze. Eamonn pushed off the doorframe, landing on legs that were spread hip width apart. "You reel me in and then cast me out only to reel me back in. I don't particularly enjoy it."

And I didn't enjoy having my indecision pointed out using a fishing metaphor. So he'd get a little bit of truth from me. "I went to Desmond's office yesterday. I sat in the chair you used Thursday."

Eamonn's jaw set while his gaze lifted and unfocused over my head. "Desmond asked me to make sure you weren't doing anything illegal in Wipuk."

My vague declaration had prompted him to admit something I hadn't known. Maybe he'd spill all the beans if I stared at him as though I knew more than I was letting on.

"His concern was that you were a spy for de Sole," Eamonn said.

I *was* a spy, but not for a vampire. Why would Wipuk's First need a sorceress for a spy when he lived in the colony himself? That made no sense. Maybe I'd ask Ryan about it later.

"I was supposed to see if you were enthralled," the Dark witch said.

Yeah, right after he checked out my breasts. I folded my arms over them, leveling an unimpressed expression on his face.

He met my gaze without blinking. There was haughtiness to his tone now that hadn't been there before. "I am not going to apologize for asking you on a date. This could have been as pleasurable as it was enlightening."

His shy attitude had all been an act. I'd almost fallen for it. Stupid, stupid girl.

I forced my clenched jaw to relax. I wasn't angry with Eamonn, not truly. I was angry with myself for failing to know better.

Well, okay, I was ticked at him, too.

I drew in a steadying breath, allowing my chin to rise proudly. "I'm not enthralled. I'm not de Sole's spy. I'm not doing anything illegal. And lies are no basis for anything pleasurable. Thanks for your offer to help, even if it was in a misguided attempt to appease your boss."

His hands slipped out of his pockets so he could settle them at his hips. "Desmond isn't my boss."

No, Pierre Cary is.

"I'm not hungry," I said. "I don't need help with my finances. And I need to get back to work." I turned my back on him so he'd know I meant business.

There was no response from him for several moments. He didn't argue or defend himself, but he also didn't leave. I gathered up the carpet padding in a trash bag so I could take it downstairs as soon as he left. Though I really wanted him to go, I wasn't going to demand he do it. I wasn't quite that foolish.

Eamonn drew in a heavy sigh, pausing another handful of seconds, and then his feet scuffed on the cement outside.

I couldn't resist one last jab while he walked down the front sidewalk. "By the way," I called out. "They're real."

I was halfway down the stairs before his French curse echoed up.

Chapter Fourteen

Someone stood in front of the window when I crested the stairs to lock the front door at midnight. The figure appeared to be male with sloping shoulders covered in a black suit. His hands were in his pockets very like Eamonn had done a few hours earlier. A quick scent of the air proved the figure wasn't Eamonn.

How had the stranger gotten *inside* without alerting me?

My heart pumped a little faster. We were on the Wipuk side of the line. This could be any manner of creature.

I really needed to build a protective net around the place when I wasn't watching it. The new crystal that had finally arrived could power the net when I was home. Why hadn't I thought of this already? Tonight I'd fix that. But first, I had to deal with whoever *this* was.

"The shop isn't open yet," I said the obvious in a careful tone.

The figure inhaled a soft breath before slowly facing me. I recognized the small lock of hair curling over his forehead first, and then noted the rest of his handsome features.

Maximo de Sole—the vampire himself.

Beneath his black suit were a plain white shirt and a thin black tie that managed to look decadent on him despite their simplicity. I wasn't sure why. He wasn't particularly broad shouldered or overly muscular. Though he was good-looking, he wasn't any more so than Desmond or Eamonn. Maybe it was the easy confidence he held himself with that didn't tip the arrogance meter.

But I shouldn't be gawking. My eyes darted around the windows, looking for the entourage he probably had in hiding.

"Ascencion isn't here," he said, answering my unspoken question. "She's still healing."

My face and neck warmed in embarrassment. I'd damn near killed his girlfriend. He should have been trying to kill me for it.

"She's been up and about for days," he said without prompting. "But her vanity has kept her behind closed doors until her skin is whole and smooth again."

I dropped my chin to my chest. "She's going to filet me."

"No."

I didn't dare ask him what I could do for him. He'd give me an answer I wouldn't like. But I couldn't stop myself from shifting my weight uncomfortably onto my left hip.

One hand came out of his pocket and draped beside his leg. "Desmond Marino tells me you received a copy of your dispensation to stay in Wipuk."

Uh oh. He'd expected me to come see him.

"I did," I said.

"I had a choice to expel you from Wipuk, keeping you safe from Ascencion's wrath or to claim you. I assumed you'd prefer to remain in the colony." He paused, perhaps giving me a chance to argue.

Torn on how to react, I remained silent.

"I have no intention of enthralling you," he said. "But rather like someone calling shotgun, my claim can be usurped by decisive action."

Was he trying to persuade me to ask him to enthrall me simply so no one else could?

I folded my arms in front of my chest without a thought for how it might appear until it was too late. "How much is this claim going to cost me?"

"Nothing," he said in an unreadable tone. Maximo massaged thin fingers over his thinner goatee. "But if you're searching for a way to repay me, there's a charity event on the nineteenth."

I held myself motionless while he continued speaking.

"Customarily we raffle off dates with Wipuk and Sedona's prominent citizens."

Was I supposed to bid on him so Ascencion wouldn't win? That would *really* improve our relationship.

Maximo quickly skimmed the walls before settling his gaze back on me. "The newest citizen, a human sorceress, would draw a good deal of money for charity."

"You want me to put *myself* up for auction?"

"It's for a good cause," he said in a suspiciously innocent tone. "The winner gets just one night with his or her date. Be it dinner and an event like a show, dancing, or picnic beneath the full moon. You wouldn't have to sleep with them."

My imagination sketched a picture of the vampire and me on a checkered blanket in the park beneath the full moon. I blinked twice, *hard*, to clear it.

"So let me get this straight," I said with careful enunciation. "If I agree to be auctioned off, you'll consider this claim thing even?"

"It will go a long way toward making the sobbing I've endured for six days worth my while."

I winced because I'd messed up when I'd set his girlfriend on fire. I could have burnt only her lips or merely hit her with the gust of air. But no, brilliant me had to hit her with a full out fireball.

I grunted. "Fine."

Maximo's lips spread into an indulgent smile. "We'll mail you the invitation." He started for the door but not before scanning dark eyes down my figure. "It's a black tie event. I trust you have something suitable to wear. If not, I know people."

I waved my hand dismissively. "Yeah. I have something suitable."

"Good." His lips spread a little broader. "I look forward to seeing you … suitably attired, Miss Walsh."

My nose crinkled as his sloping shoulders disappeared out the store door. I didn't like his hesitation before the word "suitably". What was he implying? That I was never suitably attired?

I hissed at myself for even caring.

This auctioned date thing was going to end badly. But if it were all de Sole asked of me in exchange for counting me among his faction, then I was getting off easily.

So I'd stand up and let them auction me off for a piddly sixty bucks, and then the vampire would leave me alone. If anything, it would be a good advertising opportunity. I smiled at that. And then I got back to work.
****

I hurt all over, but I was wide-awake. That was the curse of my mother's hammered silver bracelet. My brain could stay alert for three days straight, but my muscles punished me for it. I *had* done more work in four days than a team of two contractors would do in a week and a half.

Okay, perhaps an exaggeration. But it was sure as Hades more work than I'd ever done, even on my thesis. My effort had been rewarded. The shop looked great, both floors. I had warm macchiato walls with white trim and ebony colored bamboo floors. There were carefully spaced ebony stained open shelves, two glass display cases, and a clothing rack. All were stocked with merchandise on both floors.

Arrangements of dried flowers held places of honor on the edges of the show rooms. And abstract paintings of witches done in India ink had been hung in thick black frames with heavy white mattes at regular intervals on the walls. In short, the shop was a sleek, modern boutique that would only get better with time.

The sign out front matched the interior with the word "Rarities" emblazoned in an ebony, modern, sans serif font on a macchiato background. The logo was exactly how I'd envisioned it for the past two years.

There was an immense sense of pride when I breezed forward and flipped on the LED "OPEN" sign.

I doubted anyone would stop in today. I hadn't advertised in any fashion. And I'd waited to open until noon—long after the morning commute Lisping Anne had said would pass the store. My intention was to be open from noon until nine because I was only one person.

The door to the upstairs portion of the shop was wide open. There was a sign above it labeled "Employees Only"—an attempt to keep wide-eyed humans from somehow accidentally stumbling into Wipuk. Vanilla humans weren't capable of seeing the magical pocket of land. It was why the witches in the colony were so worked up about my finding my way across. If any human wandered inside the employee only area, they'd probably find a flat wall rather than stairs. But I could never be too cautious.

I'd left the stair door open so I could hear the bell jingling on the back entrance if anyone entered up there. The way my luck went, my first visitor would be Desmond Marino. I dearly hoped he wouldn't stop in until I'd had a chance to bring a few of his peers on board.

To my surprise, two female human tourists with matching wolf T-shirts were my very first customers.

They turned up at roughly half past noon with little fanfare. I greeted them warmly, and then returned my attention to the book in my hands so they'd be free to browse without pressure. The pair poked their noses near each object in the store before plunking themselves in front of me.

"Do you do aura photography?" the heftier of the pair asked.

Aura photography? Oh for Zeus's sake. That was the new age nonsense they were into these days?

I shook my head in feigned dismay rather than give into the snort I'd wanted to make. "I'm sorry. I don't."

"Do you know who does the best?"

Considering I'd never seen an aura and I was the daughter of the goddess of magic, *no* one was the best. Auras were a myth perpetrated by the supposed new age gurus. What they actually saw was a distortion of the Void generally caused by lingering spirits, not the individual in question.

"No, sorry."

A blue Mazda pulled into the lot beside the tourists' rented Caliber. A leggy blonde burst out the driver's side. She stomped over the rocky parking lot toward us with single-minded intent, her long hair flying around her in the afternoon breeze.

The quiet member of the pair in front of me glanced at my "Employees Only" sign. They exchanged a quick, anxious look that told me nothing. And then they darted toward the stairs to Wipuk like Hades himself was after them.

"Hey!" I vaulted after them.

"Get them!" The blonde's flip-flops smacked a rapid beat across the shop floor.

I'd get them all right, or I'd be in for a heap of trouble if they managed to find their way into Wipuk. Surely that would be grounds for Desmond to toss my tush into a Sedona cactus.

A loud thud sounded from ahead of me followed by another, and then a groan echoed back. I reached the supposed storage room, discovering the pair slumped on the floor at the foot of the stairs.

Huh. It looked like they'd run right into a wall like a bird flying into a glass door. That was good to know.

I stared down at them in dumbfounded inaction. What was I supposed to do with two unconscious tourists?

Footsteps flapped behind me. I glanced over my shoulder. The blonde appeared at the threshold. Her gaze darted up the stairs, and then at the pair on the floor. My stomach did a wild flip. *Could she* see *the second level?*

"They stole a crystal ball that cost half my weekly paycheck," said the blonde, who didn't look old enough to drink. "I need their keys so I can get it back."

I stepped aside so she could fish for the keys all on her own. She took one look at me, another at the stairs. "What's up the stairs?"

"Um, storage?"

The blonde shook her head in a slow motion that might have been disgust. Then she shocked the divine out of me by whispering an incantation to Aer.

The limp tourist on top levitated two feet in the air as if several pairs of fingers played the light-as-a-feather sleepover game beneath her. Yet the blonde hadn't touched her. A dry desert breeze filled my nose as the young woman, who was clearly an Air witch, floated the female's body into the shop atop a pocket of Air. She did the same with the remaining tourist until they were both in a position for her to get at their pockets.

I stared as the blonde stalked to their Caliber where she fetched a crystal ball from their back seat. She came back inside, tossing the keys at the slumped couple.

"Got it," she said and then slapped her way back to the parking lot. Her Mazda disappeared in a cloud of dust a half minute later.

I was left with two unconscious alleged human thieves and no explanation for what had happened.

This had better not be an indication of what my business had in store for me. But I supposed my first customer could have been worse. It could have been Trip in the flesh.
****

I was reading over the liability clause in my insurance when the blue Mazda pulled into the parking lot at half past one.

The tourists had woken up five minutes after the blonde had taken off with their crystal ball. Their wish to avoid incarceration had superseded the intent to sue me for putting a wall in their way in my "storage room". They'd rushed out of the store without a word of apology.

I figured it was a good idea to read over my coverage in any case. I gazed over the pages, casting glances at the blonde pulling a heavy rust-colored leather hobo bag over her shoulder as she got out of her car.

She planned to buy something this time? Why else would she need her purse? My hopes lifted. Though she was dressed like a new age hippy, she did have a nice necklace made out of stones that could have been polished turquoise. She pushed through the glass door, finally giving the store the once-over she'd neglected on her previous visit.

"Sorry about that," she said in lieu of a greeting. "My boss takes thefts out of our paychecks. And she overcharges on those useless glass globes." She rolled her eyes and then held out her hand as she neared me. "I'm Nell."

"You're a witch." My blurted statement wasn't the most gracious of responses, but she'd surprised me.

"Uh, yeah," she said with a thick snort. "And you have a shop with a floor in Wipuk. What's it to ya?"

"If you're storing energy and I shake your hand, we'll both be zapped, that's what it is to me."

"Oh," Nell said. "Well, okay then." She drew her hand back. A slight frown creased her forehead. Moments later she bopped around the store, peering at the merchandise. "So what do you have upstairs?"

"Another storefront."

"Anything good up there?"

I couldn't help but laugh a little. "If I didn't think it was good, I wouldn't try to sell it."

"Fair enough," Nell said. "But just so you know, four leaf clovers and rabbits' feet are shit."

"Usually. But those are four leaf clovers from Bridget's Grove in Ireland—potent luck charms. And the rabbits' feet are from little buggers who live in the parks of Venice. That city is built on luck and not much more."

The blonde gave me a wide-eyed look before focusing on the luck charms with renewed interest. "Can I check out the merchandise on the other side?"

"Sure."

Thanks to the vampire's visit yesterday, I'd learned my lesson about leaving the place unguarded. And with the thieving tourists' visit, I wasn't about to leave the downstairs wide open without a little help. I said a silent phrase to bring up the magical security net around the ground floor. That ought to minimize the risk of a pair of sticky-fingered tourists snatching anything.

Nell took the stairs first with quick, thwacking steps of her bamboo sandals. Moments later she stood staring at the display case where the softly pulsing crystal sat. I waited for her to ask me about it.

She didn't disappoint. Her voice broke the brief silence with a melodramatic delivery. "What. Is. That?"

"The crystal?"

"Uh huh."

She'd spotted the newest item—the crystal from Calcutta. "It's called Kali's Candle. It's kind of like a USB thumb drive for magical energy. That crystal will store any energy you put in it. The energy can then be funneled to you anytime you need it as long as it's touching your skin."

Or it could run a spell while I was absent. But I'd leave that explanation off for now until I knew if she were serious about buying anything.

Nell blurted out a question I should have seen coming. "Do you sell weaves?"

"No." My face warmed. "Many of these items could be misinterpreted as weaves, but they're not. They augment a witch's natural power rather than provide power to a non-witch. And no witch had to give up their power to create them."

The blonde gestured to the glass display case, jumping to yet another topic. "No one is working the counter up here."

"I just opened today."

"Do you do aura photography?"

My head tilted at her in confusion. She was an odd girl. "You believe in that … stuff?" I barely caught myself from maligning something she might feel strongly about.

"It was fate!" Nell tossed her massive leather purse down atop the display case. "I was meant to chase those thieving bitches to your store because you need me." She shot me a cheeky smile. "And because I just quit my second summer job in two weeks."

I let my eyebrows drift upward. "I need you?"

Nell lifted her pointy chin up and down twice. "You need an employee to run one of your floors." She gestured to Kali's Candle. "And I need that and a job at a place that isn't run by a psychopath who thinks she can read auras on parakeets."

I snorted harshly, because of both the parakeet thing and the thought that she could afford the object of her desire. "That crystal cost me five grand. You'd have to work a lot of hours to get that."

"Five grand?" Nell's shoulders slumped. "Shit."

"Yeah. These are rare items. Five grand was a steal because the vanilla human I got it from had no idea what he had in his possession. I won't be selling it that cheaply." Not when the thing truly *had* belonged to Kali.

Nell righted herself to her full height of what looked to be five foot eight, a mere inch below me. "Eight dollars an hour," she said. "An hour lunch. And I get two fifteen-minute breaks if I have to work for seven hours or more. Plus I don't want thefts taken out of my paycheck."

It was my turn to blurt out a seemingly unrelated question, "Are you one of Desmond's spies?"

"Marino?" Nell let out a low growl. "Fuck no. I hate that asshat."

"You're hired!"

Chapter Fifteen

In hindsight I probably should have done a bit more checking up on Nell before hiring her. But she simply felt so … right. We had an instant kinship. I think it was because she reminded me so much of Amphy—my nymph best friend who was stuck in the Underworld with her mother, learning the tricks of their trade … slowly.

It wasn't until Nell handed me her filled out employment application in curling bubble penmanship that I realized I had a problem.

"Kranz?" I choked on the surname scrawled on the paper. "You're related to the Air witch high priestess?"

She *was* a spy!

"Yeah." Nell gave me a sideways look. "I'm her eldest child."

"Don't take this the wrong way but none of the witches in Wipuk like me. They want me gone. So … having you work for me…"

She looked at me blankly for several long moments before a spark of life popped into her crystal blue eyes. "I'm not a spy for them. Mom's politics bullshit is crap."

I was beginning to note a defecation theme with Nell.

"I go to the University of Nevada in Las Vegas so I can get away from it," Nell said while dropping down onto the stool behind the counter. She kicked her sandals off her feet, and then tossed her legs atop the glass display case, leaning back until her frame rested against the wall. She looked comfortable in her khaki cropped pants and layered tank tops. "That and I freaking love Vegas." Nell gestured a toned arm toward the entrance. "But she makes me come back here every summer so I can hang out with all her witch friends and do witch crap. I hate it. That's why I get a summer job, so I can get away from her."

"Sounds like an awful convenient story," I said.

"You're super paranoid, you know that?" Nell folded her arms over her chest, shooting me a mutinous look of slivered blue eyes. "I can go get a job at any of the crystal shops if I want. But I'm so tired of the questions about vortexes and feminine and masculine energy that I could just puke. They're just as bad as my mother."

"I'm a sorceress," I said with a half smile. I was really starting to like her. "I'm not that different from them or your mother."

Nell set the stool back on the floor so she could drop her feet to the bamboo planking. She settled into an upright position and gave me the full weight of her suddenly sober gaze. "Look at this store." She gestured toward the wall. "It's like the Apple store for witches. It's freaking awesome. No witch would make a store like this. They'd have paintings of canyons and windswept tundra on the walls with incense burning in every corner and crappy new age music playing on old speakers."

They might if they were an Air witch.

"But this way it's inviting to every school," she said as if acknowledging her interior design bias was due to her brand of magic. "And you're not going to make me practice my telepathy until I have a migraine or ask me to sell a piece of round glass that cost you forty bucks for two hundred and fifty to an unsuspecting, struggling mother of four."

I wouldn't. But I was still paranoid. "You're going to report everything back to her." Had that been *my* whining voice?

"Shit on a stick. You got problems, chicky." Nell snorted roughly. She hopped up, grabbed her bag, and slipped into her sandals. At the corner of the display case she stopped suddenly, pinning me with a determined look of hardened features. "I'm not a spy." Her voice sobered to match the expression. "I don't like the coalition. I despise the witches in it, Desmond chief among them. I'm going to college for business so I can get the shit out of this crap hole as soon as I graduate." She jabbed her fingers toward the entrance again. "Working here, with you, would give me excellent experience for when I open my own store. I swear I'm not a spy. What do you want me to do to prove it? I'll do anything. Want me to punk Desmond? Want me to get my mom down here so she can tell you how disappointed she is in me? How about a visit from Eamonn Cary—that fine piece of evil Dark witch ass?"

My stomach tightened guiltily. Someone rather like me, though not a witch, had mentored me exactly as Nell asked. I wouldn't be here today, quite as prepared as I was, if it hadn't been for her. I had to pay it forward. But what could I do to make certain Nell wasn't a spy?

I could at least make sure she was a double agent. "You can prove it by reporting back everything you know about them."

"I don't know much because I'm willfully ignorant. It drives Mom crazy. But I'll tell you everything I do know."

This could be bad. I could be inviting an enemy into the camp and giving her the plans for the battle. But Nell still *felt* sincere.

I stared the potential mole down, hands gripping my hips in what I hoped was a mildly menacing fashion. "If anything you learn here ends up out in the wild there,

I'll fire you so fast your head will spin like a weathervane on a gusty day."

Nell's head tilted to the left. "You must be hiding something pretty big to be this paranoid." At my widening eyes, she lifted her palms in a gesture of surrender. "Okay, okay! I'll keep my big mouth shut. But it's going to cost you *nine* bucks an hour."

I couldn't help but laugh. I really did like her.

"Nine bucks," I said.

We shook heartily. And then I went to get the tax forms to make it all official.

****

Nell and I stood downstairs, going through my rehearsed product blurbs when we heard the bell jingle upstairs. My heart skipped twice in anticipation. My first Wipuk customer had arrived! Who would it be?

Nell gestured for me to go on up. We'd had four visitors since she'd signed her last employment form. She'd smoothly answered their questions about crystals, auras, and vortexes with more knowledge than I possessed. Though the tourists had gone on their way without buying anything, it had nothing to do with Nell's patient assistance. So I started up the stairs, leaving the lower floor in her care.

My stomach knotted in a combination of factors. This business was my baby, exactly as I'd told Eamonn. As such, I was anxious putting even part of it into the hands of a stranger for a few minutes. And I had no idea what awaited me upstairs apart from a lack of vampires—since it was nearly five o'clock and the sun was still high in the early summer sky.

I crested the stairs to find the store empty. Had the Wipuk customer ducked out without making noise?

No, I'd have heard that unless they'd magically hidden their retreat—a possibility.

I continued forward, meaning to check the parking lot. A dark figure caught my eye to my left. A male was hunched over the display case in front of Kali's Candle. Cropped black hair coated his skull, and a navy blue suit encased a trim body. The scent of a crisp mountain stream lingered in the air.

Desmond Marino. Of course.

I slumped but quickly rallied so I could breeze through the door, Doc Martens thudding noisily on the ebony bamboo floor. Desmond's head came up. Those fleshy lips parted slightly in surprise.

Surely I wasn't the reason behind his surprise. This morning I'd dressed in an orange blouse, jean shorts, and black Swiss dot nylons. My straight cerulean hair had been styled in its asymmetrical bob, and the mascara and eyeliner was dark around my eyes. All my customary look.

I greeted him with a neutral tone even though I wished he'd leave. "Afternoon."

Desmond stood to his full height of six feet one inch, give or take a half-inch. His chin lifted defiantly. I was clearly in for a fight.

"This store doesn't have authorization to operate in Wipuk."

"I'm fine, thank you," I said cattily on my way behind the display case. The glass would put a nice barrier between us.

He slowly swiveled toward me like water chasing gravity along a twisting glass. There was a pause before he continued. "Every retail establishment must apply to the coalition. I never saw your application."

Rather than glaring like I wanted, I gave him my beatific smile. "Someone neglected to send me the Wipuk handbook."

"Wipuk doesn't have a handbook," Desmond said in a haughty delivery I hoped was his worst. "Our ways are passed word of mouth from generation to generation."

And they were probably distorted when they came from his oh-so-pretty lips.

I tilted my head to the side in disgust, most of it at him. He was a bigot. Was that a familial thing, or had something happened to make him this way? Had some human woman broken his heart into tiny pieces? Oh, what did I care?

A drawling female voice interrupted from behind me. "No retail establishment has ever had to apply to the coalition before."

Desmond's head whipped toward the stairs. His eyes narrowed upon noting Nell in the threshold with her arms crossed over her chest. Nell leveled an unimpressed expression on him as she leaned against the frame, bare foot pressed against the wood. That look alone made me think the girl had a future as a priestess regardless of her protests otherwise.

"Creating arbitrary rules on a whim is not part of *our ways*." Nell's tone had gone caustic. "At least it wasn't until a certain Water witch became our dictator."

Oh. I *liked* her.

I glanced at Desmond and found his cheeks were red. His frame went rigid beneath his pricy suit. He shot me an accusatory glare. I lifted my shoulders in answer to his unvoiced allegation.

"Hello, Hellen," he said in a low, nasty tone.

I'd seen the name on Nell's employment forms but hadn't questioned her. Who was I to say anything when I used my middle name rather than my given one?

Desmond's lips formed a small sneer. "Does your mother know you've fallen in with a bad crowd?"

He wasn't looking my way, but I felt his attention on me nonetheless. My being part of the bad crowd was a mildly amusing thought. I was probably the most ethical person in Wipuk. If I weren't, Trip would have my soul and my mother would neutralize my magic like I'd done to dozens of witches over the years.

Was this a staged scene to prove Nell wasn't a spy? It seemed genuine…

I sent out a light empathic link to them both, working softly so as not to trip any sensors their consciousness might have. Nell was far angrier than her bored stance would have us believe. She really didn't like Desmond.

Was there bad blood here because of a failed relationship?

Desmond's emotional signature was twice as powerful as her anger. But I also noted a healthy dose of frustration and wariness mixed in. That wariness was notable, *really* notable. Was he worried Nell would share coalition secrets?

"What bad crowd?" Nell jabbed a finger toward the male witch stiffly regarding her. "You mean you? I wouldn't be caught dead falling in with you, Desmond."

Anger flashed in his eyes quickly before fading away. "No, with the weave-user."

"She doesn't use weaves," Nell said with a hard-edged voice.

I might have been surprised about her defending me with something she couldn't possibly know, but she *could* know it. Air witches were the one flavor of witch able to detect a weave.

"She might not be using one now," Desmond said. "But she used one last week when she demonstrated both Earth and Air magic."

Nell's attention snapped to my face. Her eyes widened, and then quickly narrowed. She believed him. And she looked for all the world betrayed. I let my eyebrows drift upward because I hadn't realized how attached she'd already become.

"I don't use weaves," I said. "I can access Air and Earth without one."

Desmond's gaze dropped to the ring on my finger. Only it wasn't there. I'd set it in a small jewelry box at home. The ring was safely hidden it in a corner of my closet beneath a shadow spell. A Dark witch would be able to detect it, but I hoped none would break into my apartment.

"Show us then," he said with a smug lifting of his fleshy lips.

An irritated sigh wound its way up my throat. With a glance back at Nell, I gestured toward the leather hobo purse she'd set atop the plastic cart of drawers behind the display case. "May I?"

She nodded her agreement.

I dropped my hand to the leather surface, taking in the history of the thing as I'd done to Desmond's chair and his jacket. And then I relayed that history aloud.

"You told your employer—a woman with frizzy blonde hair and a dumpy, baby blue bib dress— 'Sayonara, freak' when you quit. She tried to stop you by grabbing your purse. Before you came here the second time, you stopped for an order of onion rings from the ice cream shop on the corner. You might want to wipe the leather down because there's onion ring grease all over the back side."

"That's Earth." Nell lifted her chin in a sober nod. "Now show us Air."

I went to the back entrance where I could get at some dust. My audience wouldn't be able to *see* what I'd done if there was no dust. Desmond followed me out, taking up a spot beside the door to the left. Nell took the spot on my right.

Once they were in positions where they'd be able to see the action, I guided the Air into a swirling dust devil. Psychometry and dust devils were the two abilities Desmond already knew I could do. They were relatively safe to showcase again.

The small funnel formed in the parking lot with little fanfare. Dust had cooperated beautifully. I twisted my head, shooting a smug smile at the Water witch.

Unfortunately, he'd already adopted a triumphant smirk of his own. "You already did those. Show me something Air that *can't* be explained by a weave."

"Fine," I said between tightly clenched teeth while dispersing the dust devil's energy back into the surrounding area.

I'd show him something Air all right.

Calling on the breeze, I focused a short burst, and then shot it at Desmond with a press of my palms in his direction. The invisible force slammed into his gut, knocking him on his butt in the dusty lot. He lay stunned on the ground, staring up at the clear blue sky.

Nell's choked laugh had me clenching my lips together to keep from joining her. It was almost too much to restrain when the Water witch got to his feet with deliberately calm movements. He regally brushed the dust off the front of his suit with slow, steady gestures. Longer still was spent straightening his jacket down his middle.

"You probably have a weave to do that, too," he said at last.

Nell's snort cut short any reply I'd have thought to give. "You are such a shit-head." She shot him one last disgusted look, and then stomped back into the store. She yelled back once she reached the stairs. "She's not using any weaves, Desmond. Lay off, or she'll have grounds for mediation."

Mediation was how the different factions settled disputes. But I had no interest in settling anything with Desmond. I only wanted him to leave my shop and me alone.

The dick's voice went low and menacing. "I don't know how you're doing it. But I'll find out. And when I do, you'll be banished. Don't get comfortable."

Threat uttered, Desmond pivoted on his over-priced loafer and started for his black BMW.

Nell burst into uproarious laughter from the shop's interior. Perhaps because she'd noted the back of Desmond's navy suit. The costly navy fabric was *tan* from all of the dust it had collected during his sojourn on the ground.

My lips quivered as I struggled valiantly not to burst right along with her. I held it back until the glass door closed us inside the shop, and Desmond's car door shut him within his vehicle. We laughed until we cried it out of our system, recalling his dark glare as he drove out of the parking lot.

He'd make me pay for that. But it had been worth it.

Chapter Sixteen

"He's so full of shit," Nell said once we'd calmed down enough to breathe again.

Her good humor was gone. In its place was a ticked off expression I recognized because it had been on my face every time I'd been forced to talk to Desmond.

"No one has to apply to open a store," she said. "He makes rules up as he sees fit, and no one does a freaking thing about it." Nell gestured toward the windows at the front of the Wipuk shop. "*He's* a huge part of why I want out of Wipuk. He's manipulating the coalition using Water magic."

My pulse spiked at the prospect of having proof to bring Desmond down.

Nell dashed it too quickly. "I can't prove it, and every time I bring it up, Mom gets annoyed. But how else do you explain him showing up seven years ago and taking over Neptune's Fellowship, then the whole coalition shortly after, when he's the youngest high priest to head up a national coven?"

How else indeed?

"I don't know," I said. "I heard the Water witches were unorganized and bickering before he came along. I think he's a huge dick, too, but is it possible he's just that good at managing people?"

Nell lifted her back from the wooden corner of the "Employees Only" doorjamb, and then set it back down with a soft huff of breath. "Managing people is just another name for manipulation."

Since I'd used the line a time or two in the past, I had to give her that. "True."

She shook her long hair out of her face. "The high priests and priestesses think they're too powerful to be manipulated without their knowledge. Their pride is probably why this town is going to shit."

I didn't understand her comment because Wipuk seemed like a nice enough place to me. "How is the town going to shit?"

"The Were are running rampant," Nell said. "Desmond has let twice as many of them move here as we used to allow. They're working on his building renovations. He's refused entrance to shifters, and he ran off the last clan with his stupid arbitrary rules. Shifters always kept the Were in line. No one cares enough to do it now. And we used to have peace among the factions. Since Desmond took over we're in a quiet war with the undead."

She pushed out a puff of irritated air. "Mom won't admit that Max has been systematically taking over our suppliers. Prices are going up far higher than inflation or fuel surcharges can account for. Some items we need are discontinued on both sides of the line. But she'll give me a list of shit to buy before I come back from Vegas every time." Nell rolled her eyes toward the ceiling, a move I was beginning to think she did often.

"Are you sure it's all Desmond and Max?"

Nell's head tilted to the left. "Who else would it be?"

"What about Eamonn Cary?" She'd called him an evil Dark witch earlier. I recalled that much.

Nell's expression darkened while simultaneously flushing. Her crimson cheeks caught my attention.

"He's no angel," Nell said with a quickly souring tone. "But he's just doing what his daddy tells him to do. And I'm pretty sure Pierre's only concern is that his son has control over the Coven of Nyx."

"Why did you call him an evil Dark witch?"

"Dark witches *are* evil." Her eyes darted to the windows—a move that smacked of avoidance. "They can hide in shadows and suck away lifeforce. You can't tell me that's not evil."

I couldn't. It *was* evil what a Dark witch could do. But she hadn't specifically said why Eamonn was evil.

A few more seconds of my silence prompted a blurted response from her. "And he has a freaking harem." Nell pushed off the wall, standing flat-footed with her arms akimbo. "A harem, Kora! Witches haven't done that in decades!"

For centuries witch births had been predominantly female. The imbalance led to a male dominated culture in which the few males had kept harems of witches handpicked for their purity, beauty, and magical ability. It was one of the theories for why most witches were drop dead gorgeous.

Witches who weren't pure or beautiful enough to be chosen for a high priest's harem had been reduced to menial jobs as overworked maids or cooks. They hadn't procreated as often as the females whose sole job was to lounge about looking alluring.

But the birth rate between the genders had evened out around the turn of the twentieth century. Witches had evolved to match the rest of humanity. There were still a few who held to the old ways.

So Eamonn had a harem. And he'd been trying to get me out on a date. That jerk.

"Let me guess," I said gently. "You went out with him and found out after?"

"Yeah." She slumped back against the wall. "I was smitten at eighteen. Thought I was in love with the guy. Until one of his consorts beat the shit out of me. I think she stole a year of my life, that whore."

Consorts. They thought themselves gods or kings. It was enough to make a girl scream. And the idea of anyone stealing a year of Nell's life made me want to hurt someone. I didn't know her well, but the idea of *anyone* stealing a year from a lovesick eighteen-year-old was just plain wrong.

"He sent me flowers," Nell said bitterly. "With a tiny card that apologized. And he had the brass balls to ask me out again. I told him I'd rather go to dinner with one of Desmond's steaming dumps than go out with him again."

I couldn't help but laugh at her colorful language.

Nell shot me a bemused half smile. "That was two years ago. He's left me alone since then."

Should I admit I'd nearly gone out with him? Would it upset her to know he'd moved on to other non-Dark witches?

Since I'd sent Eamonn on his way for good, I'd keep it to myself.

"Other than that, Eamonn hasn't really done anything evil," Nell said quietly.

Being a womanizer wasn't evil in the eyes of the Olympians. How could it be when the gods were notorious womanizers themselves?

I settled onto the stool with a soft sigh. The picture I'd been sketching of Desmond and Eamonn running Wipuk together for personal gain had to be erased and redrawn based on what I'd learned from Nell. Or at least it had to be redrawn in pencil rather than India ink.

"I can't believe you knocked him on his ass," Nell said a full minute later. "He's going to be so pissed."

We were back on the Desmond the dick topic. I shrugged. "He wanted me to show him something other than a dust devil. It's his own fault for failing to specify what he wanted me to do."

"Oh, I know." She gave a sage nod several years older than she could rightly pull off. "But he's going to make you pay for that."

"He is," I said with a grumble.

"It was fated." She pushed off her back foot into the Employees Only area. "I was definitely supposed to come here today. You need me."

Nell paused on the stairs and whispered her parting words. "And I need you."

* * * *

I shuffled into the bedroom with my newly framed dollar bill in hand. It was the very first dollar I'd made all on my own. This was an immense accomplishment. That it had been made on a pot of clovers to a fat man with rank body odor—odor that had lingered for fifteen minutes after he'd left—didn't diminish my good mood. However the speakers' switching into Etta James's "Sunday Kind of Love" did.

My heart skip-jumped over three beats. Trip was here. I wasn't sure how he managed to mess with my MP3 player since he couldn't alter things on the Mortal Realm, but it wasn't the first time he'd done it.

"I thought I'd deleted that," I said under my breath.

"You wouldn't do that," said the familiar baritone voice that had haunted me for years.

I reluctantly faced him. He rested against the front door with his head lifted toward the ceiling. His arms were folded over his chest, and one leg of his jeans was bent at the knee, lending him a relaxed and bored appearance. The mist coating him proved he was safely in the Spirit Realm.

"Why wouldn't I do that?"

"Because it reminds you of me," he said without pulling his eyes down.

"That's exactly why I'd delete it."

Trip's chest lifted once in a silent laugh. "Kora, Kora, Kora." He tsked in disappointment. "You enjoy this as much as I do."

Everything about him must have been made for the express purpose of pissing me off—from his voice right on down to his appearance. Because we couldn't be in the same room without me wanting to punch him repeatedly in the head.

My voice soured to match my mood. "I enjoy you spying on me and tattling to my mother at every opportunity?"

"Yes." He formed the "s" sound with a snake-like sibilance.

I let out a quick snort. "That's why I used that penlight to capture you in the act so Catey could tattle on you to Hades."

"Which, by the way, didn't do a damn thing." He stretched an arm back while yawning. I ignored the golden skin the motion revealed beneath his plaid shirt. He brought his head down, fixing hazel eyes on me. "What have you to report?"

A dozen things popped into my head, all things that would have made him jealous. I didn't want to start a fight, not now when all I wanted to do was fall into bed and sleep for twelve hours.

"I learned the names of most of the Coven leadership," I said instead. "The Air witch high priestess's daughter now works for me at the shop. She thinks the Water witch high priest has control over the coalition, but she can't prove it."

"Desmond Marino," Trip said, proving he'd either been listening to me last week or spying this week. Neither would have surprised me.

"Yes, that's him." Without thinking, I blurted out the question that had been bugging me for days. "Why didn't you scare off Eamonn Cary?"

Trip shrugged his broad shoulders. "Maybe I was giving you a break."

I snorted in disgust. "It had nothing to do with the fact that he was spying for Desmond?"

"I didn't scare off the shapeshifter," Trip said rather than answer.

"Because he's gay!"

Trip's lips quirked into an amused smile at my indignant shout. "That might have played a part in my decision."

I found myself snarling as I had so many times in our youth. "Charon take you, Trip."

Trip switched back into a professional tone that didn't match his irritated expression. "What else have you learned?"

I gave him a rapid run-down of everything I'd learned about Wipuk, the coalition, and the vampires, including how Maximo de Sole and Desmond Marino were public figures in both Wipuk and Sedona.

"I'm supposed to auction myself off for charity in gratitude for de Sole letting me stay in Wipuk," I said.

His hooded gaze narrowed to a fine line. "If you sleep with the winner, Kora—"

I interrupted him with a dismissive wave. "I know. I'll tarnish my soul, and then it will be yours." My stomach flipped nervously despite this being old news.

And then the MP3 player began playing "Sunday Kind of Love" all over again. I inhaled a sharp breath, shooting a dark glare at him. He hadn't moved a muscle. I didn't understand how he accomplished it.

"It will be mine," he said in a disturbingly silky delivery. The delay he'd put between the completion of my words and the beginning of his made them more menacing than usual.

Trip gave me a small finger salute, and then disappeared.

My lips tingled as the lyrics reached their zenith.

I remembered that day like it was yesterday. I'd been ten and Trip fourteen. He'd been so pretty back then, but I'd hated him for his unceasing torment. He'd stolen my hair tie and a chunk of my hair along with it. I'd chased him through the Hall of Hidden Doors for what was surely a mile. He'd disappeared suddenly, and then reappeared in time to slam me into an invisible wall.

The air had been knocked out of my lungs. I'd fallen to the floor with no help from him. While I lay struggling to breathe, Trip had straddled me.

And he'd *kissed* me. Full on the lips.

One of the Furies had opened her door the moment his lips had touched mine. Etta James had filled the hall from within her chamber. He'd stayed in that position until I'd hit him with a punch of Air.

My mother had moved me to the Mortal Realm two days later.

He was right about the song reminding me of him. I'd deleted it off my computer more times than I could count.

I'd have to do it one more time.

Chapter Seventeen

After a restless night of kissing nightmares, all I wanted to do was slump behind the counter at the shop for the first ten minutes of the afternoon. But something wasn't right. A pungent cocktail of scents hung thickly in the air outside the building. And a line of black soot coated the dust a foot from the building—the exact location where my magical net ended.

I followed the soot around the structure, noting it extended all the way around and past the faint glimmer of Wipuk's edge. The tingling sensation brushed along my skin as I picked my way down the steep hill out of the magical pocket of space into Sedona.

The black line continued here, too. But what did it mean?

I spotted two red plastic containers discarded within the dried grasses to the left of the shop. Gasoline. One of the scents was *gasoline*. Someone had *attacked* my shop!

I stood in horrified inaction for what was surely a full minute. My mind was awhirl with contemplations of who would have done this.

Had Ryan Steel decided to send a message meant to silence me? While it was possible he wanted security, I doubted the shapeshifter would resort to gasoline and fire. Perhaps one of Eamonn Cary's consorts had learned of the date we'd nearly gone on. But a Dark witch would steal lifeforce rather than set something on fire, wouldn't they?

The next obvious name on my list of potential evil bastards was of course Desmond Marino. Spraying the place with gasoline would have required he get sweaty in his fine suit. The guy probably had minions to do that sort of thing. But would he? His MO had been confronting problems head on. Setting a shop on fire didn't seem his style.

That led me to the final name on my list— Ascencion Boleda. My jaw ached from how tightly I'd clamped it shut. It had to be her.

I'd set her on fire. She returned the favor.

Or she'd *tried*.

I scanned over the intact structure, relaxing slightly once I was certain my shop was fine. My magical security system had held—the net using every school of magic ran off the energy I'd stored in the softly glowing crystal inside. Tonight I'd create a second net and run it off a different magical battery just to be safe.

In the meantime I needed to wipe the evidence of anything happening before a vanilla human asked. Because I was still wary of Nell's intentions, I'd also clear the soot from the Wipuk side as well. And then I'd watch her reaction to the standing building when she arrived for her shift.

****

Nell breezed in at quarter to twelve in a pair of jean shorts, a white tank top, and a light blue plaid unbuttoned short sleeve shirt. She ditched the sandals just inside the "Employees Only" area. There was no sign of surprise at the unharmed building. A quick empathic link had verified what I'd known deep inside—Nell had nothing to do with the attempted fire.

Hours later, I sat with my laptop balanced on my lap atop the stool behind the counter in the Wipuk storefront. Nell's heavy footfalls on the stairs implied she'd soon join me.

"I'm bored," she said as she crested the stairs. "Can I bring my laptop back with me when I go to lunch?"

"Sure," I said without pause. It was only fair she be able to use hers if I could use mine. And it wasn't as if I had tasks for her to do.

She settled her narrow frame against the wall. "Maybe I can help you track down rare items."

"Maybe." I was distracted. The noncommittal answer was all I could manage.

Nell leaned over, I assumed to get a look at my screen. "You're shopping for dresses?" There was a hint of accusation in her voice as if she thought I ought to be looking for items for the shop.

And there was a hint of defensiveness in mine. "Until I sell a few of the rarities I already have, there's no sense looking for more. Yes, I'm shopping for dresses."

"Those aren't just dresses. You're looking at *gowns*!" Nell shoved off her foot. "What for? Do you have a big date?"

"Not yet." I sighed because her breath on my shoulder hinted she wouldn't let up until she had a better answer. "I said I'd let Maximo auction off a date with me at his solstice charity event."

"Oh my shit! Seriously? Why would you do that?"

I craned my neck back. She didn't look nearly as freaked out as she sounded.

"I kind of almost killed his girlfriend," I said. "In my defense, I warned her. After that he claimed me— whatever that means—so she wouldn't attack me and so I could stay in Wipuk."

Nell drew in a noisy sniff above my neck. "Shit on me! I was about to punch you for being a dirty thrall to that ass master. But you're not enthralled."

"He said this auction thing would go a long way toward making us even."

"It had better," Nell said, grumbling a word under her breath I didn't catch. "Anyone can bid. *Anyone*. Do you want to get stuck on a date with that asshat Desmond?"

"*No*." Thank Zeus, Trip couldn't appear on the Mortal Realm, or I'd be in serious trouble during the auction. "That won't happen. Desmond the dick dislikes me as much as I dislike him. Some weirdo will probably get me for sixty bucks just to see if I'm really a sorceress or if I'm a human using weaves."

"That *is* the big question on everyone's mind. It's the first thing Mom asked me when I told her where I was working now. She doesn't believe me that you don't." A wicked smile came over Nell's face. "But she did have a laugh when I told her you'd knocked Desmond on his ass. I'm gonna put it on YouTube next time you do it."

Eager to change the subject, I brought us back to the original topic. "I told de Sole I had a suitable gown, but then I saw the photos of last year's event. He wasn't kidding about it being a black tie event. I don't have anything that nice."

"Let me help." Nell snatched the laptop off my lap so she could stick it on the display case between us. "I'm a wiz at finding deals."

It took Nell forty minutes to find me a gown we agreed was suitable. The strapless full-length garment with a gathered detail on one side of the waist was classier than anything I'd ever owned. The best thing of all was the color: a deep rust orange called "cognac" that would be perfect against my pale skin and cerulean hair. I hadn't wanted to pay four hundred dollars, but when she showed me two additional sites that wanted over two grand for the designer gown, and reminded me this was an excellent advertising opportunity, I'd coughed up the money as another splurge.

I only hoped it paid off in the end.

****

The brunette in the red shirtdress was an unwelcome sight. Desmond had sent his model thin assistant. What letter would they serve me with today? A summons to appear before the coalition so I could argue to keep my shop?

Nell had verified with her mom that the whole shops-requiring-permission thing had been another of Desmond's arbitrary rules. That didn't mean the coalition couldn't have enacted it overnight just for me.

Allison's eyes immediately went to Kali's Candle in its home nestled in the display case in front of me. My paranoia kicked in. There was a gleaming shade of avarice in her gaze that set me immediately on edge. Did she *know* it was a magical battery running my overnight security?

No. She couldn't. But she also wouldn't have honed immediately in on the candle if Desmond hadn't told her about it.

Allison gave me a curt nod before sliding along the right half of the shop. She perused every item while sending surreptitious glances at the display case. Each time her gaze caught on the softly pulsing crystal, her eyes brightened a little more.

"Do you have any weaves to put volume in my hair?"

I lifted my eyes from my laptop, giving Allison the full measure of my disdain. If I sold weaves it certainly wouldn't be vanity items any Air witch neophyte could accomplish.

"I don't have any weaves," I said flatly.

"Then what is all of this stuff?" Her voice was sharp and indignant as she sent derisive glances over her shoulders to the nearby shelves.

"They're rarities like the sign outside says." I had a duplicate signs in both parking lots. She could read, couldn't she?

Her neck stretched upward in a haughty motion rather like her boss's. "Weaves can be rare."

I replied through clenched teeth. "I neither use nor sell weaves. I sell rare items that augment a witch's natural power. If you don't have natural power, then the item doesn't do a damn thing."

Except in a few instances, like the ones beneath glass in my display case. But she didn't need to know that.

Allison sent the crystal a wary glance. "Like what?"

I gestured to the shelves on the right side of the shop. "Those bracelets improve a witch's focus by clearing the mind of distractions. They improve casting time, accuracy, and impact." I paused, giving her a toothy smile. "And they come in silver for added protection against Were and undead."

Desmond's assistant glanced at my wrists. "You're not wearing one."

I shrugged rather than reveal I didn't need one.

The moment she'd decided to taunt me was clear from the grating curve of her lips. "How do I know they work if the owner of the shop doesn't even wear one?"

"You have to take my word for it. They bond with their initial wearer so you can't demo them."

"That's convenient." Allison sneered, revealing her perfect teeth.

I merely lifted an eyebrow rather than allow her to rile me. She had a problem with me, and I wasn't sure why. I hadn't done anything apart from warn her not to try Water magic on me. Maybe that was all it took.

"What about that?" She gestured to the pulsing crystal between us. "That's not a weave?"

"No," I said curtly. Though she looked like she could afford the crystal, there was something off about her. Something that made me want to keep the crystal from her. So I lied and hoped she wouldn't sense it. "That's already been sold. There's no point telling you about it."

A flash of genuine fear came over Allison's face. "Who did you sell it to? I can offer more."

Whoa. Desmond really *had* sent her for the crystal.

"Sorry. I already sold it. I can't back out now. It would be unethical." Just like lying about having sold it in the first place.

The woman's expression grew strained.

Was there more to the crystal than I'd initially thought? I'd have to take the thing out of the case and hide it at home even though I needed it here. I could make do with a different magical net and battery combination. And the crystal could run security at the apartment in case Ascencion targeted me there.

"Ten grand," Allison said, getting her checkbook out of her purse with a clear motion she meant me to see.

"I told you I sold it."

Eyes edged in hardness held mine. "Twenty."

I merely stared back.

Allison forced out her next words while leaning over the glass. "Forty grand. It can't be worth more than that."

"It's a priceless Hindu artifact." That was the gods' honest truth, but someone had put a price on it.

She held my determined gaze with a dark look of her own for an uncomfortable interval. And then she broke. Her shoulders slumped as she drew in a ragged breath. "I can't go back without it. He'll be so angry."

Desmond *had* wanted it. That dick.

"What's his number? I'll call him and tell him he isn't getting it."

Allison shook her head rapidly. "No. He'll be furious I told you I was here to buy it for him."

"Then he should have sent someone I wouldn't recognize as working for him."

The brunette nodded her agreement. Nonetheless her gaze quickly sharpened. She wasn't finished. "Fifty grand."

"Nope."

Her lips peeled back, revealing a snarl this time rather than a sneer. "You're such a bitch!"

"Look who's talking," said a drawled voice from within the stairwell. Nell hopped into the room, barefoot, a second later. "Go on back to your bridge, troll."

Allison shot my employee a murderous look, and then stalked out of the shop, two-inch heels clicking an irritating staccato against the bamboo floor. At her car's door, the brunette cast another, longing look at the pulsating crystal.

Yup. It was going in a box in my closet.

Chapter Eighteen

The crunch of gravel beneath a car's wheels still sent my heartbeat into a happy frenzy days after the shop had first opened. I wasn't sure I'd ever get used to having real customers. It was like validation for my mundane existence. And I loved it.

I loved it right up until I recognized the too beautiful face of the male outside. What in Hades did Desmond want now? The crystal? If so, why did he look like he was going to murder someone?

Nell's dinner break couldn't have come at a worse time. I didn't want to deal with the Water witch all by myself. And though Marino didn't seem to like Nell, he didn't argue with her as he did me.

The Water witch stalked across the ebony floor to the glass display case I was perched behind. He tossed a small item atop the clear surface as though the thing had been burning a hole in his hand. I allowed my eyebrows to lift quizzically as I looked down at the object.

Why was he giving me a small ceramic disc etched with a Celtic design? It was pretty, yes, with golden paint that emphasized the design sparkling beneath the incandescent light my display lamps cast. But a gift wasn't anything I'd expected from him. Certainly not when he'd looked fit to strangle.

I adopted a half drawl. "What's this? A peace offering?"

By the dark expression narrowing his features I was fairly certain peace was the last thing on his mind, but I simply couldn't help digging a little. Maybe it had something to do with how my mind had begun imagining what he looked like underneath the black polo shirt tucked into his relaxed khaki chinos. This was the first time he hadn't been wearing a suit. Damn if he didn't look hotter for it.

"No," he said between clenched teeth. And then he dropped a verbal bomb that cut short any naughty visuals in my head. "That's the weave you used to kill Steward Smith."

"I beg your pardon?" I said, pitch going shrill in a combination of confusion and indignation.

"I was speaking English, Ms. Walsh," the Water witch said in a contrastingly low voice. He stepped forward and braced white-knuckled fists against the glass surface. "I will speak slower for you this time. That is the weave you used to kill my Water witch by the name of Steward Smith."

I could hardly believe my ears. Not only had I failed to I clear up the misconception I was a weave user, but the guy was also accusing me of *murder*! Had I thought he was a bigot? He encroached on jingoism now!

My insides quivered uncomfortably. A charge of murder in the Underground wouldn't involve a lawyer or a jury of my peers. Yet I could just as easily be incarcerated for life. Or worse.

I replied in as steady a voice as I could manage. "I have never in my life touched a weave, Mr. Marino. And you and your assistant are the only Water witches I've met in Arizona."

"Don't lie to me!" Spittle formed along his bottom lip in an unattractive way as he roared—the first ugly thing I could recall in reference to him. "No one has been killed in Wipuk since I moved to the colony. Now one of mine is killed by a weave. The only change in this equation is you!"

Was that the only evidence he had in his murder investigation? No one had claimed to witness my doing the deed? None among the colony had found fiber from an orange shirt or a piece of cerulean hair at the scene of the crime?

My growing anger emboldened me to toss out a disgusted question. "So every new bad thing that happens in the colony from now on must be my fault?"

Desmond snatched up the ceramic disk from the glass. He darted around the case until his trim frame blocked my exit. Desmond then shoved the object into my face, a mere foot and a half separating us.

I found myself leaning the stool backward to get away from the surprisingly imposing body encroaching on my personal space. His mountain stream scent filled my nose with a warm tang that forced me to breathe through my mouth to avoid it.

"The only way a human can access magic is with one of these," he said in an icy voice that was tight with impatience. "You are a human. You can access magic. Ergo you are a weave user. And thus the murder of my witch by a weave is your fault."

Caution was required with the powerful male literally in my face. My voice came out with a shaky waver I wasn't able to hide. "Just as I've never touched a weave, I've also never killed anyone. You've got the wrong person."

"I don't have the wrong person." The words barely passed his clamped teeth. "You will come with me so a proper investigation can be completed."

No way was I going with him. "What evidence do you have against me?"

"I don't need evidence."

I gave voice to the questions that had floated in my head minutes earlier. "Did someone claim to witness me doing the deed? Or was a cerulean hair found at the scene of the crime?" When he only continued to glare at me in silence, I tossed up my hand. "You have to have something more to go on than just your bigoted hunch!"

Desmond took a surprised step backward. His head jerked, eyes going slightly wide. "Bigoted? I'm not bigoted. You—"

"Oh, yes you are." My new employee's voice echoed down the stairwell. Her thudding footsteps pounded down the thirteen stairs.

This was becoming a pattern, but I wasn't at all upset by it. Thank *Zeus* she was here today!

"What the shit are you talking about?" Nell asked as soon as she breezed into the storefront, taking up the spot where Desmond had been not long ago. Her sky blue gaze darted from the right to the left, eyeing us both.

Desmond's chin lifted regally as he took two slow steps out of my personal space. I was glad for the distance. Having the guy that close had been seriously uncomfortable.

"Steward Smith was found dead in his home with this in his breast pocket." He lifted the ceramic disc for Nell to see.

"So it must be Kora's fault," Nell said sarcastically. Her eyes rolled. "You're such a tool."

He refocused his attention on me, ignoring her barb. "You will come with me so a proper investigation can be completed."

Nell set her palms atop the glass and bent toward us both. My employee adopted a faux-inquisitive tone edged in ice. "What kind of proper investigation would that be? Are you going to strap her into your interrogation chair so you can politely ask her if she killed him?"

The guy had a chair with straps that wasn't in his car? That was worrisome. What would he have done to me if I'd simply gone with him as he'd demanded?

I really didn't want to know.

Desmond's eyes stormed darkly. Nell drew up into an upright position, defiant in spite of his power within her community. Her gaze narrowed into a glare that gave his a run for its money. The young woman was quite simply bad-ass.

"Have you even had an Earth witch do a reading on that thing?" She jabbed her index finger toward the disc in Desmond's hand. "How about an Air witch? Do we know if that's a weave? It could just be an art project."

Yet more silence from the Water witch implied he'd done nothing investigative apart from race here and accuse me of the crime.

Nell shoved a hand against her hip as she dropped her weight onto the opposite leg. "A *proper* investigation includes the entire coalition. I just finished dinner with my mom. She wasn't called about this. Seems to me like you've gone off half-cocked," She glanced at me. "On a bigoted hunch."

She sauntered across the bamboo floor and shoved open the glass door. "I suggest you call an Earth witch and an Air witch. When *they* give you evidence that points to Kora, then you get the coalition to agree to an investigation. Until then, get your overpriced polo shirt the hell out of here."

Desmond's nostrils flared three times as he glowered at us both. And then he stalked out of the shop to his costly sedan.

I didn't dare sigh in relief. This wasn't over. He thought I was a murderer, and I had no idea how to prove that I wasn't.

But I knew one thing—I wasn't paying Nell nearly enough.

****

I was half afraid to go home because I feared the Water priest would be waiting for me. But my anxiety had been for nothing. The only thing that awaited me at the apartment was a squashed package of incense sticks in the mailbox.

Nevertheless I found it difficult to quiet my mind enough to sleep. So with the help of my mother's hammered bracelet, I stayed up all night scouring the web for divine artifacts for the shop's inventory.

Thanks to Nell's connection to her high priestess mother, my employee had news when she arrived for work at ten until noon the next day. The good news was the death of Steward appeared self-inflicted.

However, the bad news was Alina had personally checked the ceramic disc. The thing had been a weave. But the more damaging news was the disc appeared to have been a Water-based manipulation charm. Steward could have been persuaded to off himself with a powerful enough suggestion.

The Earth witch that had been called to the scene, Dea Woods, hadn't been able to pick up on anyone other than Steward and Desmond touching the disc. Despite psychometry turning up no other culprits, Desmond was unwilling to believe one of his witches would voluntarily touch a weave.

A necromancer had reanimated Steward for his side of the story. Unfortunately it hadn't provided any help beyond learning Steward was confused about his death and also suffering from memory loss. He didn't remember the twenty-four hour period prior to his death.

Though Nell insisted my name had been pushed to the end of the list of possible suspects, I was still concerned for my freedom. And rightly so. I was no longer a citizen of the Mortal Realm. I was subject to Wipuk's laws and enforcement. For all intents and purposes, the colony's enforcement pointed straight to Desmond—the man who despised me.

I contemplated how furious he would be if I offered to help solve the case. Perhaps if I went to him personally, he'd reconsider my guilt in the matter. If I hadn't heard anything by the time I woke on my day off, I would pay the dick a visit and attempt to smooth things over with a sign of good faith.

****

I must have arrived during Allison's lunch hour because the tidy cherry desk outside Desmond's office was empty. His voice's smooth cadence rose and fell within the interior room, proving he was in even if she wasn't. But unlike the last time that I had come here, I felt out of place.

What had I been thinking? The man had accused me of *murder*! I was the last person he was going to want to see.

I'd made the decision to creep silently back out the double glass doors when the Water witch's voice halted in mid-sentence. I froze in place. Had he heard me?

My options were few. I could remain exactly where I was and risk being caught sneaking out of the guy's office. Or I could use Dark magic to shadow-walk out and hope he hadn't spotted me. If he had noted me, he'd no doubt think I'd been up to no good.

I'd play it safe by staying exactly where I was.

"Ms. Walsh." His baritone voice had gone low and icy compared to the professional tone and steady pitch he'd used for his phone call. "What are you doing?"

"Being an idiot," I said under my breath as I slowly faced him.

He stood outside his office door, clad in another costly suit—this one in a black and gray hound's-tooth fabric with an indigo shirt and black tie, all wonderful contrasts for his pale skin and dark hair. His handsome features were crinkled into a dark glare that was a measure perplexed.

That confusion manifested in his next question. "What?"

"I said I was being an idiot."

Rather than soothe the confusion, his wrinkles increased at my response. But he didn't question me again. His continued stare was question enough.

I broke beneath that powerful gaze. "I came to offer to help you discover what happened to your witch. But I realized about two minutes ago how much of a bad idea that was."

Desmond made a small sound of disbelief. "How could a *human* help?"

My hackles rose at the indignant tone he'd adopted. "A *human* couldn't. A *sorceress* could."

"Even if you weren't utilizing a weave to access magic, and you weren't a suspect in the crime, what could you possibly bring to the table that the coalition couldn't?"

I opened my mouth to tell him I had access to *all* of the schools of magic—even the extinct ones, something *no one* else in the world could claim—only to clamp my teeth down on the knowledge. My pride had nearly gotten me into real trouble. If the coalition knew I could access Time magic, they'd strap me to a tree and set it on fire.

What in *Hades* had I been *thinking* coming here?

I remembered now. It was the one thing I brought to the table that the others lacked.

"Motivation," I said.

Desmond's raven eyebrows arched, but he didn't verbalize the question filling his eyes.

"You accused me of murder," I said. "I want to clear my name."

He pushed a heavy puff of air through his nose. "I should throw you in the holding cell and call the others together."

Should implied he didn't want to do it. After his behavior Saturday night, I had to wonder why. What exactly was stopping him from demanding I be interrogated? Surely Nell's reminder the entire coalition had to be involved in an investigation wasn't the reason he restrained himself.

The Water witch's frame drew up a hair taller and straighter. "If you want to clear your name, you'll let me draw the truth from you with an empathic link."

While I had nothing to hide on the *murder* front, allowing him complete control over me would be starting down a dangerous road. I had plenty to hide from him. He simply didn't know it yet. Nonetheless, ridding myself of a murder charge was worth the risk.

I drew in a long breath to illustrate my displeasure with the request. After letting him wonder a second longer, I nodded.

Rather than invite me into his office where we could sit in comfort, he pushed his hands into the pockets of his costly trousers and braced his legs apart, entrenching himself in the spot. I assumed that meant we were staying exactly where we were. The prod at the edges of my consciousness heralded a Water witch's power, as did the scent of a crisp mountain stream that slipped into my nose. Despite how foolish it was, I opened myself to the invasion.

He'd be able to skim my emotions through the entirety of our conversation now that he'd connected to me. I didn't bother hiding my apprehension. He'd find it stranger if he felt no emotion from me than if he sensed fear.

Desmond the dick spoke in a lofty voice. "Tell me truly, what is your name?"

There was a tug at my consciousness, and then words spilled out of my mouth. "Rebecca Kora Walsh."

Ah. An initial question to ensure he had control of my answers. I was glad he hadn't asked me where I'd been born.

"When were you born?"

I barely stopped my mouth from blurting out the absolute truth. An incredible amount of willpower went into giving myself a nanosecond's worth of contemplation time.

Kore's knees! I should have known this was a horrible risk. The *year* I was born did not coincide with my actual age. According to mortal years, I'd technically been born twenty-three years ago. However I'd lived ten years within my mother's little slice of Hades where time moved on her whim—in this case at a hastened pace of eight years. So I wouldn't be able to explain how I was a twenty-five-year-old female who had been born in nineteen eighty-eight without giving up the secrets of the divine.

Using what was left of my willpower, I replied with only the bare minimum. "December thirteenth."

"Show me your driver's license."

I couldn't resist the urge to roll my eyes toward the Domain even as my hand made its way, quite of its own accord, to my purse. I pulled out my wallet and showed the dick the government approved date of birth of December 13, 1986.

"Where did you come from?"

I was glad to be able to respond with the absolute truth. "California."

"Why did you come to Wipuk?"

Again my willpower came into play. I couldn't simply blurt out that I'd come to infiltrate the coalition at my mother's request. But I could give him the other half of the explanation. "I came to open a shop selling rare magical items to the Underground."

"Weaves." His chin jabbed forward an inch and a half in an aggressive gesture that made him a hint unattractive.

Hadn't we had this argument enough times? "No. Weaves are objects that have been infused with a specific witch's power to do a specific task. My shop specializes in rare items, such as good luck charms, magic bracelets that clear the mind to make room for cleaner casting, protective armor against specific elements, and items that augment a witch's natural power. In those cases, if the possessor has no natural power then the object provides nothing but bling."

Desmond's lips twisted. "That all sounds like weaves to me."

I drew in an angry breath through my nose, contemplating how to reply to his offensive statement without making my situation worse.

He got down to business before I came up with an answer. "Tell me truly, did you kill Steward Smith?"

The answer quickly popped out of my mouth. "No."

"Were you involved with his death in any way?" "No."

He further insulted me by asking, "Did you sell someone the weave I found on Steward?"

"No!" Desmond still assumed I'd had a hand in the crime by being the weapon's dealer! I was too ticked off to hold my tongue a moment longer. "That would be kind of hard considering I've never even *touched* a weave."

Desmond withdrew his power with an abrupt funneling effect that made my head feel as if it were spinning.

And then he hit me with even more insults. "I don't know how you're able to lie to me. Another weave, Ms. Walsh?"

"You're such a dick!"

With that wholly mature response uttered, it was best I leave his office. There was no sense trying to defend myself. The guy was determined to believe the worst.

I'd simply have to solve his murder for him so he'd have to swallow his pride and apologize.

Chapter Nineteen

According to the colony's white pages, Steward Smith had lived in a small bungalow on the outskirts of Wipuk a mere half mile from my shop. A beat-up black Toyota had been parked in the driveway when I drove past the first time. It was still there when I returned on foot after dusk.

A single naked light bulb was lit above the dead witch's kitchen sink. Plenty of inky shadows clung to the room's edges with which to shadow-walk. Through the kitchen window I chose a lengthy shadow beside the rounded table.

I took a deep breath before calling on the disorienting power. The eerie swooshing sensation scrambled my thoughts for a few seconds. And then I was in Steward's kitchen without needing a key.

With no idea what had happened to the man apart from a death that looked like a suicide, I wasn't sure where to begin my search. I did a quick check of the house, careful not to touch anything I didn't absolutely have to touch.

"It was in the bathroom."

"Hera's hoppin' heart!" I exclaimed in fright upon hearing the male voice within the room.

I whirled on my heel, discovering my lifelong nemesis leaned against the witch's ratty plaid sofa as if he could actually touch it. He was clad in, of all things, an impressive black suit. I wasn't sure I'd ever seen Trip play dress up quite like this. And I was glad for it.

"You scared me half to death," I said, far more snappish than I'd meant.

"I should have tried harder." His lips lifted into his usual jaunty grin.

Yet another topic I wanted to avoid. I returned the subject to the one at hand. "How do you know where the witch died?"

Trip irreverently lifted the shoulders of his nice suit. "I have my ways."

"Hades's fine white hairs, you're such a freaking stalker!"

He tossed his surfer-boy hair out of his eyes so he could settle their narrowed gleam on me. "I'm a stalker who is about to help you beat a murder rap."

If I failed my mother's task to infiltrate the coalition *this* spectacularly, she would probably drag me back to Hades herself and hand me over to my hated nemesis on a silk pillow. So why would Trip help me? I was half afraid of what his answer would be. So I didn't ask.

"They found him in the bathtub with his wrists slit," Trip said without prompting. "The *proper* way." He let that disturbing piece of information sit for a moment before continuing. "He was one of ours. I personally judged his soul. It wasn't suicide."

The modern-day Greek mythos saw nothing wrong with suicide to escape a horrible fate. But it did frown upon death to evade responsibility. Thus if Trip had sat in judgment of Steward Smith, he would have delved into the reasons for the man's suicide. Trip probably knew the exact cause of the man's death, even if Steward himself wasn't privy to it.

"What was it?"

"Tsk tsk, Kora." His tone was twice as smug as his expression. "You know I can't say anything that may alter Fate's path."

I barely held in a curse but that didn't stop me from snapping at him. "When have you ever cared about incurring Fate's ire?"

Trip's frame drew up straight. "When have you ever been in a position to learn inside information from me?"

"Never. You've always been utterly useless."

His pupils dilated in a flash as his nostrils flared wide. I could almost *feel* the floor shake. I'd pushed him too far.

Though his eyebrows had drawn down into a deep V, Trip attempted to pull off a nonchalant tone. "Well, in that case, I shouldn't rock the boat." He shrugged a set of stiff shoulders. "Have fun fighting that murder rap without me now. I'll be waiting for your soul on the other side."

Trip's glare belied his feigned indifference the split second I saw it before he disappeared from sight. The man-shaped cloud of mist scattered in all directions. I found myself staring at where he'd been, wondering what had just happened.

Way to go me. I'd insulted away my chance at ridding the colony's suspicion of me as a murderer. What had I been thinking?

That was the problem. When it came to Trip, I didn't think. I simply acted.

I pushed my thoughts of stupidity to the periphery so I could focus on the problem at hand. Steward had been found in the bathroom. It was time to check it out.

Fortunately, the bungalow only had one bathroom. Someone had scrubbed the evidence of the death away in the days since it had happened. I glanced around the tiny room—a room that was barely large enough for the tub, commode, and sink it held. There weren't many options for someone to stand viewing the tub.

I assumed whoever had killed Steward would have been in the room with him. I simply had to find out what they'd touched while they were there. And stick around long enough to read it with my psychometry power.

This was going to be a long night.

****

Every bone in my body screamed for rest by ten in the morning. My mother's hammered silver cuff had kept my mind alert, but it had done nothing for my poor aching muscles. On the bright side, the effort had been worth it.

I'd checked the history of the toilet, the sink, the walls, and even the floor, learning nothing. What I'd stupidly ignored until the last minute was the tub itself. The cast iron object had told me everything I'd needed to know.

A vampire had killed Steward.

The Water witch had died rather peacefully, all things considered. Mesmerization had enabled the vampire to drain Steward of half of his blood without a fight. Undead mesmerization had also persuaded Steward to slit his wrists so that it would look as if he'd bled out. Best of all, the weaved disc had played no role in the death.

And I knew exactly who had done this—the ginger-haired asshole who had punched me over the head and kidnapped me days after I'd arrived in the colony. What I didn't know was how Maximo de Sole would react if he knew one of his employees had killed a Water witch. But I was going to find out.

The real question was did I go to Desmond with what I'd learned, or did I keep it to myself?

"What in the great blue sea are you doing here?"

My heart skipped three beats upon hearing the now familiar baritone voice exclaim from behind me.

This was becoming a habit—these men sneaking up on me.

I didn't lift my hand from the tub when Desmond stepped into the bathroom with me, seemingly stealing all of the useful air with his powerful presence. The images flickering in my head courtesy of psychometry were only now arriving to the good part—how the male vampire had convinced Steward to get in the tub fully clothed in the first place.

But I did reply to the question in an effort to buy myself some time. "Psychometry," I said without turning. "I'm nearly to the beginning of the incident. Just give me a few more minutes."

"Get out of my witch's house," Desmond said, snarling and taking a menacing step toward the tub.

"Don't be foolish, Marino. I know what happened now. Just let me—"

He interrupted me with yet another step forward. "Get. Out."

His timing was impeccable because the images in my mind's eye showed Steward stepping out of the tub. I'd learned all I could from it.

Drawing myself up into a standing position, I slowly faced the high priest. I wasn't sure why I was surprised to find him clad in another of his designer suits. The brown plaid fabric wasn't his best look, but he made it work by accessorizing with a yellow shirt, blue tie, and flamboyantly patterned pocket square.

"Don't you even want to know what I learned?" I aimed my beatific smile squarely at his handsome features.

Desmond's jaw set tightly with an audible snap. A half second later he relaxed it enough to speak. "I know what happened. You murdered him, and now you're here to cover it up."

Perhaps the knowledge of what had truly happened to Steward made me bold in the face of his glaring visage. "If you really thought I murdered the guy then why didn't you have the coalition toss me into some witch jail?"

The priest's retort was tight. "Because you're not a witch. You're a *human.*"

"You keep reminding me of that. It makes a gal wonder why." My mouth kept running while my brain checked out. "Are you uncomfortable with my being a human, Marino? Perhaps because … oh, I don't know, you find me attractive?"

Desmond's eyes shot wide. "What … Why … No…" He wildly shook his head as he took four giant steps out of the bathroom. "That's preposterous."

The idea I was attractive was *preposterous*? That was just mean.

I took advantage of the opening his indignation gave me to slip out of the bathroom. I continued right on through the bungalow toward the front door.

I wasn't looking forward to what lay before me. There was a half-mile walk to the car and a five minute drive to the apartment; only then would I be able to sleep until dusk. And then I had to meet with a murderer's boss.

Desmond called after me once I'd entered the kitchen. "Where are you going?"

"You told me to get out," I said without slowing.

There was no immediate response until I pulled open the front door. Desmond's long strides thudded behind me. Before I could get more than a foot onto the front step he asked, "What did you learn?"

My lips curved upward because I was off the hook. "A vampire did it to cover up illegal feeding."

He cursed under his breath. "How do you know?"

"Psychometry on the tub."

"That's impossible," Desmond said with an emphasized S sound that made my teeth grit because it reminded me of Trip. "The Earth priestess wasn't able to get anything from the tub because it's cast iron."

"Metal is a poor conductor of memories, but they're there if you try hard enough."

"How convenient."

I twisted on my heel in the middle of Steward's gravel driveway, facing Desmond, "You're going to believe whatever you want to believe, Marino. But a vampire killed your witch. Not me. And that weave you found didn't even play a role." I started down the pavement before he had the chance to comment.

Desmond pushed a puff of air out of his nose. The bungalow's door opened and closed again. Apparently he wasn't going to argue with me. For now.

Now all I had to do was confront Wipuk's First about a murderer within his ranks. I had a fun night ahead of me.
****

I sat at a booth in the only pizza place in Wipuk, nervously bouncing my legs. Maybe I shouldn't have demanded Maximo de Sole meet me in public. It wasn't as if the guy would have a hard time discovering where I lived. I'd hoped to avoid Ascencion. But would she be angrier when she heard we'd met without her? The last thing I wanted to do was give her more of a reason to hate me so she would try harder to burn down my shop.

Hades! She might have set me up for *murder*! But no. Ascencion would have been smarter than that. She would have left something of mine at the scene if she'd meant for me to take the fall.

Wouldn't she?

The spot I'd picked faced the door of the pizza bistro. From there I could watch for the arrival of Wipuk's First. There were several other customers at tables and booths scattered around, but most were a good distance from me. I had to hope none of them had supernatural hearing because what we were about to discuss probably shouldn't be public knowledge.

I drummed an uneasy pattern against the tabletop. I didn't like the idea of voluntarily seeking out a vampire. Especially to relay bad news.

The door opened, and in walked Maximo clad all in black. It was too late to back out now.

His sable hair had been slicked away from his face in a fashionable wave, but he'd left his trademark curl hanging down his olive sienna forehead. His gaze immediately homed in on me. The vampire's dusky lips curved slightly upon finding me waiting.

My tapping and bouncing ceased as fear quickly filled my limbs. I'd called a *vampire* to a public meeting so I could accuse his employee of murder. I would be lucky to step out of the restaurant alive.

Maximo sauntered across the bistro, nodding his head here and there at what were probably familiar faces before stopping beside my booth. His lips lifted the remainder of the way into an amiable smile that made him look approachable instead of runway handsome.

"Miss Walsh." He greeted me smoothly. With a gesture to the seat across from me, he asked, "May I?"

I bobbed my head in answer because just then I couldn't have spoken to save my life.

The vampire slipped onto the naugahyde seat, smiled for a beat, and then took hold of one of the menus that had been stuck behind the condiment basket. He flipped open the trifold brochure as if he planned to actually order something. I had to admit that it had gone a long way toward easing my nerves.

"Thanks for meeting me," I said quietly without meeting his eye. "I don't have good news."

Maximo's head tilted to the right. "You changed your mind about the auction?"

Moments passed before I recalled the solstice charity ball. "Oh, no. I'm still doing that ... if you want me to."

"I want you to."

"This has nothing to do with the ball, or really me at all."

The vampire waved a dismissive hand. "Then there is nothing you could say that would be bad news."

We'd soon see about that.

I pulled in a breath for bravery, and then began the explanation. "Desmond Marino has accused me of murder."

Maximo's milk chocolate colored irises went cold and hard in an instant. "Clearly he does not know you."

I'd opened my mouth to agree but halted. *How exactly did de Sole think* he *knew me?*

"I found out what happened," I said, glancing around to see if anyone was watching us. The groups gathered were deep into their own conversations. "He still doesn't believe me. Unfortunately it was a vampire."

"I gathered that." Maximo's response was oddly calm. "Do you have a description or a name of this individual?"

After drawing in a long breath, I nodded. "I'm fairly certain it was the red-haired vampire who hit me over the head and dragged me to your home weeks ago."

The only indication that he'd heard me was a tightening of his jaw.

Nonetheless I continued with the explanation. "I set out to solve the crime to clear my name. Using psychometry on the witch's tub, I found the vampire had used mesmerization to get the witch into the tub where he drained him half to death. And then he mesmerized the witch into slicing his wrists to finish the deed. He wiped the witch's memory of his visit. I'm sorry that you had to hear it from me."

"No," Maximo said in a surprisingly soothing tone of voice despite the stormy look in his eyes. "I'm sorry you were involved at all. Desmond is a fool. I'll take care of this, Miss Walsh. You'll experience no fallout. I guarantee it." He gave a deferential bow of his head. "Thank you for coming to me. Let me to buy you dinner to show my gratitude."

Eating dinner with a vampire was not high on my list of things to do. And I had the perfect excuse to get out of it.

"I'm sorry, but I can't. I have a meeting scheduled in fifteen minutes in Sedona to discuss radio advertisements for the grand opening."

He gave me his amiable smile, but it didn't reach his eyes. "Another time then."

I nodded rather than verbalize the agreement as I slipped out of the booth. "Have a good night." I hightailed it to the door.

All in all that had gone exceedingly well. And that worried me. But that was a worry for another day. I really did have a meeting to get to.

Chapter Twenty

I closed and locked the Sedona door at nine on Wednesday night. Nell let out a long yawn while stretching out her limbs. We were both tired. It had been a full week since I'd opened the shop. And a full day since I'd met with Maximo to tattle on his employee.

While the Sedona side of the shop had seen a hopping influx of tourists who bought good luck charms and a few sets of Tarot decks I'd collected in Europe during one of my mother's favors, the Wipuk side hadn't sold a single item. Several witches had passed through, I assumed simply to be nosey.

I hadn't recognized any of them, but Nell had. She'd given me their names for my logbook after they'd left. I gave the excuse that I wanted to keep track of repeat customers. In reality it was all part of spying for my mother.

A single nameless Water witch had come in looking for Kali's Candle in the display case that afternoon. He'd left without checking out anything else when he'd noted it missing. I was glad I'd taken it home. Nell hadn't been able to I.D. the guy based on his license plate alone, so I'd never know who he was, apart from the scent of brine he'd carried implying he was a coastal Water witch.

I'd met with the local radio and television stations to set up advertising for the shop's grand opening on Friday. Nell had taken petty cash so we could get finger foods for the customers to munch on. Downstairs would be a veggie platter because most of the new age crowd was vegetarian. She suggested a meat and cheese tray for upstairs. I trusted her judgment on both.

"Night, Kora," she said as she pounded up the stairs to the Wipuk side where we'd parked our cars.

My thoughts grew troubled while I shut off the lights one by one. Though no fallout had occurred today as a result of my meeting with Maximo yesterday, I wasn't stupid enough to think I'd heard the last of that incident.

However, the business of the Water witch's murder had quickly moved to the back of my mind upon learning something new today. Nell had seemed to be in an "off" mood. I'd asked her about it halfway through the day. She'd slumped down to the floor against the wall, set her head in her hands, and then told me all about her "horrible life".

According to Nell, at least one witch tradition had survived into modern times. Though Alina Kranz lived with a Healer, the Healer was not Nell's father. Nell's father was the previous high priest of the Aer Association—an eighty-three-year-old man who had retired ten years ago.

While pureblooded Air witches were free to love and marry whom they liked, they were obligated to have one pureblooded child. Nell was that pureblooded child. And as a pureblooded child, she was obligated to have one of her own. It was a vicious cycle Nell had no interest in joining.

But her time was running out. Alina had procreated with the previous high priest when she was eighteen. Nell was twenty and was being pressured into spending time with Curtis Hawksley, her mother's co-leader. Curtis was one of the reasons Nell had gone to school in Las Vegas and wanted desperately to get out of Wipuk. She assured me he wasn't a bad man, but that he was at least in his fifties, far too old for her. She insisted the real issue was she wasn't ready to have children until she'd begun her career.

The lengths the witches went to keep their race powerful sickened me. But there wasn't much I could do about it apart from being a sympathetic ear when she needed to talk.

My drive to the apartment and the walk inside were fraught with lethargy while I put all of my focus into a solution for Nell's predicament. The growling in my stomach had me grabbing an apple off the breakfast bar after I'd dropped my purse and keys down. I lifted the apple to my lips and halted.

I hadn't bought an apple in years. A glance at the breakfast bar showed me that it was the only piece of fruit in the apartment. Had a hag-like old witch had dropped a poison apple for me to eat and fall into a deep sleep?

I examined the apple for holes, turning it over and over in my palm. Etta James crooned from the bedroom. I hurried toward the sound.

The MP3 player wasn't plugged into the alarm clock docking station as it ought to be. It was connected to my portable speakers. Someone had turned both on and tuned it to the beginning of the iconic song. I swiveled on my heel and found Trip standing within two feet, a smug look creasing his handsome face.

"How…" My words trailed off in horror. I pulled up my hand, staring at the rosy red apple that held the impression of my teeth in the waxy skin. "Hera, help me," I whispered.

"So close, Kora." Trip crooned almost as smoothly as Etta James. "I almost had you."

I dropped the apple onto the floor as if it had bitten me, staring mutely at the spot it had landed. Ten seconds passed before I was able to draw enough air into my lungs to speak. "How did you do it?"

"Kronia has just past." Trip shook a leather wristband at me. "My mother gave me a present for surviving another year."

Kronia was one of the first festivals in the Olympian's year, but that wasn't the disturbing news.

My whisper went ragged. "You brought that apple from Hades's personal stash."

"Happy Kronia, Kora."

"If I'd eaten it…" I couldn't finish the statement. It was too horrible to consider.

Trip's smile spread into a wicked grin. "I would have been able to cart you right back." His voice dropped into a deep pitch. "Where you belong."

"I don't belong there. I was always destined to be here."

He stalked toward the front door. "What have you to report?"

I couldn't think of anything but the apple on the floor and how close I'd come to being shackled in the Underworld. While eating the food of Hades wouldn't have tarnished my soul, it would have made me fail my mother's task.

Trip shot an impatient look over his shoulder.

I pushed through the tar of my worried thoughts so I could come up with my report. "The Water witch high priest really wants Kali's Candle," I said woodenly. "I hid it in the closet because I don't trust what he'd do with it."

From there I reported each witch who had visited. Somehow I managed to share everything Nell had told me about pureblooded witches and their mating habits. And I even explained the outcome of the Steward Smith murder even though I suspected he already knew.

When I was finished, Trip tracked back and stopped a foot in front of me. The wristband was visible in my peripheral vision. That item was a symbol of how the game had changed in a massive way.

Could he touch me now?

My pulse spiked. Trip's gaze dropped to my lips. A shiver of heat wiggled down my arms. His chest rose and fell at a steady pace as if none of this bothered him, while I could hardly draw in air in anticipation of what he'd do. I could step back, put space between us, but that would be admitting I was scared of him.

He tipped forward. I inhaled a sharp breath only to release it when I worked out he was dropping into a crouch near the apple. His wristband glowed momentarily, and then the apple was coated with mist. Trip lifted himself to his full height of six foot whatever. Apple in hand, he brought it to his lips for a noisy bite. Trip chewed the fruit with unhurried lifts of his jaw. His long throat worked, swallowing the bite down seconds later.

"Mmm." He softly moaned. "So sweet."

Once more his gaze dropped to my lips. He rocked forward on his heels every so slightly. I held my breath, not daring to move a hair on my head.

With a mocking smirk, Trip rolled away, gave a finger salute, and then disappeared.

Etta James warbled "Sunday Kind of Love," in the bedroom for the last time as I slumped to the floor in panting shock.

****

Trip's new toy had me jittery and sleepless all night. I put on my mother's hammered silver cuff so I could get *something* accomplished rather than stare at the ceiling in horror. The first thing I'd done with my extra time was toss out every item of food in the apartment. I could no longer trust anything that had been out of my hands for any length of time. Now that Trip could hide in the Spirit Realm *and* at the very least manipulate objects on the Mortal Realm, I had to be especially wary of everything.

I needed to talk to my mother. Something had to be done about my nemesis. He'd never tried anything this dangerous in the entire decade and a half since I'd been on the Mortal Realm. If I hadn't caught myself in time, that apple could have potentially destroyed everything we'd worked toward. Given the task I'd been handed, Hades might extend me some leniency for eating Underworld food, but eventually he'd make me go back. Whether that would be tomorrow, fifty years from now, or only during the winter months, no one truly knew. If Trip had his way, I'd be transported back sooner rather than later.

But the subject of Trip had been a sore spot with my mother for so long that I dreaded mentioning his name. Later … I'd summon her later when most souls were asleep and I'd built up enough courage to face her wrath.

A visit to the grocery store saw to the replacement of some of the food. For an added layer of protection, I set a spell to note tampering of *any* kind on any object in the place. The spell was powered off of Kali's Candle hidden in the closet. And I'd made triple sure Trip wasn't watching as I set it. But he'd been known to get past my spells even when he hadn't seen me cast them. I'd still have to be vigilant.

Nell noted my grumpy mood almost immediately and took steps to minimize catfights. She stayed on the Sedona side, keeping the noise to a minimum, and suggested I work on documentation for the web site in the Wipuk storefront. After lunch she brought me chocolate. After grilling her about where they'd come from, I relented and took a piece. But I didn't eat it until after I'd done every test on it imaginable. The packaging had a history that was all within the Mortal Realm. And it didn't hold the scent of pomegranates and aether that Hades did. I had no idea how I would function at events where strangers served food unless I could come up with a better way to detect things Trip had placed in our realm.

Nell and I worked hard to get the shop in tiptop shape for the grand opening tomorrow. During the second half of the evening I ran through my blurbs for her again so she'd have them fresh in her mind. We swept the floor and polished the shelves before we left for the night so we'd have less to worry about in the morning.

She vowed to arrive early with the party platters and made me promise to be in a better mood. I hoped I'd be able to deliver on that. It would all depend on my mother's advice.

Eager to get home so I could call her, I sped the short distance from the shop to the apartment. A sticker on the door told me a package had been delivered and awaited me at the main office. I pushed it into my purse so I'd remember to fetch it in the morning.

I needed an offering if I planned to summon Hecate. It didn't matter that she was my mother. I'd need to provide coffee, or she'd be a bigger grump than I was.

The fifteen minutes it took to make a pot of dark roast gave me enough time to change and choose my outfit for the grand opening. From my stash of clothes, I drew out a russet blouse with tiny cornflower blue daisies, a jean skirt, and a pair of nylons with blue dots at regular intervals. They would look good with my chunky heeled mary-janes.

I settled onto the futon with two mugs of coffee in my hands minutes later. Pressing my eyes closed over a long breath, I visualized my mother, and then I whispered, "Hecate, I summon you."

A lone dog baying in the distance heralded her appearance. She sat nearly upside down in my beanbag chair clad in jean overalls over a Red Sox T-shirt with red three-quarter sleeves. Without asking for permission, she grabbed one of the mugs and began sipping despite her awkward pose.

"Two sugars and two creams," I told her even though I hadn't needed to. She'd gripe if I'd done it improperly.

My mother closed her eyes while making a sound of contentment as she wiggled her tush to get a better position in the cushioned chair. They flipped open a moment later. "It has been some time since *you* summoned *me*."

"Something happened. Andronika gave Trip a bracelet—"

She let out heavy sigh and rolled her eyes. I barely kept from growling. She was weary of hearing about Trip. I got that. But this wasn't his usual taunting.

I relaxed my tightened jaw. "It lets him manipulate things on the Mortal Realm, or something, I'm not sure. But he put an apple on my breakfast bar. I almost ate it."

Her steady gaze hinted she didn't quite understand the problem.

"It was an apple from *Hades*," I added.

My mother shot upright. Coffee sloshed onto the thigh of her overalls. "Did he *say* it was an apple from Hades?"

"I asked him if it was from Hades's personal stash. He said that it was."

My mother let out a stream of obscenities in an ancient tongue—one only the gods spoke. I understood ancient Greek and Latin, and that wasn't either.

"I can't have his gift taken from him without help from on high," she said with a grim delivery. "But I'll bring it to their attention. In the meantime, I'll commission an item that will detect items brought over from the Divine Realm."

Her image shuddered, the marker she'd temporarily been in the Underworld. There was no telling how long she'd actually been gone or what she'd done while she was there. When it smoothed out, her free hand held a leather wristband rather like the one Trip had been wearing. This one was tooled with a wave pattern much like the ring she'd given me. She tossed it at me.

"Wearing that wristband near your pulse point will detect objects brought from the Divine Realm," she said. "They will softly glow when detected. It won't detect mundane objects he's tampered with. But at least you won't have to worry about eating a forbidden fruit."

Yeah, at least.

I nodded my understanding. "Thank you, Mother."

She ducked her head in acceptance. "I must get back. I'll update you as I can." My mother held out the coffee cup. I took it, holding it lightly at my side. She hugged me tightly, a gesture I wasn't able to return because of the twin mugs in my hands.

"Good luck with your grand opening, Kora," she said with a peck on my cheek, and then disappeared. The baying of the dogs outside immediately ceased.

I wrapped my new bracelet around my wrist. After setting the mugs aside, I checked the fridge and cabinets. A single carrot softly glowed within the bunch. I stared aghast.

Trip was a truly devious bastard. I never would have suspected a single carrot among many. And it was the best looking of the bag. After tossing the entire bag in the trash, I made my way into the bedroom for a much-needed nap now that my latest problem had been softened.

Chapter Twenty-One

"Do you sell dragon's blood incense?"

I drew my attention away from the pair of Canadians dressed in pale green Crocs and foam visors. They'd been demanding I show them exactly where Brigid's Grove was in Ireland on a map. The new question gave me an excuse to leave them. I faced the customer at my back.

"The only incense I have is clove-scented," I told the woman with the thick braid that reached her tush. "But the scent isn't the important thing; it's what it can do for you."

"What can it do for you?" A fourth customer who had been hovering on the edge of the room asked. He was in his late thirties with wild hair and eyes to match. He'd personally finished off the celery sticks ten minutes ago.

"It focuses the mind so that it's easier to get into a meditative state." In any other shop that would have been new age mumbo jumbo to sell ten cent incense for a buck a stick. But that wasn't the case in my shop. "One stick of my incense is better than a dose of Ritalin." I didn't know that for sure, but it was probably true.

"What's in it?"

"It's a secret blend my supplier won't share with even me," I said.

That was the truth. They didn't need to know my supplier was a Healer who lived on a remote Balkan mountain. I'd helped her fight off a Dark witch two years ago during one of my mother's favors.

"Here." I snatched up one of the sticks. "I'll burn one so you can see. If your mind doesn't focus, then don't buy any of it."

The incense went into a sleek ebony holder atop the glass display case. The four customers who had been huddled around me took up spots around the incense's finger of smoke. Though my stuff was the real deal, half of them would probably claim to feel the focusing effect simply to prove how in tune they were with energy.

The three sets of customers bought sticks as well as a few stragglers who had overheard us. I sold out of what I'd had on display within five minutes. Fortunately, I had a stash hidden in the true employee only area—a closet halfway between the first and second floors.

So far the shop's grand opening was a hit on the Sedona side. Our finger food had been annihilated after the first hour. Nell got more during her lunch hour so we'd have something for the evening crowd. We both kept our ears open for the bell on the Wipuk side of the shop but didn't hear it a single time all afternoon.

We did, however, get visits from several crystal shop owners. Most left in disgust, but one stopped long enough to buy a stick of my special incense. I suspected she'd analyze it in an attempt to duplicate it. She'd fail. The stuff took a Healer to make, and she was no Healer.

Nell's salesmanship saw to the sale of every luck charm I'd had in the store and a third of what had arrived yesterday. After my show with the incense, she'd also sold a large amount of what I'd had left.

But I made the most expensive sale of the day so far when I persuaded an overweight woman to try on the leather belt that was an appetite suppressant. She'd complained of wanting to eat the entire party tray of vegetables and get ice cream on the way back to the hotel. Once the belt was around her middle, a shocked expression had filled her pudgy face. She then declared she had absolutely no urge to eat. But when the belt came off she'd wanted iced cookies.

After exchanging her signature on a legal waiver and a price tag of six hundred and eighty dollars, the tourist headed out with her belt snugly holding up her jeans. I'd made sure to give her a set of instructions to follow, with a small magical nudge to follow them so she wouldn't die of anorexia. I certainly hoped the young man with her would be able to persuade her to eat since the belt would squelch the urge.

I spotted a cropped head of raven hair at the front of the shop at half past five. When it turned, I found myself staring into a familiar set of aqua eyes. Desmond had slipped into the Sedona side of the shop.

Eyes still on me, he leaned over and spoke into the ear of an unfamiliar male with salt and pepper hair. Rapid-fire questions from a pack of Connecticut tourists snagged my attention away. I focused my thoughts. There was work to do, and *he* didn't figure into it.

"No, the incense doesn't immediately induce a meditative state." I gave them a half smile. "If it did, we'd all be flat out on the floor. It only helps to clear your head so you can focus on a single task."

"I don't like the scent of cloves," one said. "Do you have it in any other scent?"

"I'm sorry, I don't." I shook my head in an approximation of dismay. "My supplier says cloves work best for concentration."

"Do those cigarettes work?" The hawk-like male in their party asked.

Did I sell cigarettes? I didn't think so. A moment passed before I worked out exactly what he was asking. "Clove cigarettes?" At his nod, I said, "I don't know. I stay away from tobacco and the like."

"Good girl," the first of the Connecticut tourists said.

I gave her a closed mouth smile, distracted again. The smooth cadence of Desmond's voice spoke a few feet away. Nell's stilted replies were rather accommodating considering how much she disliked him.

The tourists demanded my attention again. "Do you have any incense holders made of crystal?"

"I don't carry crystals here because there are several crystal shops already in Sedona."

Desmond's gaze fixed on me around the heads of my customers. It went to the display case to my left. No doubt he was looking for Kali's Candle. Was that why he'd come in on the Sedona side? The man was obsessed, and he didn't even know what the object did.

"I do have a few redwood incense holders if you're in need of something in a pinch," I said.

The redwood incense holders were probably the least magical things in the shop. They had no latent power and weren't divine or rare at all. I'd bought them so I'd have something to hold my special incense, but then I'd found the ebony holder.

"Do you have anything in the shape of a wolf?" another of the Connecticut tourists asked.

I softened my smile. "No, sorry. The other crystal shops have wolf items. I didn't want to step on their toes, and I specialize in rarities."

"Rarities," an unfamiliar male voice said. "Do you have any rare items to ensure the outcome of the next election?"

I made a quarter turn until I faced the speaker—the man with salt and pepper hair. Desmond stood behind his right side, watching me with a tightlipped stare. The Water witch relaxed his lips so he could speak. "Mr. Mayor, I'd like you to meet Kora Walsh, the proprietor of Rarities."

He was introducing *me*? Like we were old friends? Like he'd had something to do with my opening a shop? Like he *hadn't* accused me of murder days ago? By Zeus, the man was a dick!

The mayor's eyebrows drew together in confusion. "Cara?"

"Close," I said patiently. "But it's with an 'O'."

"Kora?" At my nod he said, "That's a strange name."

"It's a literary name with ties to mythology," Desmond said.

I shot him a pointed glare even as my shoulders stiffened. He was damn *close* to the truth. Who in Hades did he think he was?

He held my angry expression with feigned calm. It had to be feigned because I could almost see the waves of frustration wafting off his back—an extreme emotion I could easily pick up without an empathic link. Was that frustration because he was behaving like a jerk and he knew it?

The mayor's profile tilted toward Desmond. "Mythology?"

"I believe it is a variation of 'Kore'," Desmond said, chilling the blood running through my veins. I worked very hard not to show anything in my body language and to tamp down any emotion he might be able to pick up without an empathic link. "Kore was one of Persephone's nicknames."

"Persephone," the mayor said. "That's the Norse love goddess."

It took every ounce of control to keep from laughing or showing my deep disgust with the man. "I believe that Persephone is the Greek goddess of spring growth. She is also the wife of Hades and queen of the Underworld."

And my godmother.

"That's it," the mayor said as if he'd known the answer all along. The tight smile he gave me was a dare to disagree. I wasn't that foolish.

Instead, I smiled lightly. "Is there anything I can help you with, apart from a charm to win elections?"

His graying eyebrows shot up. "Can you do that?"

Hades's hair! The mayor was a believer in all the new age mumbo jumbo!

"No, sir." I gave a wide shake of my head. "I can't charm people."

"But you're charming me," he said with a twinkling eye.

My cheeks flushed warm before I could stop them. The ridiculously corny answer should *not* have gotten that response from me.

"You have a delightful blush, Kora." The mayor leaned in, whispering, "I'd love to see what else is delightful."

My back went ramrod straight. There was a ring on his ring finger, the cheater. I shot a disgusted glance at Desmond for bringing this jerkwad into my shop only to find *him* glaring at the mayor. That was strange enough that I was able to soften my ire in time for the mayor to rock back onto his heels.

"There are many delightful things in my shop," I said amiably while keeping my distance. "Maybe a lucky four leaf clover would help you campaign."

I really hoped he wouldn't buy anything for luck. I didn't want him as Sedona's mayor for another term. He followed the direction of my hand to the shelves holding the potted clovers as well as the ones packaged for purses and wallets.

I continued with the sales pitch I wasn't really feeling. "They're from Brigid's Grove in Ireland—a plot of land sacred to the Celtic goddess. They have been known to bring great luck to any who possess one."

The mayor rolled onto the balls of his feet for another lewd comment. "Great enough luck I'll be able to find out if the carpet matches the curtains?"

Oh, for Zeus's sake.

Desmond noisily cleared his throat. "Ms. Walsh, I believe your employee has been attempting to get your attention at the register for the past few minutes."

"I'm sorry," I said with a nod to them both. And then I ran headlong for Nell behind the glass display case.

She shot me a confused look,

"Hide me," I said under my breath.

Minutes later the mayor and Desmond left the store without buying anything. Relief flooded me. At least it wouldn't be my fault if the guy were reelected.

Nell and I continued our brisk trade until seven when the flow of customers slowed for the dinner hours. We had time to restock the dwindling displays and clean up the mess the influx had brought. I sent her off for a break because neither of us had had a chance to catch our breath.

A black limousine pulled into the lot minutes later. Out of the back stepped Maximo de Sole. He assisted a companion out of the back seat. My fingers tightened on the price gun.

Ascencion, his newly healed vampire girlfriend, stood to her full height beside the car. She'd dressed in a spaghetti strap summer dress with bold purple flowers hand-painted on the white linen fabric. A pair of matching purple sandals completed her look. The outfit was prettier than anything I owned and made me feel a little shabby in my opening-day best.

She breezed into the shop past the door Maximo's driver held open for them both. Ascencion sent a mere glance at me, as if I were beneath her notice. "How charmingly bourgeoisie."

My teeth snapped together. She meant to rile me. It had worked.

If my shop was bourgeoisie, then did that make the other crystal stores ghetto? I had no aspirations of being a high-class shop, but I didn't think it was decidedly middle class in the sour manner Ascencion's tone implied.

Maximo lingered on the edge of the store perusing the merchandise as if he actually cared what I sold. He greeted me once he'd reached the shelves nearest the display case.

"Good evening, Miss Walsh." He nodded his handsome head. His gaze touched on the ring I'd slipped on this morning. After Trip's game-changing move, I needed all the help I could get.

The vampire's attention returned to my face. "You have transformed a dreary space into something really quite magnificent."

I flushed beneath his praise because it sounded genuine, unlike the mayor and Ascencion's words. I *had* transformed the dated interior into something modern and beautiful.

He gave me an indulgent smile as if he felt *he* had something to do with my success. Would he remind me it was his claim that had allowed me to remain in the area?

"Your grand opening has gone well?"

"Yes, very well." Half my focus remained on Ascencion. Her fingers hovered over an expensive glass vase. The object was one of the divine pieces I'd picked up—this one extended the life of any plant stored inside. If she broke the costly item, Maximo would pay twice as much as it was worth.

"I hear you have Nell Kranz in your employ," Maximo said without looking for the leggy blonde.

"I do."

"Good." His smile increased. He was really starting to bug me. "Perhaps you will help each other."

I wasn't about to touch that statement with a ten-foot pole. Instead, I brought the topic back to a professional vein. "Is there anything I can help you find?"

"Ascencion insisted we pay a visit to your shop," Maximo said, earning him a dark look from his woman. "We are merely browsing."

"You don't have any crystals," Ascencion called out from the front corner. Her tone was triumphant, and the smug expression on her face matched. "How can you have a new age shop in Sedona and not have a single crystal?"

Two customers across the store turned, perhaps to hear my response. I took in a small breath for courage.

"Sedona is saturated with crystal shops," I said at a volume they could all hear. "My shop serves a niche—those customers searching for unique gifts that are truly beneficial."

Ascencion let out a harsh laugh. Her tone dipped into deep condescension. "What do you have that is *beneficial*?"

I scanned the shop for a single object that would be beneficial to a vampire. A cloak hanging on the rack at the middle of the left side of the shop caught my eye. The black fabric was lined with Nyx's netting—a fine woven fabric that kept out the sun's rays. The last thing I wanted to do was put something that powerful in the hands of a vampire, especially one who had tried to eat me. My lips curved into a wicked smile upon spotting the garment beside it.

"The red duster there." I gestured toward the ripstop, ankle-length jacket. "That can withstand flame up to fifteen hundred degrees Fahrenheit for up to five minutes."

Ascencion's expression turned murderous. She darted a look at the hovering customers, and then, perhaps realizing she couldn't eat me without the media hearing about it, she stomped out of the shop. Maximo's driver had the car door open in time for her to slip inside.

I'd probably made a misstep, but I didn't care. She'd asked for it. I snuck a look at her boyfriend. His indulgent smile had turned to amusement rather than hate. He wasn't ticked I'd taunted her?

Maximo bowed his head courteously. "We wish you luck in your grand opening weekend, Miss Walsh."

"Thank you," I said uncomfortably.

Thank Zeus, the limo was long gone by the time Nell got back from lunch.

Chapter Twenty-Two

"Pardon my French, but I don't know what the *fuck* you're doing to these cords. I can't get this one undone for the life of me. How the shit am I supposed to plug this in?"

I looked up from the budget program on my computer. Nell stood in the door to the employee only area. In her hand was a hopelessly snarled black power cord, one that was attached to a lamp I used to light the shelves. I hadn't touched the cord. Nell had turned off all of the lights last night.

"It's not me," I said uneasily. My mind already raced through the possibilities of who had done such a thing.

"Uh, if it's not you, then who is it?" she asked the question on my mind. "I found six like this yesterday, four on Friday, and two on Thursday. Well, not this bad, but bad enough it took me a few minutes to get them untangled. I kept quiet because I thought maybe it was some weird O.C.D. thing you got goin' on, but every cord downstairs is like this."

While a few names had popped up—Ascencion, Allison, Desmond, and Eamonn—the one I returned to again and again was Trip. He had that bracelet now. If he could place an apple in the Mortal Realm and then bring it back into the Spirit Realm, then he could conceivably take a lamp into the Spirit Realm so he could tangle it all up.

But why? I couldn't believe he'd do it simply to annoy me, especially since I hadn't realized it had been happening until Nell pointed it out.

"I don't know who it is," I said.

"No one would break in just to tangle up power cords and not steal anything." She tossed the cord up in frustration. "Someone wants to piss us off."

"Yeah."

Someone did. And someone succeeded.

I followed her down to the Sedona portion of the shop to help untangle the lamps. My mother's leather wristband with the wave pattern didn't reveal any new glowing objects. But she'd told me it wouldn't detect things Trip had merely manipulated. We were still untangling when the first customer came in at five after twelve.

The crowds had been twice as large yesterday. We were dangerously low on all the hot ticket items. I'd put in more orders with my suppliers, earning me a mixture of irritation and pleasure. They enjoyed the money they were making off me but not the effort they had to put in to fill my orders. I was counting on the traffic to slow dramatically after today.

"I am so glad we have tomorrow off," Nell said once the customer moseyed back out to their car without buying anything. "I've never worked so hard as I have these past two days."

I nodded in agreement. "Me either."

I'd scheduled the shop to be closed on Mondays and Tuesdays based on the research I'd done on the area and that I'd wanted a "weekend" of my own. We'd need the break to rest and restock.

I got the last of the lamps untangled without breaking a nail, and then headed back upstairs. There were numbers to crunch and Underground contacts to call. So far the sales we'd made surpassed my hopes three-fold. If we sold nothing today, it would still be a successful grand opening.

I stalled at the top of the stairs. The lamps on the Wipuk side—the lamps that had been turned on when I'd gone downstairs—were a tangled mess in the middle of the shop floor.

"Charon take it!" I stomped my heel into the ebony floor. "Trip! Show yourself!"

He shimmered into existence in the corner of the store, leaned against the window in an arrogant pose. I wished I could have thrown something at him and have it hit.

"This is so childish." I stabbed a finger at the floor where he'd left the pile of lamps.. "There's no point to it!"

Trip's eyebrows lifted in amusement as he picked at his plaid shirt. "There is a point to it. The point was to piss you off." His lips curved into a shit-eating grin. "And it worked beautifully. You're redder than Geryon's crimson cattle."

"You have unlimited time and resources and now a gift that allows you to manipulate items here, but instead of working on something beneficial, you use your gift to screw with me!" I let out a sound of disgust before dropping to the floor. It would take all afternoon to untangle the hopelessly knotted cords. I continued my tirade at a muttering volume. "And they're going to put you in charge of *judging* souls? You, who wouldn't know an altruistic gesture if it knocked you on your butt? It's a travesty!"

His torso shook in fury—visible out of the corner of my eye. I'd gone too far. I knew that.

Trip was my Underground contact no matter how many times I'd asked my mother for someone different. He'd make my life more of a nightmare than it already was if I didn't apologize. There were more important things than my pride.

"I'm sorry," I said quietly without looking up.

Trip let out a rough laugh. "No, you aren't. You meant every word."

I remained quiet rather than confirm or deny it.

He snorted in disgust because he knew me well enough to know why I hadn't replied. "You don't know what I do the other twenty-three and three quarter hours of the day, Kora. I could be stopping floods and famine in Third World countries for all you know."

Bravely I lifted my head, capturing his angry glare. "Are you?"

Trip drew in an unsteady breath. His chin lifted defiantly. "I could be."

"Then why aren't you?"

"Because it would be altering Fate's plan."

My pride took a back seat. I snarled, tossing my hands up in frustration. "Oh, don't feed me the party line. Especially not when you put that apple on my counter!"

"I knew you wouldn't eat it."

I didn't dare comment, not when I'd barely avoided entrapment by apple.

"It could have been a regular apple," Trip said with a sullen mien.

"Was it?"

His lips set in a tight line. The answer was clear without him speaking. No, it wasn't a regular apple. He really had brought fruit from the Underworld.

With a negligent shrug of his shoulders he said, "You got a gift out of it. Now you can use your wristband to track down more rarities."

My vision went hazy when I realized he was right. It quickly narrowed on him once again. "You didn't do that to help me, so don't even try."

"You have no idea why I do the things I do."

"So you're not trying to get me to screw up so you can torture me when I die?"

His jaw set tightly. "No."

"Then what in Hades's little white hairs are you trying to do, Trip?"

"Nothing." Trip stared at me for a beat and then whispered, "Nothing."

He disappeared. Mist that had once clung to him shot in all directions. I rolled back onto my tush, slumping beside the mess of electric cords.

He was a liar. He'd always been a liar. He'd always be a liar.

But now he was a liar with a way to make real trouble in my life. I only hoped I'd offended him into leaving me alone. After decades of torment, that was unlikely.

****

I lifted an eyebrow at Nell the third time she sent me a questioning look across the shop. It was Wednesday. I'd slept nearly the entirety of my days off. And I'd eaten like a horse. Not worrying about the origin of my food was nice. Better still, I hadn't heard anything about the Water witch death and my supposed hand in it. Apparently Maximo had really taken care of the situation.

"What?" I asked sourly when Nell shot me a fourth not-so-surreptitious glance. "Did I put on weight? Great. I'm not going to be able to fit into that Gucci gown that is supposed to arrive any day now."

"No," Nell said. "I was just pondering if that fight you had with yourself upstairs on Sunday was the reason why none of the cords are tangled up today."

My face heated. She'd heard me yelling at Trip. I should have closed the door.

Nell made light of the situation. "Did you smack your other personality around?"

"Yeah," I said because it was safer for her to think I was insane than the truth.

I'd been reckless by speaking to Trip with someone within earshot. My soul would be forfeit if I revealed the secrets of the gods. And he'd said he *wasn't* trying to get me to screw up. What a load of Minotaur crap.

"Your Gucci gown hasn't come yet?" Her tone was alarmed, but at least she'd changed the subject.

I hadn't been particularly worried about the gown situation, but after hearing her voice and seeing her horrified expression, maybe I should be.

"No," I said.

She whipped a mobile phone out of her pocket with the ease of a Wild West gunslinger. "Gimme your order number. I'll call and bitch."

I clicked through my e-mail until I found the receipt.

Moments later she was on the phone with a customer service representative declaring that my service was "unacceptable" and "utterly disappointing."

She had a broad smile on her face when she pushed her thumb down on the disconnect button. "They're refunding your shipping cost, sending a new gown overnight, and giving you another fifty dollar discount. You just have to refuse one of the packages."

How would I do that when I wasn't the party accepting the packages in the first place? Sanda over in the front office usually did. Maybe it was time to have them delivered to the shop.

"Thanks," I said with a light flush. "I never would have called."

"Well, then." Nell shot me a toothy smile. "Maybe we can help each other." She must have noted my surprised expression because her forehead crinkled. "What?"

"Maximo was here on Friday," I said quietly. "He said that exact thing. That we could help each other. I didn't think anything of it until now. What do you think he meant?"

Nell's eyebrows drifted upward. "He said you and I could help each other?"

"Uh huh. He said he'd heard you were in my employ now. When I said you were, he said, 'Good. Perhaps you will help each other'."

Nell slowly shook her head. "I don't like the sound of that."

"I was too distracted by his bitchy girlfriend insulting the shop to put much thought into it."

"God. I hate her," Nell said. "I wish someone would just set her on fire."

I choked on my next breath. I wished I could tell her I *had* set Ascencion Boleda on fire. But I didn't want to advertise I could manipulate more than Air and Earth magic. The news would come out eventually, but I didn't have to be the one to tell. Maybe, just maybe, she wouldn't hate me for betraying her when it *did*.

Chapter Twenty-Three

I paced my apartment, unable to sit still for any length of time. Trip would arrive for my weekly check-in any moment now. What would he have in store for me *this* time?

Nothing good, I was sure. Not after I'd insulted him. And certainly not after I'd tattled.

Surely something would be done. He *had* nearly thwarted Fate's plan with that apple stunt. But would the big guns agree?

The digital clock on my microwave flickered from eleven twenty-nine to eleven thirty. I waited, tense from the inevitable altercation ahead of me.

The apartment building was too quiet—the kind of eerie stillness before the monster attacked in a horror film. Wouldn't it be fitting for *my* monster to appear now?

But he didn't.

I finally sat at a quarter to twelve only to pop back onto my feet so I could fetch my laptop. The thing booted up and opened my e-mail at a snail's pace.

My daughter.

I jerked, gasping at the feminine voice I heard from literally out of nowhere. My mother hadn't spoken directly in my head in years. Why now?

Your presence is required, she said.

"I can't go there," I said, aloud because I was out of practice with divine methods of communication. "I can't realm jump."

We know. Scry.

I didn't have a crystal ball or a black mirror. How was I supposed to do that?

Water.

A picture of a black bowl of water flashed in my mind's eye as if she'd sent the suggestion. I didn't own a black bowl. I had titanium plates … they wouldn't hold much water. Would it be enough?

I walked to the kitchen and rummaged through my cabinets for a suitable vessel. Nothing I owned would do.

They are growing impatient. My mother's essence felt impatient, too.

I ran the water, while grabbing the first bowl I could find. An image flashed out of the corner of my eye. I glanced down, noting a *figure* in my sink.

Of course! The sink's interior was dark enough to work as a scrying surface.

I shoved the stopper in the drain and let the water fill the bottom. More details became visible as the water smoothed along the metal. The image of a tall corner, large chair, and vaguely familiar woman shifted as though a camera's viewfinder had moved to the left. I soon found myself looking at an intimidating male figure reclined in a larger chair. Was I seeing what my mother saw?

Yes, she said in my head again. *Focus closer on the images. You will begin to hear their words.*

I focused closer. Out of the murky water the image sharpened, revealing a chamber very like those I'd grown up visiting in the Underworld. Seemingly never-ending walls lifted to the sky. The marble floors were polished like glass. And the furniture was built as though giants often sat among their smaller counterparts.

"Things to do," a female said as if I'd missed the first part of her statement.

I darted a glance to my right, half expecting to find someone standing there merely based on the location of where I'd *heard* the sound. My cabinets hung silently. No female was there.

"Is she ready?" the male asked. His voice was the last thread I needed to knit my memories together. The male in the throne ahead was Hades himself.

Oh no. I was in trouble, wasn't I?

"She is ready," my mother said, startling half of the divine out of me because it had sounded as if she'd spoken from on top of me. This was seriously disorienting.

"Rebecca Kora Walsh, speak."

I gulped at the King of the Underworld's command. "I'm here."

"We've heard the testimony from the accused. Kora, as the accuser, please share with us your recollection of the apple incident."

My heart stalled.

A *trial*? And I was the accuser? Trip was *finally* being called on the carpet?

I couldn't breathe. This couldn't be real. I had to be dreaming.

Speak. Tell them what you told me, my mother said in my head.

I tried to work out exact dates and times but could only come up with approximations even as I called on Air magic to form a protective bubble around me. I'd get my very own trial if anyone in Wipuk overheard me having an entire conversation with creatures in the Underworld. At least with Air magic's help, no one but a nosey Air witch would.

"Last Wednesday I arrived home and found an apple in my apartment," I said.

"Your human apartment on the Mortal Realm," a female said to my right.

The image in the water shifted as my mother glanced to her right. Clotho held the seat beside my mother. Clotho had adopted her guise as the gnarled Fate spinner complete with her Rapunzel-esque snow-white hair. This was *official*.

"Yes," I said, setting my palms on either side of the sink so I could lean closer to the image. "In my mortal apartment on the Mortal Realm."

Clotho nodded at me to continue. The water's focus returned to Hades.

"I almost bit into the apple, but I remembered I hadn't bought any apples in ages. I dropped it. The radio in my bedroom started playing a familiar song. That's when Trip appeared—"

"State for the gathering the accused's full name," Hades said.

It had been so long since I'd called Trip by his full name that I hardly remembered it. "Triptothemus, son of Triptolemus and Andronika."

"You posit this apple came from my personal stash," Hades said.

"I accused Trip of that, yes."

Murmurs broke out in the room. I didn't have a feeling for how many individuals were there beyond Clotho, Hades, and my mother, but there couldn't have been more than a dozen.

"What did the accused say when you accused him?" Clotho asked.

I took a moment to recall the events of that terrifying night. "After I dropped the apple Trip said 'I almost had you.' I asked him how he did it—how he had gotten an apple into the Mortal Realm. He said his mother had given him a present for Kronia, and he showed me his bracelet. I said, 'You brought that apple from Hades's personal stash.' Trip wished me a happy

Kronia. When I said 'If I'd eaten it', Trip told me he would have been able to cart me back where I belong."

"Where do you belong?" an unfamiliar male voice asked from our left.

My mother turned that way, giving me a view of the other portion of the chamber. Beautiful Persephone sat to her immediate left, a flowing gown spilling over her ornately carved chair. Several faces I barely recalled from my childhood held seats beyond her—Nyx, the Furies, Charon, Trip's father, and the other Underworld judges. And in the middle of them all stood Trip himself. His attention focused too squarely on my mother, as though he *knew* I could see him. I tried to look at everyone but him and ignore that he even managed to look tall and imposing among *gods and goddesses*.

Answer them, my mother said.

"I believe Trip meant the Underworld," I said. "But I can only assume that I belong on the Mortal Realm."

"Why do you assume that?"

The image in the sink waved back to Hades, no doubt because he'd asked the question.

"Because of the task I was given to infiltrate the magical community's ruling body, hold them responsible for any and all crimes against nature, and also keep them from going public with the secret of magic until the gods deem it appropriate."

"Hecate and I gave Rebecca Kora this task," Clotho said, her voice echoing cleanly against the chamber walls *and* my Air bubble. "Through Hecate she does our bidding on the Mortal Realm as part of our human army."

My teeth ground at the word choice. But it was the truth. I was little more than a servant to the gods—a conscripted soldier.

"Has she succeeded?"

"She's only just begun." My mother's voice hardened. "She *will* succeed, provided she's not trapped into returning here."

"Triptothemus, you admit you did bring one of my apples to the Mortal Realm but maintain it was meant as a joke for Rebecca Kora. Given the testimony from your accuser, do you have anything additional to say in your defense?"

Trip had *admitted* that? I supposed the alternative—lying to omniscient beings—was unwise. Still, I hadn't expected him to tell the truth.

"No," Trip said, quiet and more than a little sullen.

"Triptolemus, what have you to say on your son's behalf?"

"My son is young."

The water rippled as the image shifted. A tall, blond male stood motioning toward Hades as though imploring him to be merciful. He shared many of my nemesis's features but lacked the menace I usually associated with Trip.

"He doesn't have the weight of experience behind him that we do. He knows what he did is unacceptable and will never interfere in the Fate spinner's plans again. We ask that you take his youth into account."

Trip was nearly thirty! I was younger by almost five years, and yet I never would have done half of what Trip did to me. Youth was not his problem.

The image bounced as my mother focused on Hades again in time for his nod of understanding.

"This boy's actions nearly rendered a critical member of our human army useless," Clotho said, speaking above the murmurs that had broken out. "*We* ask that you take *that* into account."

"Hecate, what have you to say on the matter?"

"Young Trip has served me well these last years," my mother said.

I barely kept myself from hurling obscenities aloud. She'd catch them in my mind. For once, I was okay with that. Trip may have served *her* well. But he'd been nothing but a tyrant to me.

"My daughter has needed someone to keep her in line when I was otherwise engaged," she said as if I weren't listening in. She glanced between Trip and Hades. "Trip has always been available in that regard. He willingly assists with anything I ask no matter how small the task or how little warning I give. That said, he and my daughter have had a strained relationship from childhood."

That was a tactful way of saying he was my nemesis.

"Neither is more responsible than the other for this strain," my mother said—a verbal dig I couldn't miss. "I believe he brought the apple from the Underworld as Kora has accused and he's admitted. I don't believe he meant real harm to befall her or her task."

"I am ready with my judgment."

My hands gripped the counter as my breath held. Given my mother's final words, I highly doubted anything would come of this. No wonder Trip always got off with a slap on the hand. She *championed* him!

Hades gestured toward the left. "Triptothemus, you will serve a punishment of one week in Tartarus where you will consider your failure to uphold the One Rule."

Clotho tutted to our right—perhaps the reminder that the One Rule was *hers*. We were never supposed to screw with her plans.

I held my breath, wondering how bad Trip would be after he'd completed a week of punishment in the worst part of the entire universe. My mother turned, giving me a view of my nemesis. He'd bowed his head, implying he'd accepted the punishment.

But had he really?

You have your justice, my mother said in my head. *Be content. Summon me on Wednesday nights at your convenience.*

The water cleared, and the voices bouncing off my Air bubble faded. I stepped away from the counter and inhaled a long breath.

I had my justice. So why didn't I feel any better?

****

"I'm sorry, but we're closing early tonight for the solstice ball," Nell told the last customer a second time. Her tone was edgy with some emotion I hadn't been able to name. "We'll be open at noon tomorrow."

I might have scolded my employee for running off a paying customer, but the girl had stood in the corner typing on her mobile phone for the past fifteen minutes without so much as glancing at any of the merchandise. She had no intention of paying for anything.

Nell pushed out an annoyed puff of air when the girl finally left. "You have the address?"

"Yes," I said, knowing she meant the address for her hairstylist.

I'd been content to attend the ball with my hair in the same style I wore every day. Nell had other ideas. She'd threatened to track me down like a vanilla deadbeat dad if I didn't agree to stop at the Wipuk salon at eight.

"I swear to God." Her eyes rolled upward, emphasizing her melodramatic delivery. "I'll come find you if you don't show."

"I'll be there barring any unforeseen emergencies with tires." *Or my mother.*

Tonight would be the absolutely worst time for my mother to ask for a favor. Which was probably why she would. Then again, she might leave me be since tonight was a major event that would have me "rubbing shoulders" with Wipuk's elite.

"If you have tire trouble, you call me," Nell said in a firm, maternal tone. She impatiently waved toward the door. "Hurry up. You only have an hour to shower and get into that gown."

I needed longer than an hour for that? Perhaps I should have tried it on when it arrived yesterday morning. It was too late now.

I hedged a little nervously. "Is the sign about closing early on the door downstairs?"

Nell pushed out a martyred breath. "Yeah."

Had I asked her that already? Probably. I was getting anxious. I hadn't been to a formal event since my senior prom. And that had been a disaster.

Maybe this wasn't a good idea.

Maybe Maximo had asked me to auction myself off simply so he could get me on stage where Ascencion could attack me. I'd have to keep Catey's ring on just in case.

"God, you are so slow for a skinny chick," Nell said at the Wipuk door.

My neck warmed at her grumble because I despised being skinny. I wished I had curves like her.

I hurried simply so she wouldn't have a reason to complain again. She waited until I got in my car before she moved to hers. Did Nell have latent Water empathy? She certainly seemed to sense my growing reluctance to go to the solstice ball.

It had started when the invitation arrived. Two weeks ago I'd received a letter from Maximo stating though I'd agreed to attend the event and take part in the auction, I wouldn't receive my invitation until the night prior to the solstice ball at the earliest. Apparently they'd had problems with scalping and counterfeiting. None of that had particularly bothered me.

What had bothered me was that the invitation I'd received yesterday had my name engraved in it. And there was no spot denoting I could bring a guest. When I'd asked Nell about it this morning, she'd told me her invitation had mentioned a guest. That de Sole had specifically taken away my choice rankled me.

Was it because I'd agreed to be auctioned off? Auctionees had to attend stag?

Nell's car was nearly on my bumper on the way out of the parking lot. She stayed directly behind me all the way to the apartment complex entrance. I was a little surprised she hadn't turned into the drive with me given her zeal the past few hours.

Maybe if I lived through tonight I would have to give her a gift for helping me out. The gown in my closet really was beautiful. And she was calling in a favor to get my hair done professionally on a night when everyone else would want an up-do. Yes, I'd figure out some way to show my appreciation.

Provided I saw the sun on Sunday.

Chapter Twenty-Four

The curls floating on the warm breeze were annoying the human out of me. Those two hot-iron spiraled locks of hair at either side of my face looked like little piggy tails. The little piggy tails had poked me in the eyeball no fewer than three times since I'd left the place.

But Nell's stylist, Hannah, had threatened to cut off my fingers if I pushed them behind my ears. I'd have to suffer through more eyeball poking until the breeze died down. If it died down, my armpits would start to perspire from the anxiety pumping through my veins. It was a catch twenty-two.

I resisted the urge to tap the heel of my chunky mary-jane on the gravel sidewalk. The woman holding my invitation took forever. She'd looked me over no less than three times, as if she thought I might be carrying a concealed weapon into a black tie event. I drew in a deep sniff, checking what manner of creature she was. The smell of a crisp northern wind answered that question. Air witch.

Had they stationed her here to look for weaves? My mother's ring was on my finger and the leather wristband was around my ankle, but neither would be detected as a weave because they were divine objects. I hoped.

I shifted my weight onto my left hip nervously. What was taking so long?

"First is coming to personally escort you inside," the fanatically professional Air witch said, no doubt noting my impatience.

My stomach plummeted. First? Did she mean Wipuk's First? I hoped that meant Maximo had last minute instructions for the auction and not that he

225

expected me to mingle with him. I didn't need his girlfriend trying to eat me as a canapé.

"Miss Walsh." The vampire's resonate voice greeted me from behind.

I didn't turn because the last time I'd swiveled quickly, I'd almost fallen on my tush thanks to the gown pooling at my feet.

The Air witch handed him my invitation rather than giving it back to me as she'd done with the others. Maximo appeared at my side a half second later. He held his tuxedo-clad arm toward me.

I discreetly scanned his figure. His outfit was a standard formal black silk tux with the crisp white shirt, black bow tie, and black satin cummerbund. But as with everything else I'd seen him in, Maximo made standard look exceptional. His hair was particularly spiked and wild tonight. I had the fleeting urge to run my fingers through it to see if he used gel to make it stand up.

"You look radiant," he said with a smile that was warmer than the breeze passing over my skin.

"Thank you." I battled down a flush as he walked us up the pebbled walkway toward the music. That was the nicest compliment I'd ever been paid even though he was simply being polite.

Gesturing to my gown, he asked, "What color is that?"

"They called it 'cognac'."

"It complements your hair superbly."

It did. The gown fit me like a glove, and the bunched detail on the waist made my hips look curvier than they were. Based on the photograph on the website, I'd been a little concerned about the bodice falling off, but it was snug around my breasts. In short, it was perfect. I really owed Nell for helping me find it.

In a softer volume, the vampire said, "I hadn't realized just how beautiful you were until your hair was away from your delicate face."

Maybe he wasn't simply being polite. My hand stiffened on his sleeve. Maximo sent me a sidelong glance but didn't comment.

We crested a hill and found a torch-lit courtyard with several tables holding wine glasses and stacked china. There was a grassy area off to the right surrounded by hanging Chinese lanterns. A DJ booth was setup beside it with large speakers belting out Heather Nova. A handful of younger people, witches most likely, danced on the grass in their finest. The remainder of the attendees had gathered in small groups around the tables in the flagstone courtyard.

"As a member of my faction, it's my duty to introduce you to Wipuk," the vampire said quietly as we neared the party.

I let myself relax. The explanation made perfect sense. He was only being polite.

Ascencion was the first person I recognized. She stood directly across from the walkway in what looked to be a position of honor. She was the host's lover. But she was obviously overcompensating for something. Why else would she need to wear a gown that barely covered her body?

The black knit fabric spread across her shoulders in a straight line boosted by obvious shoulder pads. Five thick black gems decorated each shoulder. From the shoulder the bodice plunged straight down in a deep V that ended past her navel, dangerously close to something that would have been indecent. Generous portions of her breasts were bare for all to see while still managing to cover up the parts that counted.

On the opposite end there was a slit that cut her skirt wide up to her mid-thigh—a creamy, leggy thigh she took no pains to hide. Her glossy dark hair was pulled over one shoulder to skim the bottom of her breast, perhaps a coy reminder of what it was hiding. The most unattractive thing she wore was the glare she'd adopted just for me.

Seemingly unaware of his lover's ire, Maximo guided me to the first group of people and into a hole that formed for us, fortunately out of Ascencion's line of sight. He nodded his head politely to those gathered. "My apologies for interrupting. I thought you might want to meet our newest citizen. This is Kora Walsh, the owner of Rarities."

A woman stepped forward. Her mocha hair was pulled into a French twist style exactly like mine. Her amber eyes were nothing like my pale gray hue, but at least they weren't glaring like Ascencion's. A soft smile curved her pink lips as she extended a hand from her airy blue chiffon sleeve.

"Alina Kranz," she said in a quiet volume. "My daughter can't say enough good things about you."

Alina was exactly what I needed right now. I gave her a bright smile and concentrated on blocking her energy as I took her hand so we wouldn't be zapped.

"Nell has been a life saver," I said, making no effort to hide my gushing. "I wouldn't have made it through my grand opening without her. She has a bright future before her." I was careful not to mention Nell's interest in business because I recalled the talk of Alina's disappointment.

"Yes," Alina said warmly. "I believe she does."

While I made silent comparisons between the mother and daughter from my memory, Maximo gestured to the figures around the circle. "This is Dea Woods, the ambassador plenipotentiary for the Earth Witch Monarchy."

Dea was a youthful woman with dark blonde hair that had been plaited into a soft braid. Her wide eyes were an earthen brown that might have put me at ease if I weren't terribly nervous. The woman nodded her head in light deference matching her mild smile.

The next two names were a daughter of the previous Air high priestess, who looked weary but pleasant, and Dea's Guardian, a gentleman with an obvious chip on his shoulder if the glare he gave everyone but her were any indication. Next came a man with a salt and pepper beard, kind eyes, and nondescript styled hair. His standard tuxedo looked just that, standard, unlike the vampire beside me.

"This is Curtis Hawksley," Maximo said. "The high priest and co-leader of the Aer Association."

While Curtis nodded politely, I worked on not glaring at him. So this bland, aging male was the witch Nell would be forced to sleep with. I couldn't find anything particularly wrong with him, apart from the fact that in a society of beautiful people, he was only attractive. He offered to shake my hand as Alina had done. I took it reluctantly though I made sure to block the zap I might have received from latent energy.

The final person introduced was quite obviously the Healer high priest. In lieu of a bow tie beneath his tuxedo he wore a silver choker inlaid with coral and turquoise stones. The choice emphasized his Native American appearance. And he'd left his long, straight brown-black hair down around his shoulders.

"Viho Hiamovi heads up the Healers of America this quarter. Again," Maximo said.

They all smiled and there were a few chuckles.

Viho nodded his handsome and surprisingly youthful head in deference. Long hair rippled up and down over a broad chest. I'd expected the coalition to be filled with old people, but that simply wasn't the case. His dark eyes held mine directly for several beats too long, but he didn't smile. The scent of aloe filled my nose on my next inhale. Yes, definitely Healer.

The vampire patted my arm as if to say it was time to go. I nodded to them and said, "It is a pleasure to meet you all."

"We must continue with the introductions." Maximo guided me to the next group of people.

"Difficult to get dues." A gravelly voice I vaguely recognized grumbled when we pulled alongside. The wild shoulder-length hair atop the man's head was also something I'd recalled from somewhere else.

A moment passed before I was able to place it. This was the spastic man who had been sitting in Desmond's chair the morning I'd visited.

He stopped his rant when we appeared on the edge of their group, shifting uncomfortably in his navy suit. He was the only man we'd come across thus far who wasn't wearing a tuxedo. But his suit and the lack of a tie seemed fitting for his wild, middle-aged look.

"Gentlemen," Maximo said by way of a greeting. "Allow me to introduce our newest citizen. This is Kora Walsh, the owner of Rarities."

His words were met with mute stares. I resisted the urge to tuck my curl behind my ear.

Still the vampire smiled in his indulgent way. He gestured at the wild haired man I'd recognized. "This gentleman is Andoni Arima, Osiris's steward in the Cult of Osiris."

A Death witch had been collecting dues from Desmond? Dues for what? Were the necromancers running a protection racket? Hmm, it was something to look into.

Maximo turned me toward my right. A blond with deep blue eyes and wrinkles a plenty peered back at me. He looked to be in his mid fifties or a well aged sixty, perhaps the same age as Curtis. He was handsome in the same way most male witches were. I even liked the black shirt he'd worn beneath his tuxedo to give him an air of difference. What I didn't like was his haughty expression.

The vampire nodded politely. "The gentleman to your right is Rhys Martland, one of the thirteen council witches in the Western Phoenix Coven."

Ah, a Fire witch. That explained why Maximo was especially nice to him.

Rhys merely nodded at me, but it was more than I'd gotten from the Death witch.

The remaining members of the circle were assistants to the priests as well as the Alpha of the local werewolf pack. He was a gruff, hairy guy who had kept his eyes lowered and focused on the cellular phone in his hand. It probably had a lot to do with the looming full moon.

Maximo drew me toward the last large group on the Wipuk side. Unfortunately the group held his lover. Ascencion related what she believed to be a humorous vignette at a loud volume. She punctuated her tale with broad gestures in which the predominantly male gathering watched for nipple slips like dogs following a treat with greedy intent.

If it bothered Maximo to see his lover flirting with a rabid pack of males, he didn't show it. Instead he patiently waited for her to finish so he could speak his line about introducing the newest citizen.

"We've met," Ascencion said sourly.

Maximo ignored her as he began the introductions.

I already knew one of Ascencion's hanger-ons. Eamonn Cary managed to eclipse most others in his half tuxedo. He'd worn the trousers, white dress shirt, bow tie and silk vest printed with a blue and green plaid design, but he'd left his jacket behind. And he'd folded the sleeves of his shirt up to his elbows. As usual his shoulder length hair was tousled around his face negligently, and there was a few days' worth of stubble coating his cheeks.

I managed to pull my attention away from him so I could greet the person Maximo had recently introduced. I hadn't heard the name. I'd heard enough to know it wasn't a high priest. They were one of Rhys Martland's assistants. The next gentleman appeared to be the werefox Alpha. He was a wiry man of thirty with red-brown hair and a twinkling eye he hadn't been able to extract from Ascencion's chest. Two more assistants filled out the ranks until Maximo made it around to the Dark witch.

"And this is Eamonn Cary, high priest of The Coven—"

"We've met," Eamonn said. His gaze was intent on my face.

I nodded in agreement rather than greet him.

"And of course you've met Ascencion Boleda," Maximo said.

She sent me a smirk. "His *fiancée*."

Maximo's muscles stiffened beneath my arm. Frustration rolled off him like a heat wave, nearly threatening to choke me in the caustic stuff.

Hmm, maybe it was more than frustration.

"Fiancée?" The werefox Alpha echoed with a nervous laugh. "You popped the question after all these years?"

Maximo didn't reply. A glance at Ascencion's ring fingers showed both had massive stones. Her smile was wide enough to split her face when she caught me eyeing them.

A scene was brewing here I wanted very much to avoid. I lifted my hand from Maximo's cool sleeve, turning with the intention of thanking him for the introductions. He reached out, taking my palm in his. The startling temperature of his chilly skin made me forget what I'd been about to say.

Until that moment I'd managed to gloss over the knowledge that this man was *dead*. Carefully I shuttered my expression so he wouldn't note the queasy turn of my stomach.

"Allow me to escort you to the real party," he said with a smile nearly as broad as Ascencion's.

The female inhaled a sharp breath. We stepped away from her pack of admirers, drawing a shrill squeal from her. I had no choice but to remain a pawn in their game. At least I was no longer within clawing distance.

Chapter Twenty-Five

The "real party" was at the end of a hidden sidewalk in a nearly identical courtyard and lantern-strewn lawn. The real party had a real band with real instruments and real people. I recognized the mayor of Sedona, several of the crystal shop owners, and a few of the customers who had come in on opening day.

And I recognized Desmond standing beside his assistant. He shone more brightly than any of the Sedona citizens in his luxurious black velvet tuxedo. Rather than the traditional bow tie, Desmond wore a mandarin collar with softly glimmering opal buttons atop the silky white material. The outfit complemented his handsome features. The soft fabric simply begged to be touched. Not that I would. Touch him, that is.

I had the misfortune of spotting him at the exact moment he'd spotted me. We scrutinized each other, each settling on surprise. I'd known he looked good in a suit, but I hadn't realized quite how good he looked until now. He was mouth-watering. It was such a shame he was a dick.

Desmond's dramatic eyebrows lifted in surprise before settling to their usual hooded position seconds later. And then they formed a deep V when he noted whose arm held mine.

"I'll spare you the introductions here." Maximo's voice drew my attention to the left. "I merely wanted to save you from Ascencion's ire and show you the way to Sedona's party."

I turned my head, giving him the first genuine smile of our association. "Thank you."

The indulgent expression on his face faltered for a moment before switching into an emotion I couldn't name. He hesitated a moment before he said, "It's no problem, Miss Walsh."

I was beginning to buy his nice-guy act. That meant I needed to keep my distance.

A feminine gasp in the distance drew my attention. Nell hurried across the flagstone courtyard with the skirt of her ivory chiffon gown in her hand. She exclaimed about how nice my hair looked long before she reached me.

"I leave you in capable hands," Maximo said while drawing away. "Someone will fetch you for the auction later. In the meantime, enjoy the refreshments and the Sedona auction. The event always proves to be amusing."

Nell's soft features glowed beneath the torchlight as she made her way through the gathering. Someone had applied natural makeup to her face and pulled her long blonde hair back into a Grecian style of plated braids. The gown she'd picked was straight out of one of my mother's red figure Kraters—ancient pottery displaying the goddesses. She looked more beautiful than every female in attendance, and most had noticed. Her competitors shot envious glares while the males barely hid their drool.

"You look beautiful!" Nell grabbed hold of my shoulders so she could spin me around. "The gown is amazing. It was totally worth it. Wasn't it worth it? Tell me it was worth it!"

I laughed heartily but withheld my answer until she'd allowed me to face her again. "It was worth it. I owe you."

"You sure do. But oh my shit, your hair!" She reached out, tugging at the piggy tail on the right. It sprang back up in time for her to repeat the action. "It's so pretty up like that. And shit, Kora, I had no idea you were a knock-out. You should dress nice more often."

"Me?" I snorted while rolling my eyes to the star drenched sky. "Look at you!" I held my hands out in front of me like a game show prize girl showing off the latest car. "Your crops and tanks don't do you justice."

We both broke into quiet laughs, a shared kinship that brought us closer together.

"I was beginning to think you weren't coming," Nell said. "Did Maximo monopolize you?"

"Hannah took a little longer than she'd planned because she insisted on doing my makeup to match the dress. And then Maximo claimed he had to introduce me." I explained at a lower volume. "Because I'm part of his faction."

Nell's expression soured, but she didn't comment. "You met my mom?"

"Yeah. She was real nice. The only nice person over there."

She nodded. "Good. Good. Come on, I want you to meet my friends."

Nell's friends were young witches like her. There was a daughter of an assistant within the Aer Association, a daughter of an Earth witch, and even two Water witches. The youngest was sixteen with Nell being the eldest. They had names like Terran, Logan, and Avery, and they were laid back and fun, a far cry from the witches on the Wipuk side of the party.

I straddled two age groups. I didn't have the maturity to fit in with the witches in middle age, nor was I young enough to hang with the teenagers. But I preferred the easy conversation of music, movies, and fashion the girls discussed to the hostile looks I'd earned from the "grown ups".

When the girls decided to dance to the swing band's lively song, I moved into the crowd of vanilla humans to mingle and publicize. My strange hair color was the topic of conversation in nearly every group. I used it to segue to the topic of my unorthodox business. Several questioned me on my merchandise and promised to visit sometime.

I studiously avoided the group that contained Desmond and the mayor during my rounds of Sedona's finest. It became easy when I found the group of attendees who had won their tickets on the local radio station. They looked as uncomfortable being among Sedona's elite as I felt. We carried on a lively conversation about new age hooey and the quirks of the tourists for several minutes.

"Ms. Walsh." Desmond's smooth cadence interrupted a tattoo enthusiast's tale of rear-ending a tourist when the visitors had stopped their car in the middle of the road for a sudden photograph of Airport Mesa.

I glanced over my shoulder, pretending I hadn't recognized his voice. He stood looking far too gorgeous and smelling of a fresh mountain spring. I lifted my eyebrows in question.

"May I speak to you?"

He *was* speaking to me. If he wanted to speak elsewhere, then it was probably something the vanilla humans wouldn't understand. I gave him a curt nod then turned back to my new friends.

"It was so nice chatting with you all," I told them.

"Aww, you leavin', Kora?" The tattoo enthusiast pursed his pierced lip.

"Unfortunately," I said with a slight nod toward Desmond. Before anyone could comment, I withdrew from the circle and stood in front of the Water witch.

He gestured for me to walk ahead of him on the gravel path toward Wipuk. I moved forward, walking slowly as he fell into step beside me. He was quiet until we felt the tingling pressure change between Sedona and Wipuk.

Now that we were safely in the magical pocket, unseen and unheard by the vanilla humans, he slowed to a stop. I remained where I was while he drew off the path and onto the grass. Desmond clasped his hands behind his back in a gesture I might have thought was nervous if I hadn't known him better.

"I wanted to inquire about the crystal you had in your shop a few weeks ago," he said rather predictably.

I stood mutely waiting for him to actually inquire. While I waited, he sent out a tendril of power that tickled my consciousness. He was trying to set up an empathic link. I let him get as far as the periphery of my consciousness where he'd get little in the way of emotion.

"Is it still for sale?" he asked.

My spine stiffened because he already knew the answer to this question. "As I told your assistant, the crystal has already been sold."

"Has the buyer picked it up?"

I eyed him suspiciously. Did he know it was sitting in my closet?

Rather than lie, I pushed it back on him. "Why are you so obsessed with it?"

Desmond's dark eyebrows lifted. "I didn't realize I was obsessed."

"You've been in twice to look at it. You sent your assistant to buy it. You sent another Water witch who didn't introduce himself. And now you're asking me about it."

His lips thinned as his irritation jabbed at my consciousness. "Why are you hiding it from us?"

"I told you, it's been sold." My answer was cooler than I'd intended.

"Who bought it?"

"Why should I tell you? So you can steal it from them?"

Desmond took a menacing step forward. "I'm not a thief, Ms. Walsh."

"No, you're just a manipulative dick." I took the opportunity to snap his empathic link back at him.

He blinked back surprise. Fleshy, beautiful lips parted, revealing the tips of his perfect teeth. I didn't worry until he took another, larger step toward me. He grabbed my arm in a firm grip. But he stopped mid-movement, dropping his hand to his side. The indecision went unexplained until the crunch of gravel beneath a shoe rung out from behind him.

"I thought I heard you." Eamonn's gently accented voice echoed through the darkness.

When the Dark witch emerged from the shadow, his attention was on my face. Slowly his gaze switched to Desmond, and then back to me. I felt, more than saw, Desmond's retreat. Clenching frustration and hot anger hit me in stereo, seemingly from both males.

"The auction is about to begin in Sedona," Eamonn told Desmond. He spread his lips in a mockery of a smile. "You don't want to be late."

Had I been wrong about the relationship between these two? This wasn't a leader and a follower. These two were equals. So just who was running Wipuk behind the scenes?

"Thank you," Desmond said tightly. His shoes were soft on the grass as he hurried down the hill.

A pleasant smile formed on Eamonn's face. He offered me his arm. "Can I escort you down? The auction is an opportunity to see Sedona's finest making fools of themselves." After a pause he said, "For a good cause, of course."

I nodded rather than tell him to take a flying leap into the river Styx. He'd saved me from a scene with Desmond. I could be accommodating for a few minutes. Once we were in Sedona, I'd find Nell and her friends and hope Eamonn would find one of his harem members to bug.

To my surprise that was exactly what happened. He escorted me to Nell's side, nodded politely, and then strode off into the crowd until he spotted a female he'd recognized.

I made myself focus on the stage where the mayor emceed the event. The poor men and women being auctioned were paraded across the platform in a line. The gathered company got a look at their choices before the "merchandise" hid behind the scenes. I didn't recognize any of them apart from Desmond.

One by one they were brought up with the mayor calling out their vitals and accomplishments. The males posed like body builders, and the females adopted pin-up poses. The price of auctioned dates made it into the hundreds by the time the fourth person appeared on stage. Each time someone called a higher number, the crowd gasped and clapped, and the individual posed a little more provocatively. It was as amusing as they'd warned.

Desmond was the final person auctioned. The delay before he stepped on the stage meant the crowd was rowdy in their formalwear. Champagne had been flowing for hours.

In contrast, I'd grown tired. My shoes pinched my feet. I wished I'd worn my Docs. No one would see them beneath my floor length gown anyway.

"The final date up for grabs this evening is with a man who needs no introduction—the illustrious Desmond

Marino," the mayor called out. "He vows to prepare a home-cooked meal at his beautiful Sedona home, complete with a dessert from scratch following an event of his date's choosing. Desmond suggests boating, swimming, hiking, bowling, skating, dancing, or perhaps a show. Let's start the bidding at a thousand dollars."

The last date auctioned had gone for fifteen hundred dollars. They were *starting* Desmond at a thousand dollars?

Someone shrieked behind me.

"Do I hear a thousand one hundred?"

The mayor indeed did. Soon the bids jumped to fifteen hundred. Then two thousand. Women shouted over each other with viciously sharp voices. The price reached four thousand. Violence threatened to break out between two friends who had differences of opinion about who ought to get the "businessman". Meanwhile, Desmond stood stoically watching it all without posing like an idiot or mugging to the crowd.

Beneath the stage lights he looked somehow more beautiful. Gazing at the vivid aqua eyes staring out across the crowd almost hurt. I turned my attention to the women wildly calling out numbers to avoid having to see it. Good looks were just another weapon in a dick's arsenal.

The auction ended when an aging woman toward the back bid ten thousand dollars in an authoritative tone. I didn't know if the others clammed up because of the high number or if she were merely a woman not to be crossed. Neither would have surprised me.

Desmond folded his lower half toward her in deference then walked to the edge of the stage. He carefully took the stairs to the ground. I didn't realize I'd been gawking until someone touched my arm, startling me half out of my skin.

"Miss Walsh." The Air witch who had been manning the entrance to the Wipuk party stood just behind me. "You're needed on the other side."

Chapter Twenty-Six

For once I wished the phrase "needed on the other side" had been in reference to Hades. Right then I'd have given just about anything for my mother to show up with an emergency. She, of course, didn't.

I nodded woodenly for the Air witch. My nerves stretched thin. I didn't want to be paraded around in front of the witches with their hostile expressions, the Were with their leering gazes, and the vampires who wanted to kill me. But I'd agreed to this weeks ago. I couldn't back out now.

I followed the Air witch up the shadowed path, glad Desmond and Eamonn were on the Sedona side of the party still. I'd be spared the humiliation of them seeing me sold off like a slave.

Of those being auctioned, I recognized only one—the Healer high priest. He seemed at ease with the situation, but he did glance at me several times. I was too worried about what was to come to put much thought into socializing.

The group of us emerged behind the stage where I was handed into the care of a male vampire I hadn't met. He was civil without being either warm or cold. He spoke directions for the Wipuk merchandise in a quiet voice while the emcee for the evening riled up the crowd.

The voice coming over the speakers was tenor-pitched, boisterous, and familiar. I placed it as soon as someone called out the name "Henry". The emcee was Ryan Steele's boy-toy!

Moments later we were paraded up on stage. I was fortunately distracted from the catcalling crowd as I got a look at Ryan's lover. He had medium length chestnut hair that fell four inches below his shoulder blades. The dark mass framed a handsome face with two piercing dark eyes. He looked positively youthful when he smiled, so much so that I couldn't place his age. Perhaps he was a shapeshifter, too.

"And our final date of the night is Miss Kora Walsh of the new shop, Rarities," Henry called out as we walked across the platform.

My cheeks flushed because I hadn't known I would be the last auction. It would be a rather boring finale. They should have put Viho after me.

Henry sent everyone but the first person off the stage. I paced in a narrow circle behind the festivities while the gathering called out numbers. Much like Sedona, the dates began with rather low numbers but reached into the hundreds by the middle of the offerings. From the continued rowdy noises, I gathered the dates were making fools of themselves with poses, silly expressions, and fake stripteases.

Quickly my companions disappeared for their own auctions until I was left alone, pacing the grass and no doubt getting stains on my beautiful gown. Wisps of hair had come down from my carefully styled up-do, and I was sweating anxiously in the cooling breeze as I listened to the catcalls for Viho. I didn't want to do this. I wanted to go back to the safety of Berkeley where the only thing I had to worry about was if I'd studied for the latest test or if the inter-library loan books I'd borrowed for my thesis needed to be renewed for a sixth time.

The vampire waved impatiently at me. He'd been doing that for some time, hadn't he?

I had nothing to distract me on this trip onto the stage. It meant I easily saw the leering gazes and glaring expressions when I stepped up beside Henry.

"Our final date tonight is with Miss Kora Walsh. She is our newest citizen and entrepreneur," Henry called out. "She recently graduated from U.C. Berkeley with an

MBA. Anyone who has visited her store knows Miss Walsh's design sense is unparalleled. Win a date with her and she can probably improve your budget and your wallpaper all in one night. Let's begin the bidding at a thousand dollars."

The soft rubbing of crickets met Henry's suggestion.

Exactly as I'd expected. Maximo had been horribly wrong about my popularity. Even as an oddity, I didn't rate a thousand dollars.

A female voice called out from the back of the crowd. "A thousand!".

"A thousand to Miss Kranz," Henry said.

I stared in shock when I worked out it hadn't been Alina Kranz but *Nell* who had bid on a date with me. If she had that kind of money, she wouldn't need to work for me at nine dollars an hour.

I soon understood why she'd done it when another person outbid her.

"A thousand one hundred to Jim Phillips," Henry said.

A wince was stifled when I realized the leering werefox had bid on me.

Someone else called out. A name I didn't recognize was announced into the microphone.

"A thousand three hundred," a slightly accented voice I *did* recognize said.

"A thousand three hundred to Eamonn Cary,"

I searched Eamonn out in the crowd, annoyed he'd trekked back to Wipuk in time to see my humiliation.

Another voice I recognized topped the bid. "Fourteen hundred."

There was a sharp feminine gasp a moment before Henry announced, "Fourteen hundred to Maximo de Sole."

The vampire had bid on a date with me? In front of his fiancée? Did he *want* Ascencion to drain me of blood?

"Fifteen hundred." It was Eamonn who countered.

Henry shot me a wry look, and then turned it toward the crowd. "Fifteen hundred dollars back to Priest Cary."

Maximo bid next. "Sixteen hundred."

"Seventeen." Eamonn gave the rapid-fire response.

The vampire topped him. "Eighteen."

Eamonn chuckled loudly enough that it was audible from the stage. Then he called out, "Nineteen."

Maximo's lips broadened into a startling smile of bright white teeth. "Twenty-five hundred dollars."

Ascencion shot us both murderous looks. I lowered my shoulders, trying to make myself look smaller in the hope they'd give up the bid war.

Not to be outbid, Eamonn said, "Three grand."

"Four."

"Five thousand dollars."

Both males turned in surprise toward the whip-sharp female voice .

"Five thousand dollars to Ascencion Boleda." Henry called out my fear.

My stomach did a mighty flip. Ascencion would try to kill me if she won a "date" with me. That couldn't happen. I willed someone to top her.

"Six thousand," Eamonn said.

To my surprise Maximo called out, "Ten thousand dollars."

It was where the bidding on Desmond had finished in Sedona. It would be where we finished. No one would go over that.

Eamonn proved me wrong. "Fifteen thousand dollars."

Now I was really growing uncomfortable. I leaned toward Henry so I could be heard over the speakers. "I'd like the record to show I can't cook," I said in a self-depreciating tone and gave a nervous chuckle. A light ripple of laughter passed through the crowd.

"Twenty thousand." Ascencion's snarling voice was clearly recognizable.

This time it was her lover who outbid her. "Twenty-five."

"Seriously," I said into the microphone even while Ascencion hissed a curse in Spanish. "I can't even make macaroni and cheese."

Eamonn took advantage of the lovers' quarrel. "Thirty thousand."

Then, much like the Sedona auction, an authoritative voice called out, "Fifty thousand dollars."

The gathering clammed up. Maximo, Ascencion, and Eamonn eased back, refusing to outbid the speaker.

I stared in shock even as Henry spoke. "Do I hear fifty-thousand one hundred?"

Silently I willed Eamonn, Maximo, or even Ascencion to make a bid. *Someone* had to save me.

"No?" Henry scanned the audience. "Then it's fifty-thousand dollars to Desmond Marino."

****

I thanked Hera Nell rescued me when I stepped off the stage on rubbery legs. I would have fallen otherwise. We shared a silent, horrified look in the shadows beside the stage.

Desmond the dick had just pledged fifty thousand dollars for one night with me. The only thing that would have been more disturbing than that would have been if Trip had been the winner.

"He just wants the crystal," I whispered to Nell. "He's obsessed with it."

She said nothing, staring over my shoulder into the crowd of supernatural creatures behind me.

"I need to go home." I'd croaked the words. A cough did little to fix the problem. "I did my duty. I can go right?"

Nell drew her attention back to my face. Her hard expression softened into a smile. "Yes, hon. You can go home. Let me walk you to your car."

I was grateful because I didn't want to risk a visit from Ascencion, or worse, Desmond. Right then I felt ten years younger than my twenty-five, and Nell seemed ten years older than her twenty. She'd grown up here in this land of politics and supernatural intrigue. I'd been fairly sheltered in the Underworld with only Trip and a few young nymphs as companions. We'd rarely dealt with the gods themselves. Maybe I should have. It might have prepared me for this.

Nell hugged me before letting me get in the car. She made me promise to come to work in the afternoon. As if I'd duck out of my responsibility simply because of a bad night. But her promise to bring coffee would make it a little easier.

I tested Wipuk's law enforcement by speeding twenty-five over the posted limit all the way home. Then I walked barefoot from the parking lot to the front door because my feet were sore. Fortunately no one was in the courtyard to catch me in my designer gown and spiffed up hair. Without turning on the lights in the apartment, I tossed everything onto the bed so I could jump in the shower.

Only when I was back to myself did I allow my brain to think about how I was going to get out of this. What in Hades would I do on a date that had cost Desmond fifty large? He'd expect the crystal without a fight. And that was exactly why I was going to give it to someone else first.

Chapter Twenty-Seven

I pulled my piping hot coffee back from my lips, gazing at Nell the morning after. "I need another favor from you."

She settled against the wall beside the employee only door on the Sedona side of the shop. "Okay. What?"

"If I give you something, will you promise never to give it away or sell it no matter how much you're offered?"

Nell's head came up as her coffee dropped to her side. "Kali's Candle?"

I nodded slowly. "I need to be able to claim I sold it. Just give me a dollar and we'll call it even. I'm not going to tell anyone who I gave it to. That's up to you. But the heat on it is beginning to be too much. You're the only person I trust because you could have taken it any number of days and you didn't."

Without a word she fished a dollar bill out of the pocket of her cropped jeans. I reached into my purse so I could pull out the carefully wrapped item.

She held her palm out for it and then hesitated. A wary expression knit her features. "It's more than a glorified USB device for energy, isn't it?"

"I don't think so." But I wasn't one hundred percent positive. I only had accurate information for items created by gods in my own pantheon. I had no idea about Hindu items. "I've pushed power through it and didn't notice anything odd about it. It can be used to run spells when you're not present. But batteries aren't considered dangerous or evil, even magical ones."

That wasn't explanation enough. Nell gave her head a little shake. "Why are you giving it to me?"

"For starters I owe you for helping me. But the main reason is because I don't want Desmond to have it."

"And I hate him as much as you do."

A nod was all the answer I was willing to give.

"I promise I won't sell it or give it to anyone, especially Desmond," she said while handing me her dollar bill. Nell took the item to complete our trade.

I'd lost a depressing chunk of change, but Desmond's obsession with it made me question the thing's power. My Air witch employee's lack of interest in coven politics made her the ideal person to give it to.

She carefully unwrapped the crystal. Her eyes went narrow, perhaps in confusion. "What happened to it? It's not glowing any longer."

"I discharged the power I'd had stored in it." I failed to tell her I'd had Fire energy stored in it. "The way it works is you visualize energy moving from the aether into the crystal. Think of it as a really fat straw with stoppers at both ends. Lift the stopper on the bottom to fill it and then lift the stopper on the top to take it into you. Got it?"

With her attention focused on the crystal, she nodded absently. A moment later a cool breeze passed by us scented like dry desert air. Nell made a sound of surprise when Kali's Candle began pulsing a soft white glow.

"How come it isn't orange like it was when it was in the display case?"

"Different energy has different colors," I said while popping up from my seat. I was going to use the excuse of checking the inventory in the storage closet to avoid any additional questions about the energy I'd stored in the crystal. Nell didn't know I could wield Fire. I wanted to keep that quiet for now.

Her exclamation echoed up the stairwell. "This is *so* cool!"

I truly hoped she wouldn't show her mother or anyone else, but I wasn't going to stop her. Though I'd asked for her promise not to sell it or give it away, the object's fate was in Nell's hands. I hoped I'd made the right choice.

****

I dug my fork a little deeper into my taco salad when I spotted the BMW pulling into the lot. The only consolation for Desmond's arrival was that Nell had left with Kali's Candle ten minutes earlier. She'd wanted to put it in a safe place before the evening crowd arrived. I was ridiculously glad she had. But I would have liked her as a buffer.

I released my fork because my appetite would be nonexistent at least until he'd left. My stomach already burbled sickly, and he'd yet to get out of the car. I pushed the salad aside when his stately figure unfolded itself from the driver's side.

My attention went to the car, noting it was empty of other travelers, rather than look at his outfit. But I had to see his clothing when he pushed through the glass entrance, pulling his aviator sunglasses from his nose. He slid them within the interior pocket of his beige suit. An azure blue dress shirt was buttoned primly beneath it, a complement to the brown and green patterned tie he wore.

His gaze settled on me as he walked across the ebony floor with a steady padding of his soft-soled shoes. I held my breath when he came to a stop two feet from the glass display case I hid behind. Desmond scanned over the offerings. He soon met my gaze. I'd been caught staring. How embarrassing.

"You escaped before I could get your phone number," he said in a softly accusatory tone. The smooth cadence of his lovely voice was almost soothing despite it.

I made myself laugh lightly even though I was the farthest thing from amused. "The shop's number is all over the place."

"I'm not going to call the shop regarding a date with you."

My face and neck warmed. He'd called it a date. But that wasn't what he meant.

The awkward reaction prompted me to latch onto my baser emotions, in this case, irritation. "Why not? The only reason you did it was to get your hands on that crystal."

Desmond's full lips pressed tightly together at my bitter taunt. But even tight they were wider than most were pouting. He relaxed them so he could speak. "Your shop is closed tomorrow and Tuesday. I assume you are free those nights? Which would be better for you?"

I stared at him blankly. He wasn't serious, was he? So I asked him.

"You're not serious, are you?"

His frame drew up just a little taller while his expression darkened. Each feature crinkled or pouted until it was obvious he was offended. A spike of an unnamed emotion shot through me when I compared the look to how Trip had looked when we'd fought here. Because of it, I foolishly answered him.

"Tomorrow would be better."

"Three o'clock?"

My head tilted to the right as if I'd find an explanation for so early a time engraved on his ear. Monday was a workday for him. He was going to leave early to go on a fake date with me? That didn't seem right.

"Uh, sure," I said with an uneasy drawl.

Desmond lifted his head in a brusque nod. With a last lingering look at the display case, he walked to the door. I watched in mute surprise as he folded himself back into his luxury car and then pulled out of my lot.

I didn't know where he was going to meet me at three o'clock tomorrow. I didn't know what I was supposed to wear. And I didn't know why I cared.
****

Nell took one look at my harried expression, the spoon sticking straight up from my taco salad, and then immediately switched into maternal mode. "What happened?"

"Desmond stopped by," I said woodenly, still staring out the window at the spot his car had been thirty minutes ago.

Her eyes narrowed darkly like a mama bear ready to tackle a wolf for taunting her cub. "Did he threaten you for the crystal?"

"No. I kind of wished he had." I pushed a puff of air through my mouth. "All he wanted was to set up a time for our date."

"Really?" She stared over my head at the wall that only held the framed dollar bill and a calendar.

"Does he have a harem?"

The Air witch's focus switched to my face. "Not that anyone has seen. In fact, besides the annual auctions, no one has ever seen Desmond on a date. The rumor is he's gay and in the closet."

Gay. I could handle that. He *was* well dressed, gorgeous, and meticulous.

"But what about Allison?" The words burst from my lips without thought. I couldn't seem to stop myself. "There's some obvious tension between them. Do you think he's bi-sexual?"

Nell lifted her narrow shoulders. "I don't know. He could be. Allison has worked for him since he became part of the coalition, but they're not dating. She's living with a werewolf."

So whatever made Allison fearful of Desmond's ire had nothing to do with a relationship.

"You should make sure you go some place public," Nell said. "And call me if you need help."

I inhaled a breathy laugh. "Thanks, Nell. But I'll be safe."

"He's a high priest." Her brows knitted in what looked like worry.

"And I'm a sorceress. I'm not powerless. I'll be fine."

I just had to get through one date-for-charity without permanently ticking off one of Wipuk's most powerful. Maybe I had my work cut out for me.

Chapter Twenty-Eight

I wasn't dressed up anymore than I would have been for the grand opening of the store. The black and white pleated skirt, orange short sleeve V-neck T-shirt, wide diamond-weave fishnet thigh highs, and Doc Martens were a careful mixture of casual and dressy goth. My hair was styled in its usual bob, and the only make-up I'd bothered with was my black eyeliner and mascara plus a little lip-gloss to keep my lips from chapping.

I'd been in my closet organizing my box of tights, nylons, and stockings when the doorbell rang. My spirits plummeted. I'd secretly hung onto the hope Trip would frighten off Desmond. But my nemesis had either washed his hands of me or he was serving out his punishment in Tartarus. But that was what I'd wanted, wasn't it?

My feet were heavy on the way to the front door. I didn't want to do this. I wanted to relax at home with some tunes and scour the Internet for potential rarities.

To my surprise, it wasn't Desmond standing on the other side of my door. The peephole showed me a male of moderate height blocking the view. He looked three extra inches taller thanks to his spiked brown hair. A beige T-shirt hung loose over his trim body, and even his blue jeans appeared to be too big. He reminded me of the werefox that had stolen my boxes except he didn't look sullen.

I opened the door enough to poke out my head. "Hi?"

The guy's deep brown eyes widened, and his lips parted as if he hadn't expected a female to greet him. I did a quick scan of his face, noting it would have looked youthful if it hadn't been for the coating of dark hair. Without the hair he'd have looked nineteen. With it, I guessed he was in his mid to late twenties.

He cleared his throat nervously. "I'm Keith Tykal, Kenny's dad."

Then again, he had to be at least thirty-two or so to have a fifteen-year-old kid. He looked damned good for a thirty-two-year-old guy.

"I came to apologize for my son. I understand he took a few of your boxes? I'm really sorry he took your stuff. And um…" He ran his left hand through his hair while the right one tugged something from his pocket. "I think these belong to you?"

I glanced at the orange scrap of silk in his fingers. My face burned upon working out what hung from his fingers. Those were my panties! The little bastard had stolen a pair of my underwear!

"At least I h-hope they are, and that he st-stole them," Keith said in a stammering voice. "I don't want to deal with … that yet."

Confusion was my predominant emotion until I made the connection to sex. He didn't want to deal with his son being sexually active at fifteen, or however old Kenny was.

I took the silk from him, blushing furiously as I did. The blush went into crimson territory when I caught the history of the fabric thanks to my psychometry ability. Kore's knees! He'd had them to his nose! He'd done it track the fabric's scent back to its owner, but it was mortifying all the same. And Kenny— No. I pushed the imagery into the periphery. I did *not* want to see that.

"They're mine," I said. "I certainly didn't give them to him or leave them behind."

But there was no way I was thanking the guy for bringing them back.

"Again, I'm really sorry my kid did this. He's at that age…" Keith's voice trailed off while his eyes shifted to the right. I was pretty sure his blush was almost as dark as mine. He shrugged. "He's taking the divorce badly."

Werefoxes got divorced? I thought they claimed mates for life and that marriage was a superfluous tradition only vanilla humans cared about.

I nodded as if I understood. Unfortunately it only made him feel like I was being sympathetic.

"And then the infection." Keith shook his head in dismay. "It was a horrible thing for a kid of ten to deal with on top of his mother taking off."

Hades's hair. He was making me feel bad for him. Worse, he was making me want to invite him in and feed him cookies until it earned me a smile. I couldn't do that because it was nearly three, or past three. I'd been too anxious to check.

I needed to say something to Keith since he'd shared this with me—well, *over-shared* this with me—but I couldn't decide what. I didn't want to tell him it was okay because it wasn't. His kid stealing my undies was definitely not okay.

I could say I understood, but that would be mildly offensive. I would never understand what it was like to be infected with a virus that made a person turn into a wild animal three nights a month … unless it happened to me. I didn't know if my human half meant I could be infected, definitely did *not* want to find out. I also didn't understand what it was like to be divorced. So it would doubly be a lie.

There was only one thing I could say. "I'm sure you're doing your best. Thanks for bringing me this."

Desmond's tall figure was visible at the entrance to the courtyard nearly outside my peripheral vision. How long had he been there, and how much had he seen? Silently I prayed it hadn't been much.

Keith's face flushed brighter before mine could. "I shouldn't have said all that. I'm sorry. Um. I'm just going to go now before I make myself sound any stupider." He turned, took one step, and then looked over his shoulder. "If my kid bugs you anymore, let me know, okay?"

Based on what I'd briefly seen in the history of my orange panties, I'd steer clear of little Kenny Tykal. But I nodded for Keith anyway.

His shoulders slumped for no apparent reason. And then he slunk off across the courtyard to his apartment without looking back once.

I pretended I hadn't seen Desmond as I slipped my panties behind me and withdrew inside. I could at least get them out of sight before he knocked. And Hera help me, I'd cool the mortified blush on my face, too.
****

The tight expression on Desmond's face told me he was ticked I'd made him ring the doorbell. I didn't care. He couldn't prove I'd noticed him.

I didn't invite him inside. Instead, I grabbed my purse and emerged onto the porch with him. He glanced down at the weeds surrounding the cement steps, perhaps worried I'd make them attack him like I did the last time he'd visited me here. And then he looked at my boots. When a disgusted expression took up residence on his face, I pressed my lips flat to keep from grinning.

What had he expected me to wear? Gucci and thousand dollar heels? He'd bet on the wrong girl if that were the case.

But beside his black pinstriped designer suit, I looked like a gangly, disaffected youth. His perfectly knotted tie was tight around his pale neck, and the white shirt beneath with its shadow stripes was primly buttoned to his chin, as always. I held in a sigh because it was unfair the dicks got all the good genes.

"Are you hungry?" he asked when we reached the parking lot.

I shot an arch look across my shoulder. "If I say yes, will I get off the hook earlier?"

Desmond's pretty lips turned down, but he didn't look away from the car ahead of us. "No."

"Then I'm not hungry."

He was glaring when he unlocked the BMW's passenger door for me. It made the gentlemanly gesture almost bearable. I smoothed my skirt over my legs atop the seat while he walked around the car. In the side mirror, his attention appeared to be on the area in front of him rather than me.

Even without him inside it, the vehicle smelled of a crisp mountain stream. I peeked at the compact disk cases in the console. What kind of music were dicks like Desmond listening to these days? There was a Massive Attack greatest hits album among the Muse, Radiohead, and old school Cure. He was supposed to listen to something nauseating like country, not bands I actually liked.

Desmond caught me looking at his CD collection when he folded himself into his seat. He started the engine, quickly turning down the volume on the stereo before it could burst my eardrums but not before I caught it was the Massive Attack album. Desmond eased the car out of the space with mechanical grace as though he took part in some sort of vehicular ballet.

He sent me a sidelong glance as we reached the stop sign at the mouth of the lot. "Do you listen to the radio?"

I'd seen the action out of the corner of my eye but was unwilling to look at him. Having him just over the center console was too close. I didn't need the masterpiece of his face swaying my opinions.

Self-preservation had me flippantly answering his question. "Only when I'm too lazy to plug in my MP3 player."

"What is on your MP3 player right now?"

My eyebrows lifted. I knew this game. This was the getting to know you game. He and I weren't supposed to be playing it.

"Uh, you know, music."

Desmond pushed out a martyred breath but didn't press me for a better answer. Instead, he turned the volume dial up on the Massive Attack song "Protection". Tracy Thorn's throaty voice sang about a girl who needed shelter.

I settled further into the seat when the singer sang about having no fear and taking on any man. My lips curved at the thought of Desmond listening to this song daily while he drove to his next mark—a mark he'd bully, intimidate, and manipulate into doing whatever he wanted them to do. Didn't he note the irony?

"You like this song," he said.

Why hadn't I sensed his empathic link? He'd been skimming my consciousness while I'd been distracted. I pinned him with a glare. "Can you even relate to a person without using your power?"

He shocked the Hades out of me by flushing red. "I'm sorry. It's second nature." The empathic link withdrew rapidly.

Soon I sensed his embarrassment without a link. Then again it might have had something to do with the fanatically focused gaze he had on the windshield.

I'd vowed to set him on fire the next time he manipulated me with his power. This was the second time since I'd given the vow without acting on my promise. I was usually good about keeping my word. But he was only trying to get a feel for my mood rather than anything nefarious. Of course, some of the worst things started as something benign.

When it came down to it, I really couldn't afford to set the high priest of Water witches on fire. I needed him on my side if I wanted to enact my mother's plan.

"So where are we going?" I asked because I no longer recognized where we were. The back road out of Sedona was one I'd never had the need to use.

"The Arboretum at Flagstaff."

He was going to drive me the half hour up to Flagstaff and then make me walk around an arboretum? It was a good thing I'd worn my boots. But I wished I'd worn shorts.

Wait a second. He was going to walk around in his suit?

Desmond's expression suddenly soured. I concentrated to see if he'd renewed the empathic link but found nothing. So why was he suddenly giving off waves of clenching frustration?

"You're new to the area and an Earth witch," he said by way of an explanation. "I thought you'd like to see the gardens and nature walks."

I'd have snarled at him if he'd said that to me a few weeks ago. But given the context, it was actually surprisingly thoughtful … for a dick. So my response was neutral.

"I'm not an Earth witch."

A heavy breath exhaled out of his nose. "You can manipulate plants." Then in a sharpened tone he said, "Would you rather go somewhere else? A movie?"

"No, the arboretum is a nice idea." But I couldn't let that sit as it was. "I just would have dressed differently if I'd known we'd be outside."

"Do you want me to go back so you can change?"

That he hadn't immediately huffed or puffed made me turn toward him. "Are you going to be traipsing about the grass in that suit?"

Desmond dropped his gaze to his chest as if he'd forgotten what he'd pulled on this morning. "I'll probably take off the tie and jacket, but yes. I hadn't planned to change clothing."

Hera, help me. I pictured him without the coat and tie. And with a few buttons undone. Maybe the shirt loose around his trim waist. Charon take it! What was wrong with me?

I forced my attention forward. "Then I should be fine."

"Are you sure? I've only gone five miles. I can turn around."

I sent him a questioning look. Was he sincere? Why did he care about my comfort? He wanted me to take my alleged weaves and leave Wipuk but not before I gave him Kali's Candle.

His expression was blank—a professional visage I suspected he wore when working. However he did sneak a few glances at me while he drove, further confounding me.

I pulled a totally girly move. "Do you think I should change clothes?"

He laughed softly. "I'm not touching that."

"Why not?"

"Because if I tell you no, it will be my fault when your tights get snagged on a bush. And if I tell you yes, you'll think I didn't like your outfit."

My lips quivered from restraining a smile. I didn't know what possessed me, maybe it was that he was behaving like a decent human being, but I heard myself teasing him. "So are you saying you like my outfit? Or you just don't want me to know you don't like it?"

He held a palm out toward me. "This is exactly what I wanted to avoid."

"I'm just funnin' you, Marino. I don't care what you think of my outfit." After a beat I said, "If I did, I'd have worn a peach pantsuit and sensible shoes."

"What makes you think I like peach pantsuits and sensible shoes?"

I hadn't expected the question or the strange, cautious tone he'd employed. It showed in my stutter. "Uh, y-your assistant wears them. I assumed it was a dress code thing."

"It is." His shoulders might have squared just a little more, but it was hard to tell when the guy was uptight to begin with. "There are certain expectations in a business environment."

"So what do you do anyway? Apart from ruling Wipuk."

"I don't rule Wipuk," he said far too quickly.

I made sure he saw the dubious lifting of my eyebrows, but I didn't argue. The afternoon was still young. I'd have plenty of time to anger him later.

"I work in wetland conservation," he said.

"In the middle of Arizona."

My flat tone earned me a sharp look. "Obviously much of the work is done in other states," he said.

"So how do you explain being headquartered in Sedona to your shareholders?"

"They think I was born here."

A portion of my question had been fishing for information. I hadn't researched him or his company and thus hadn't known if he had shareholders. It was surprising to hear he did.

"You weren't?"

"No. I was born in Colorado."

"The Rockies," I said without thinking. "That's why you smell like a crisp mountain stream."

His lips parted in surprise. "You can smell that?"

A nod was the only answer I gave him.

"You were born in California?"

I could have smacked myself for getting us on that subject. Now I had to lie because there was no way I could tell Desmond I'd been born in Hades.

I nodded rather than verbalize the lie, and then I pushed the topic back to him. "So did you move to Wipuk specifically with the goal of one day single-handedly running the colony?"

Okay, so I'd given up on waiting to anger him.

He inhaled and exhaled in quick succession, the huffing and puffing sounds I'd begun to associate with him. "I don't single-handedly run the colony."

"Is that because de Sole won't let you?"

His jaw set with another noisy breath. "I would ask you what I did to piss you off, but I think I know."

"You had *better* know," I said rather than remind him of how he'd tried to run me of out of the colony, shut down my shop, and had also accused me of murder. "But you're avoiding the question."

"I'm not running the colony. Wipuk is ruled by the Centralized Coven Coalition."

"Fine then." I made a dismissive gesture with my fingers rather like a jazz hand. "You're ruling the Centralized Coven Coalition."

Desmond enunciated each word carefully as if I needed the assistance to understand him. "I don't rule the Centralized Coven Coalition. I don't rule Wipuk. Before you accuse me of it as well, I don't rule Sedona. The only thing I can be accused of running is Neptune's

Fellowship, and that leadership was offered to me, not taken by brute force."

"Oh, I doubt you do anything brute force. It might mess up your precious suit."

He dropped his head against the headrest with a heaved sigh. And then he clammed up.

Chapter Twenty-Nine

Desmond must have been thinking about our conversation during our five-minute lull because the next words out of his mouth picked up right where we'd left off. "Everything I've done was to protect Wipuk."

I could have laughed, but I didn't. Instead I arched my eyebrows at him mockingly. "So Wipuk was the reason you sicced Eamonn Cary on me?"

His pale skin flushed pink. "I didn't sic him on you. He offered."

"But you did strike a bet as to the validity of certain portions of my body. How exactly was that for Wipuk's protection?"

"Christ." Turning as much as he could in the seat while still driving, he said, "I'm sorry. Okay? I am an ass. Are you happy now?"

An actual apology from him was shocking. I didn't like it. Not one bit. He was pushing past the mold I'd put him in, and that made for complications.

I adopted a catty tone. "You're a dick. Not an ass. Desmond the dick has a pleasant alliteration. And no, I'm not happy."

"You aren't supposed to *exist*," he said with breathy emphasis on the final word, ignoring I'd just revealed the little pet name I'd created for him. His fingers clenched and unclenched on the steering wheel. "Humans aren't supposed to have magical ability. They're not supposed to *see* Wipuk let alone enter." He gestured at me. "Yet here you are, screwing with our carefully regulated entrance requirements."

I opened my mouth to mention the influx of Were Nell had mentioned, but it didn't seem like the appropriate time. He was trying to apologize and offer an explanation. For some reason, I wanted to let him.

"I wanted you and your store out because no one controls you," he said. "You're a loose canon, like a rogue Were, only worse because no one understands what you are or what you can do. You can't fault me for wanting to protect my home."

"I can fault you for your tactics."

He nodded mutely.

"I know you won't believe me, but I care about the welfare of Wipuk and its people, too," I said. "I'm not here to threaten anything."

"No, you just want to sell us sparkly charms."

Was that sarcasm? Had Desmond ever pulled that tactic before?

Whatever the case, it rankled me into a defensive response. "I've got bills to pay and no big time corporation to pay my salary, Marino. I've got to make a living somehow."

"Why come to Wipuk?" He snuck a glance at me. "Why not open your store in Los Angeles or New York?"

"For starters, have you seen the price for retail space in L.A. or New York?" I whistled for effect. "I can't afford that. But the true answer is that Sedona is basically the new age capital of the United States. It's the perfect place to open up a shop like mine."

"If you were living in Sedona, with a shop in Sedona, we wouldn't be having this conversation."

"No?" I fixed him with a challenging stare he'd note the next time he glanced over from the road. When he didn't recant his position, I forged onward. "I think it would have taken a bit longer if I hadn't announced myself by leasing an apartment in Wipuk, but eventually we would have had this same exact conversation."

He didn't immediately argue. And for some reason I was disappointed. It was too quiet in the car, almost boring now that I had nothing to dispute.

It wasn't until I'd taken to staring out the window at the passing red rocks that he quietly said, "The tone of our conversation would have been different."

"How so?"

"You would have been another crystal shop owner on the Sedona landscape rather than a potential threat."

I let out a sardonic laugh. "Right," I said sarcastically. "I wouldn't have pushed your buttons by being all independent, mouthy female, and you wouldn't have pushed mine by being all haughty, dominating male—even without the Wipuk element involved."

"I have no problem with independent, opinionated females," Desmond said. "And simply because I am a leader doesn't automatically make me dominating."

"But the fact you manipulate everyone into doing your bidding does."

He exhaled a long, slow breath, perhaps while counting from ten backwards. I was pushing him to his limit, but he'd had plenty of chances to simply sit there and shut up. He hadn't.

Desmond must have dealt with people like me often in his line of work because when he spoke next, it was in his usual blank professional tone. "Apart from minor empathic sensing, I haven't manipulated you, Ms. Walsh."

My arched brows said otherwise. "You don't consider intimidation to be a form of manipulation?"

Once again he muttered a quiet curse to his god. I thought he'd finally learned his lesson and that he'd remain quiet. I was wrong.

"Can we make a deal?"

I held myself still because I had a pretty good idea what he was about to say. Could I remain vague without implicating Nell in the ownership of Kali's Candle?

Desmond glanced at me to see if I was paying attention. I gestured for him to continue.

"We'll go back to square one," he said, proving he was just a little unpredictable. "I'll forgive you for being an unauthorized human operating an unwelcome shop in Wipuk who has invaded my privacy with at least one count of uninvited psychometry, assaulted me with a show of Air magic in front of one of my colleague's daughter—an incident, I might add, that cost me an expensive trip to the cleaners—and who has also mocked me at every opportunity. And you can forgive me for being a manipulative, intimidating, haughty, dominating dick whose concern for his home prompted him to bully you with threats, accuse you of a crime you didn't commit, and also attempted to sense your intent using his power."

"With a presentation like that, how could I possibly refuse?" I said with a dramatic roll of my eyes.

"The point is we've both done things to anger the other. In fact, I would argue for each offense I've made against you, you've countered with one against me. We are even. It should be a matter of simply calling a ceasefire so we can enjoy the rest of the night."

He'd *admitted* we were even. For a man like him—a man who had taken a mere five years to become the leader of not only Neptune's Fellowship but also a powerful figure in the entire country's coven leadership—it took guts to swallow his pride and admit that. Then again, I suspected he was following a chapter in one of those how to win over and influence people books.

"You're the one who bid a ridiculous amount of money for this," I said. "Why should I bother with a ceasefire when you're just going to wait a few hours until

I'm full from dinner and relaxed to ask me about the crystal you saw at my shop?"

Desmond made a noise at the back of his throat while dropping his head against the headrest. His eyes closed momentarily. "You're not just mouthy. You're incapable of being pleasant."

Though my tone wasn't sharp, I meant every word I said. "I take offense to that. I am perfectly capable of being pleasant with pleasant people."

"I didn't bid on your date so I could ask you about the crystal. You told me multiple times you sold it. I believe you."

"Then why did you bid on my date?"

"The bid war had to be stopped," he said in his professional tone. "I didn't think either Eamonn or Maximo would back down. Both could afford to bid virtually any amount. And had I allowed it to continue, Ascencion might have become violent." He sent me another sidelong look. "I heard about the disagreement with her."

I snorted in disgust. "Disagreement? That's a nice way of saying I set her on fire."

The BMW's engine revved dangerously without warning as Desmond's body smacked against the seat in his attempt to twist toward me. He must have deemed himself unsafe to drive for he quickly maneuvered the car onto the nearest scenic pull off, a mere two hundred feet ahead. He twisted his torso in my direction after he put the vehicle in park. The rounded aqua eyes and parted pretty lips weren't promising.

"You set her on fire," he said woodenly.

I inhaled a long sigh because I'd screwed up. The screw up wasn't in telling him I'd set the vampire on fire, though that hadn't been bright. I'd messed up by setting Ascencion on fire in the first place. It was really quite shocking the news hadn't made it around Wipuk already. Perhaps she was embarrassed by it.

Since there was no sense in hiding it now, I nodded. "Yes."

Desmond's gaze lowered and hooded. "Did you pour gasoline on her and flick a lighter?"

I slowly shook my head. "I called up Fire magic and hit her with a fireball when she tried to eat me. In my defense, I warned her I'd do it if she touched me with her fangs."

"You told Ascencion Boleda you'd set her on fire if she touched you with her fangs, and she did it anyway?"

The careful word choice he used and the obvious repetition had me on my guard. But I answered him anyway. "I believe it was something to the effect that I'd annihilate her before she could draw a single sip if she so much as touched a fang to my skin."

He sat staring at me with eyelids slowly easing shut only to open equally as leisurely. Ten seconds of silence passed before he broke it. "What happened?"

Desmond's eerily sedate reaction made me terribly uneasy. "She set her fang to my skin," I said impatiently. "I hit her with a fireball. I just told you."

"I mean why isn't she dead if you threatened to annihilate her? Why hasn't Maximo killed you for it?"

"I put her out using Air magic." That much wasn't giving out any trade secrets since he knew I could manipulate Air. "I don't know why Maximo hasn't killed me. Not only didn't he kill me but he also claimed me as part of his faction right after."

"You warned her not to touch you, so why would you put her out if she tried to feed on you without your permission?"

I drew in another heavy sigh because I was once again going to have to admit this to someone who was a threat.

"I don't kill people." I gestured at the wrinkled expression that took up residence on his face. "And you really don't have much room to look all disgusted with me. I said I'd show you why a vampire claimed me the next time you tried to use your power on me. That was two attempts ago and I didn't hit you with a fireball."

"This isn't my disgusted look," he said under his breath.

I needed something to get us off this subject before he wondered how I was able to access three schools of magic. "Fine, we'll go back to square one. You have your ceasefire."

Desmond's wrinkled expression slowly opened into surprise.

"I'll even attempt to be pleasant," I said with a mocking smile.

It was Desmond's turn to lift his flat, dark eyebrows mockingly. His lips curved into the beginnings of a smug smile. "It might be worth the money for charity just to see you struggle with that."

Chapter Thirty

Somehow I managed to carry on a civil conversation with Desmond the rest of the trip to Flagstaff. I learned he'd gone to college in Colorado, he'd earned a Ph.D. in international business with a Master's degree in environmental geoscience, and he'd moved to Wipuk following his mother's death from a sudden embolism.

His father—the high priest of the Rockies Water witch covens—had died years earlier. I didn't ask, but it sounded like a case of a young witch forced to breed with an older priest. However, I did gather he'd been a spoiled only child who'd had a deep fondness for his mother.

And he'd made me admit I was also an only child. I'd given him the partial truth when I'd said I'd lived with my mother until I was ten. The partial part was that I'd told him she'd passed on to the other side. Technically I was the one who had passed on to the other side.

It had indeed been a struggle not to make catty comments about his need to control everything, the rumors he was gay, and his stuffy fashion sense. I made it easier on myself by persuading him to tell me all about his thesis and dissertations. The rising and falling of his smooth voice discussing geoscience and business in Africa was an unexpected treat. I almost cared about the pollution in the Niger River Basin simply because of his emphatic points.

The arboretum was empty of visitors when we arrived at quarter to four. Desmond stood from the car without a word and stripped off his jacket, carefully arranging it over the back of the driver's seat. I hopped out of the vehicle so I could avoid getting hit with another fragrant cloud of mountain stream scented air. He stared off into the distance as he loosened his tie's knot, slowly drawing it down in an unintentional striptease. I forced my gaze to the landscape, taking in the smell of pine and the outdoors to cool the warming of my skin.

It had been some time since I'd gone to any sort of nature preserve. While I could tap into Earth magic, I was no Earth witch. I wasn't particularly eco-conscious. I didn't recycle unless forced. I wasn't concerned with balancing my carbon footprint. But I couldn't deny there was a small pull to wild places. Maybe this wouldn't be a complete waste of time.

Desmond appeared around the front of the car, gesturing a newly revealed pale forearm to the arboretum's entrance. He'd rolled his sleeves up past his elbows and even unbuttoned the first two buttons on his crisp white shirt. But he hadn't pulled the shadow-striped garment free from his trousers. It meant I had to see the shape of his body beneath the slacks.

Fortunately he gave me something else to concentrate on when he immediately guided me onto a secondary path beneath massive pine trees to a shaded garden. I stopped to read the signs, feigning interest because it was better than looking at his nice tush—a feature I couldn't seem to avoid staring at whenever I had the chance.

There was a nervous impatience to him as he hovered without standing still for longer than a half second. His mood was notable enough that I craned my head back for a look at him. "What?"

His eyebrows lifted in question. "Hmm?"

"You're antsy like you're supposed to be somewhere and are late."

"It's the wetland," he said quietly. "It's pulling on me."

I couldn't help but laugh. "Okay then. Let's go get it out of your system."

Desmond's mouth parted as if he might argue. He seemed to think better of it, for he nodded twice, and then started toward the wetland. I couldn't smell any water apart from him so I sent off a tiny bit of Water sensing magic to find it.

Something went horribly wrong because instead of sensing the wetland, my magic immediately homed in on Desmond. He let out a low growl, coming to an abrupt halt. Desmond pinned me with twin dark orbs. "I *feel* you!"

I held up my palms in front of my chest in a sign of surrender. "It was an accident. I'm sorry."

A surprisingly powerful roar emitted from him. "You can access *Water,* too?" His aqua eyes were tiny slits of dark color worthy of a storming frothy sea, his lips had peeled back to reveal tightly clenched teeth, and his entire body shook with fury.

I swallowed down heavy unease. Until then, he'd only been miffed; now he was truly angry.

What would the high priest of America's Water witches do when he was angry?

He took a menacing step toward me. "Earth, Air, Fire, and now Water," he said in a low, icy voice. His attention dropped to the ring on my finger—the ring that *could* access every school of magic with the correct incantation. "No witch in history has ever claimed more than two schools, and yet you have access to four." His tone soured into a disgusted range. "You cannot honestly expect me to believe you aren't a weave user. Just admit the truth and stop using the damn weaves so we can move on from here."

I began shaking with fury, too. "I'm not using weaves! I am so tired of this!" I stomped toward him, tugging the ring from my finger.

Desmond recoiled as though I might hurt him. I didn't let it offend me because he had a right to be concerned. I'd demonstrated my ability to hurt things.

"Hold this." I shoved the ring toward him.

He lifted his palm and took it. I concentrated on his expression to see if he noted anything strange about the powerful piece of jewelry. There was no change to his angry yet cautiously curious expression.

Next I untied the leather wristband. It went beside the ring on his palm. I unhooked the mundane silver maple leaf earrings that hung from my earlobes. Those were dropped within the hole the wristband created on his hand. I bent down to unlace my boots—an item of clothing that was ever-present and thus would be suspected as a weave, I was sure. I yanked them free from my feet, tossing them onto the ground one by one with deliberately loud thumps.

Then my hands went to the thick black leather belt that served as a decorative element around the low-rise plaid skirt. Desmond's eyebrows lifted just a little higher when I pulled it free from the belt loops. I unceremoniously dropped it beside my boots. I ignored his questioning look as I crouched so I could unroll the fishnet stockings down my thighs before he could accuse them of being Air magic weaves. They were balled up and shoved into the openings in my boots moments later. When nearly everything was removed, I stood barefoot in three items of clothing, glaring at him.

"The only things I have on now are this T-shirt, this skirt, and my panties," I said in my most confrontational of tones. I was done being pleasant if he persisted in accusing me of being a weave user. "And just so you have less of a reason to accuse me of wearing a compound item, I'll remove one more of those. Your choice."

His neck worked, as though swallowing down a lump. I gave him a vicious smile, fully aware of what I'd done to him. I'd given him the power to make one of us very, very uncomfortable.

"Panties."

I was mildly impressed he'd managed to speak the word in his blank professional voice. But it gave credence to the rumors he was gay.

I reached down and wiggled out of the panties without showing any skin. The scrap of silk was tossed into the boot with my hosiery. Now my plaid skirt suddenly felt daringly short with its mid-thigh length. Every tiny breeze was grounds for stress. I thanked the gods he wasn't an Air witch.

However, Desmond reminded me of why I'd created a mean pet name for him in the first place. "How do I know that T-shirt isn't composed of a left sleeve for an Air magic power, a right sleeve for an Earth magic power, and front and back pieces for the other two? Or that each pleat in your skirt isn't a weave for a specific power?" His voice grew more confident. "And maybe you're wearing piercings I can't see that are weaves for funnel clouds and plant control."

"You got to choose an item. You didn't pick the skirt or the shirt. I bought this shirt at Old Navy, and this skirt came from Hot Topic. They're not weaves. And the only things pierced on me are my earlobes. I have no magical tattoos in places you can't see. You'll just have to take my word on that." I inhaled a sharp breath, knowing I'd regret my next statement. "But I'll let you choose the four powers from the four schools you want me to demonstrate for you."

Because a weave was one specific power distilled into an object, allowing Desmond to choose which powers I demonstrated should dispel his suspicion once and for all.

The Water witch glanced around the space for inspiration, and then down at himself. "Tell me everything you can about these trousers," he said a moment later.

The level of psychometry I'd already exhibited was that of a powerful high priestess, which, of course, I wasn't. I could understand why he'd demand I show him that power again despite having proved I could do it time and time again. He wanted to know if I could do it without my ring.

I closed the six feet between us, feet scraping on the rough ground. My forehead knitted in irritation. "Where do you want me to touch?"

Desmond hesitated before patting the side opposite the hand that held my jewelry. "This hip."

Easing forward, I set my palm on his hip exactly where he'd patted. The first thing the trousers told me was that they had recently become *tight*. I noted the problem and immediately flushed hot. I turned my head away to avoid seeing anything more.

Soon I traversed through the trousers' history. They showed me the ride in the car to Flagstaff, Desmond picking me up, and him in the car on the way over to the apartment. Once the history I hadn't personally witnessed began, I started speaking my findings aloud.

"You ate an early lunch at your desk—a watercress salad. One leaf fell on your right thigh, but it didn't stain. You stopped at your assistant's desk on the way back from someplace shortly before lunch. She wanted to know when you were leaving for the day. She was unhappy when you told her it would be early, so she hit the desk. You felt it against your knee. You took several calls during the morning and tapped your thigh with your knuckles during each one. On the way into work this morning, you stopped for an espresso that you held between your legs until you could get the money out of your wallet. You tapped your leg while you waited for the drink. I think the barista might have been chatty?"

His gave me a tight-lipped nod.

"Is that good enough, or do you want me to go back further?"

"That's disturbing enough."

I pulled my hand back and then immediately put several feet between us. He was no longer showing evidence of arousal. Anger must have cooled it. That was a good sign. Wasn't it?

"Telepathy," he said next.

Telepathy was within the domain of the Air school. Neophytes could throw their voices on the wind, and thus many ventriloquists were Air witches. But it took a powerful witch to be able to demonstrate true telepathy—speaking within the mind. Desmond wasn't throwing any punches. Not only was he checking for weaves, he was also trying to get a feel for my mastery of each school.

I used one of his lines on him. "You are fishing for information in dangerous waters, Mr. Marino."

"Would you rather get naked?"

My eyes went squinty at the smug curving of his lips. So I called Air and asked it to carry a message to his mind. *"You are such a dick, Marino."*

He quickly lost his smug smile.

And I gained it.

"Next," I said with an irreverent toss of my cerulean hair over my shoulder.

In a whip sharp voice, Desmond said, "Quicksand."

While quicksand wasn't the most powerful Earth witch power, it was a destructive one. If a witch could turn earth into quicksand, she could topple buildings.

I'd had it with Desmond's bullshit. So I hit him with a double whammy rather than pointing out I'd already demonstrated an Earth power. I loosened the land directly beneath his feet. While he scrambled for firm ground, I persuaded several plants to grab hold of his calves. All at once, I put the land back to rights. Desmond shot me an annoyed glare when he noted the grass stains on his fine trousers.

"Relax. It will come out in the wash," I said.

His voice came out frosty and stilted. "Blue flame, from nothing, one foot by one foot, without burning the surrounding environment."

I stared at him in mute shock for what must have been a half a minute.

Starting flame from nothing was a mid-range Fire witch power. Starting a fire that was one foot by one foot large from absolutely nothing was just shy of impossible. But making it a blue flame, the hottest of all fire? I wasn't sure there was a witch in the world that could accomplish it.

Seeing my hesitance, he taunted with a frustrating smirk. "You can just give up and tell me where you're hiding the weaves."

"*Dick*," I said under my breath while calling on the aether to send me Fire energy.

I backtracked to the pebble walkway for the assistance it would give in controlling the flame. He'd taunted me, so now I had to rise to the challenge. I let the energy trickle into me, slowly filling the magical seed beneath my heart. In order to pull this off, I'd have to store up a good deal of latent power in addition to siphoning directly from the Earth.

"You might want to step back," I told him. "I don't know what is going to happen."

I barely saw him move because my vision had already grown hazy from the influx of power. And then I lost control. Fire exploded out of my chest above the T-shirt, blue as my hair. I let out a terrified yelp as I struggled to control the blaze. I needed a barrier between the flame, my clothing, and the surrounding area at the very least.

Desmond's hands lifted up in a familiar gesture.

"No!" I shouted before he could douse me with rain. "Don't! I can handle it!"

"You're on fire!"

I ignored his shout as I willed the inferno into a sphere between my outstretched palms. Flame slithered over my body like thick sludge into the space I'd allotted until it formed a dense blue ball of crackling power.

Desmond inhaled a sharp breath. "Jesus Christ! Your clothes aren't even singed!"

Voices in the distance had us exchanging worried looks. I quickly called Fire back into me, and then asked it to disperse to where it had originated.

The Water witch's jaw dropped open clear to the pale skin of his chest. A moment passed before I'd realized I'd made a terrible misstep. Most witches were unidirectional conductors. I'd demonstrated I was bi-directional. Now he had more evidence of my power.

I turned my back on Desmond. Time to put some distance between us. I snatched up my boots and belt. Without a word, I stalked barefoot toward the wetland before the other visitors could interrupt us. He was close on my heels.

"Are you satisfied yet?" I heard myself snarling over the stomping of my bare feet on the cool ground.

"You haven't demonstrated Water."

I muttered several curses under my breath. If I didn't calm down soon, I was going to lose control of my emotions and possibly harm him. So I concentrated on the mountains in the distance, willing their steady figures to calm my ire.

I would show him whatever Water power he asked and then I'd make him take me home. Surely proving I was as powerful as four high priestesses all rolled up into one was worth the money he'd given to charity. He never would have learned any of that otherwise. I'd been truly foolish for getting myself into the situation in the first place.

He quickened his step. I didn't understand why until he stood in my way. "Right here is good."

Of course it was good. I sensed the wetland in front of us. He felt secure now that he could quickly tap into his element.

I dropped my boots and belt onto the path then shoved my hands onto my hips. Desmond's gaze darting to my thigh reminded me I didn't have a scrap on beneath the short skirt. I pursed my lips to keep from insulting him.

"Manipulate me," he said in a rumbling pitch.

I dragged in a ragged sigh. Of course. I should have guessed that would be his demand. There was only one Water ability trickier than manipulation and that was another form of manipulation—one done through dreams. He didn't have time to make me demonstrate that ability or I was certain he would have tried.

"Fine," I said between clenched teeth.

Inhaling a long, steadying breath, I drew in power from the nearby pond and wetland, making certain he sensed it in the aether. I didn't soften the connection. Instead I hardened it so he'd be certain to feel it sliding along his consciousness. Once we were connected, I soaked in the emotions he gave off. Anxiety tinged with fear was chief among them joined by a heavy wash of frustration and, Hera, help me, the smoky tang of lust.

Warmth spread out across my shoulders, tingling my skin. I understood it was a shared sensation when his frame lightly shook. He rolled onto the balls of his feet toward me. Had I unintentionally drawn him toward me, or had he done that all on his own? I needed to finish this up quickly so I wouldn't have to find out.

"What were you planning to do next on our date?" I asked softly, skimming his emotions without pressing my will upon him. He could lie if he wanted to, but I'd sense it.

"Dinner," he said, equally as softly, as if he were trying to match my tone.

"Where?"

"My house."

I didn't detect anything lusty about the answer. He had no intention of putting the moves on me despite the arousal I'd noted earlier. "Why?"

"Because I don't want to be seen in public with you."

He might as well have backhanded me. Never had anyone been so embarrassed by me that they'd been fearful of being seen in my company. All of this had truly been so he could fish for information and track down the damn crystal.

Fury rose within me. Some of it spilled out onto him, quickening his breath. I struggled to pull it back and tamp it down.

And then I hit him with all of the manipulative power I could drudge up. "You want to take me back to my apartment as fast as is legal. You don't want to bring me to your house. You want this date to be over." I waited a beat. "What do you want, Marino?"

"I want to take you back to your apartment as fast as is legal. I want this date to be over." he said robotically.

I snatched my things from the ground and then stalked toward the parking lot as fast as my legs would take me.

Chapter Thirty-One

I should have paused my angry charge long enough to put on my panties. Now it was too late. I wouldn't be able to shimmy into them in the BMW's leather seat without showing a serious amount of skin. At least my mother's gifts were safely around my wrist and knuckle again.

Arms folded petulantly in front of my chest and eyes firmly on the passenger window, I waited until the car was several miles out of Flagstaff before I released Desmond from my steady manipulative link. Now he'd have to fight the lingering suggestions. That could take anywhere from an hour to weeks depending on his power level and conviction.

He silently shook for the first two minutes of freedom, and then he pulled the car over to the side of the road. The heat pouring off him meant he was either furious or furiously fighting my will. Perhaps both. But I was more concerned with how *fast* he'd thrown off my will.

Exactly how powerful was Desmond Marino?

I spoke up before he could shout at me. "You told me to manipulate you. You can't be angry now that I did."

"I can be whatever the hell I want to be!" Desmond drew a handkerchief out of the pocket of the jacket draped over his seat. He dabbed at the beads of perspiration that had formed along his forehead.

"I want to go home."

Desmond's trim body gave the impression of taking up more space as he leaned forward with a menacing glower. "I spent fifty thousand dollars for a night with you." His whip sharp voice took over. "You don't *get* to go home yet."

I'd stood toe-to-toe with more intimidating foes. This one wouldn't cow me. "Why did you bother if you didn't want to be seen with me in public?"

"You *made* me tell you that."

I shook my head. "I was only skimming your emotions then. You told me that all on your own."

A rough snort ripped through Desmond's throat. "You don't even know your own strength." He made a louder sound of dismay. "You're a toddler with a nuclear weapon!"

I rolled my eyes. "You're just angry because you're no longer the most powerful manipulator in Wipuk."

"I wasn't the most powerful manipulator before. Maximo de Sole has that title, *your* benefactor. You're teaming up to take us down, aren't you?"

He'd said "us"—as if it weren't simply him holding the reins. Could I believe that?

"I'm on my own team, Marino, team sorceress. I don't want to take anyone down." Thinking better of it, I said, "Unless they deserved to be taken down."

He quaked with anger but was no longer in my personal space. I clamped my mouth shut because I'd caused enough trouble to last me years. He was going to demand I leave Wipuk, with or without Maximo's claim. A very real slice of fear lanced up my body from the pit of my stomach. I'd fail at my mother's task if he kicked me out of Wipuk. Failure wasn't an option.

I slumped back against the seat, exhaling moodily. This was going to take an immense swallowing of my pride. But the alternative was unthinkable.

"Please," I whispered. "Don't make me leave."

His head jerked a half-inch toward me. I didn't know what that meant. No new emotions floated on the air to explain it.

Several silent moments passed before he said, "I told you that you couldn't go home until the night was finished."

I gave a small shake of my head and continued my whisper. "Not the night. Don't make me leave Wipuk. Please. This is where I belong."

Desmond's frame drew up into a stiff, regal pose. His chin lifted into his haughty stance. These movements focused my brain onto one shining fact—I'd made yet another misstep. By pleading with him for understanding, I'd admitted he had the ability to eject me from the colony. I'd inadvertently handed him control.

"You can't stay." He arrogantly drew his pause out. "Unless you agree to voluntary probation and persuade a coven to take responsibility for you."

All things considered, it was a reasonable request. That was essentially the deal we'd agreed upon the first day we'd met. But the second part worried me.

"No coven will be willing to take responsibility for a sorceress with access to multiple schools."

His dark eyebrows drifted upward. "No?"

I shot him an impatient look. He might be somewhat unpredictable at times, but now wasn't one of them.

Desmond nodded, a sign he wasn't going to insult me by continuing the coy responses. "I'll take responsibility for you provided you agree to certain checks and balances."

He wanted *me* to agree to checks and balances? That was my job. I was the check for every witch on the planet, or at least the ones my mother pointed me toward.

But I needed to earn the trust of each coven, and Desmond's was the first and largest roadblock. If agreeing to this would clear the way through that block, then I'd simply have to swallow my pride.

He'd think something was odd if I agreed without questioning him, so I adopted an uneasy tone. "What checks and balances?"

"No using magic." I opened my mouth to argue, but he cut me off. "Unless it's in self-defense. And you need to learn to control your abilities. You can start by working with me on the granular control of your manipulation power."

He was going to help make me a *better* manipulator?

"You want to use me," I said suddenly, only just realizing he'd been planning this for some time.

"I'd be an idiot not to. Who else knows you have access to Water?"

I shook my head wearily. Hera, help me. I was so stupid.

"Only you," I said.

"Let's keep it that way. And keep your Fire ability to yourself. Ascencion and Maximo haven't seen the need to share it. We won't either."

"Marino," I said warningly. "I have morals. I'm not going to do anything for you that is contrary to them even if it means risking you'll kick me out."

He chuckled softly. "We'll worry about that when we come to it."

That rankled but not enough to call an end to this.

I stared out the windshield for a moment before I got up the nerve to ask the next question. I wanted to hear it from his lips—to know I wasn't simply making assumptions. "How did we go from you thinking I was a murderous weave user to you wanting to use me?"

"I wanted to use you even when I thought you were a weave user." His attention drifted to the windshield. "Though you are universally distrusted in

Wipuk, no one expects you to be a threat. And yet you are. You are the perfect mole."

I *was* the perfect mole. He just didn't know I was a mole for my mother, not for him.

Could I live with myself if I agreed to be his minion? I would be fulfilling my own agenda while I worked on his, but would it be worth the slimy feeling I'd get for being a dick's lackey?

I needed his support to stay in Wipuk. And beyond that, I needed his support on the coalition. There really was no choice but to accept the slime.

"It would work best if we didn't alter your dispensation form." He pretended to be deep in thought. I suspected he'd been formulating this idea for days, perhaps weeks. "Together we can work on slowly cutting your duties to de Sole."

"De Sole hasn't given me any duties."

Desmond's attention snapped back to my face. "But he claimed you without enthralling you. He's having you spy for him."

"If he is, he's never told me and he's never asked for a report."

The Water witch's eyes drew into slivers, and his fleshy lips thinned impressively. The tone that came out of his mouth was sharper than a serpent's tooth. "You've slept with him."

A sound of disgust bubbled out of my nose. "I told you what happened, Marino. I didn't sleep with him. The only favor the vampire has called in for claiming me was the charity auction." I gestured at Desmond. "And look where that got him."

Just as quickly as the dark look had come over him, it faded into a smug smile. Then he let out a hearty laugh. "His charity may be fifty-thousand richer, but his faction is one sorceress poorer." Desmond's smug smile worked its way into a broad grin. "And he'll never suspect a thing."

****

Desmond drove past my apartment complex. Intentionally, I was sure. He'd probably done it to tick me off. But perhaps a small portion of it was because he didn't know if he could. My manipulation had been strong. If he'd been anyone other than a powerful Water witch, he probably wouldn't have been able to resist my will.

Discomfort had me fidgeting when he pulled his vehicle to the security booth at the entrance of a ritzy gated community on the other side of the colony. The man on duty saluted him and lifted the mechanical gate. The paved road wound through a heavily wooded area abutting the shimmering Wipuk-Sedona line. We drove for two miles before Desmond pulled off onto a narrow driveway. The back end of a split-level house appeared between the trees with a garage on the upper portion—the Wipuk portion—that was even now opening for his BMW.

The interior of Desmond's garage was as meticulously maintained as he was. Tools carefully hung from hooks upon a sleek metal workbench. A mop, broom, and dustbin hung from a labeled stand. The quick glimpse gave me an idea of how the rest of the house would look.

He eased the car into its spot, turning it off and opening the car door with a smooth move. Even his garage door slid down in time with the rest of his efficient motions. I carefully pulled myself out, minimizing the amount of skin I showed. The air on my tush didn't bode well, but Desmond was already at the garage's man door with his jacket and tie folded over his forearm. I doubted he'd seen a thing.

"Can I use your bathroom to fix my …
stockings?" I hesitated on the final word because I hadn't
wanted to remind him of what I wasn't wearing. I'd
failed because his cheeks flushed as pink as mine.

"I'll show you," he said while studiously looking
anywhere but at me.

I followed him through the curious house—a
structure in the shape of a semi-circle. The interior had
walls made of floor-to-ceiling glass with a garden view.
Rooms not constructed of rustic stacked rock walls or
massive windows were painted in a modern cream color.

Desmond's garden was a lovely plot of land with
a small pond, stream, and working waterfall. The first-
floor location of it implied the garden existed in Sedona.
Whoever had designed the place had curiously carried the
garden's flagstone walkway inside the house—perhaps to
give the building an outdoors inside impression.

He gestured to a door on his right while
continuing the walk through the rounded space. "The
restroom is in there. I'll be in the kitchen. Follow the
corridor forward past the living room and you'll find it."

I ducked into the restroom, glad to have a door to
close. The flagstone floor and cream walls in the
bathroom made for a modern but cold feel. I supposed
that was indicative of its owner.

A glance around the room showed me his sink
was a glass bowl with a metal spout for a faucet. It was
like I'd stepped into a modern art museum. I quickly
pulled on my panties, tugged up the fishnet stockings,
and then laced up my boots good and tight. Knowing I
wasn't half naked made me feel a measure better. I'd
been about to leave the room when music seeped through
the walls from further in the house—the Massive Attack
song I'd heard in the car.

Was Desmond trying to impress me?

No. I shook my head wildly, hair flying around my face. No. He wasn't trying to impress me. He couldn't bear to be seen in public with me.

I shoved off my back foot and went in search of him. He'd made us continue this evening when I'd demanded to be brought home. So I'd push him to the limit of his patience only to pull back again. I was good at that.

The walk around the semi-circle house was slow because I couldn't help but look at everything. Desmond's living room had a spectacular view of Mingus Mountain, but the waterfall burbling down the wall behind his flat screen television drew my attention most. I followed the line of water from the ceiling, down the surface and to the honest to Hera two-foot wide stream edging his living room. The flagstone floor had a trench encased in glass that stretched from the wall to the semi-circle's windows. Water flowed through the trench where it created another cascade that emptied into the stream outside. Listening intently, I could make out other sources of liquid in the house. This was surely a Water witch's dream home.

I swept past the French gray furniture in the next portion of the semi-circle shaped home toward the dining room. A glass topped table on a heavy black pedestal held the position of honor. Six padded cream chairs stood at precise intervals around the table. Another interior waterfall flowed from the wall to the indoor stream and on to the windows.

The Massive Attack song pouring from the kitchen switched to The Cure's "Love Song". I made my way to the source where I found the homeowner behind a black granite kitchen island.

He appeared to be sautéing onions in a frying pan over a large grate on his giant gas stove. One hand held a spoon while the other poured water into a saucepan. With the stacked rock wall framing his handsome figure, he could have been a celebrity chef on a cooking channel. Though he was hotter than any chef I'd seen on television.

Since he'd told me to find the kitchen, I assumed he wanted me to see him at work. I settled against the wall dividing the dining room and the kitchen to watch. Like everything he did, Desmond cooked with meticulous care. He measured liquid to the drop, using a rubber spatula to scrape every last bit into his pan. The steak he'd pulled from the refrigerator was weighed and cut to the exact dimensions he'd needed. Mushrooms were sliced with fanatical precision, ensuring each had consistent widths.

I hadn't been kidding when I'd said I couldn't make macaroni and cheese, but watching Desmond in the kitchen didn't make me want to change that. He made it look painful. Most people enjoyed cooking, didn't they? How could this level of detail be fun?

He hadn't bothered to ask me if I ate meat, mushrooms, or onions. That bugged me. Especially since he'd be furious if I failed to eat his carefully prepared meal. It was a good thing I wasn't a vegetarian.

I rapidly grew disgruntled. I'd stared, silently willing Desmond to drop something all over his shirt so he'd have an excuse to take it off. But I didn't want him shirtless. Not really. I moved toward the windows so I could take in the view of the mountain rather than the male.

"Would you get a bottle of the Alcantara Cabernet Sauvignon out of the rack?"

My first impulse was to snark about him getting me drunk, but I kept my mouth shut. Posh people drank wine with dinner as par for the course. Since Desmond had paid to get me here, I'd do his posh dinner thing.

I glanced around until I found the wooden rack within the stacked stone wall. I had to crouch to read the labels because they were near the floor. I didn't know the first thing about wine, let alone what Alcantara's bottle looked like. Desmond's cheeks were pink when I set the bottle atop the kitchen island.

My jaw set in irritation. Had he made me get the wine because he knew I'd have to bend in my short skirt? Or had it been an unintentional perk?

I turned on my heel and stalked back to my spot by the window because I didn't want to be near him for longer than I had to be. Behind me Desmond worked on tugging at the softly creaking cork in between stirring his concoction of steak and 'shrooms.

A sizzling sound and then quieting of the mixture meant he'd poured something into it. I glanced over my shoulder in time to see him lift the wine bottle away from the pan. He'd needed it to cook. He probably hadn't been trying to check out my tush. I inhaled an annoyed breath because I was beginning to think he was right. I couldn't be pleasant with him.

"Here," he said in his blank professional tone.

He'd set a wine glass atop the stone island. Within the glass decorated with a single gold ribbon meandering up the side was a half glass worth of deep red liquid. And he had one of his own already pressed to his lips. He wasn't looking at me, instead concentrating on his preparation.

I hesitated for several seconds before fetching the glass he'd set aside for me. Then I headed right back to my spot. A minute passed before I was brave enough to take a sip. Sour flavor assaulted my taste buds, drawing a shudder. I held the wine in front of me rather than admit I didn't like it. Yet another thing he could be contemptuous about.

Desmond's softly tapping loafers retreated into the dining room. He returned so he could gather up utensils and the bottle of wine.

"It's ready."

I reluctantly followed him, slowing when I noted he'd set the spot at the head of the table and the one immediately to its right. Only the promise of going home after this made me take the seat he'd pulled out for me.

Desmond didn't speak while we ate the food—steak tips and mushrooms cooked in butter, onion, and wine. There was a bowl of salad on the table he'd pulled out of the refrigerator. A clear decanter of vinaigrette sat beside it, a sign he'd perhaps made it from scratch.

I had the sudden urge to claw him.

Desmond looked up then, catching my eye with a rounding of his. "What?"

I didn't sense any brushing of his power, but I didn't doubt he'd sensed the sharp turn of my mood anyway. "I'm kind of miffed you're so good at everything," I said between clenched teeth.

His lips curved ever so slightly, perhaps an attempt to hide a smile. "But I'm a dick." "That you are." But if he were to be believed, he'd only been a dick because he'd been trying to protect Wipuk. If that were the case… "Why does Nell hate you?"

Desmond's lips thinned again as his frame grew stiff. "She thinks I'm a dictator." He sent me a pointed look that implied he knew I shared her opinion.

I set my fork atop the cream-colored plate. "You act like you run the place. I understand why she'd think that." With a sly smile I said, "Come on, Marino. Admit it."

His aqua gaze held mine intently. I struggled not to squirm under the strange warmth of it. He wasn't supposed to merely stare. He was supposed to go squinty-eyed and puff in irritation.

Finally, he gave a reply. "As I've said before, I don't run Wipuk."

While I was sighing, he poured me another glass of wine. The stuff tasted better with the food. I hadn't noted my glass was empty until he'd filled it.

I took another sip. "Then why do you need a mole?"

"Because there are plenty who want to run Wipuk. I need to be prepared if I want to stop them."

One glass of wine in me and steak coated in the stuff had me relaxed enough to bring up a topic I'd avoided earlier. "What about the Were? Nell says you've let in a bunch of them do … something, I can't remember. And that you ran off the shifters so there's no one left to keep the Were in line and they're causing all sorts of trouble."

I was surprised when he failed to stiffen or huff and puff, again. His tone was his usual blank professional sound. "Wipuk's town hall and the pre-school are in need of renovation to bring them up to standard code. As I argued, simply because we aren't subject to human code doesn't mean we ought to disregard their wisdom. The companies that bid the lowest on the coalition's RFPs are Were owned. The shapeshifter clan was angry we didn't accept their grossly inflated proposals simply because they were already here. They chose to move rather than submit a new proposal."

That sounded entirely reasonable. Was it really, or was that the wine talking?

I remembered more of what Nell had said. "She thinks there's a quiet war going on with the undead because of you."

"The quiet war with the undead predates me." Desmond eased back into the chair with that arrogant shift of his weight onto one hip. It put him just a little farther from me, which was good. What wasn't good was how the pose made it easier for him to stare at me. "But I intend to end it." He paused. "With your help."

So now I was a pawn in a quiet war. Great.

I lifted my glass to my lips and chugged the rest.

Chapter Thirty-Two

I could barely recall how we ended up on Desmond's sofa. I vaguely remembered bringing my plate to his sink and him pouring me another glass of wine. He'd suggested a walk outside. It had been a nice, albeit quick, circuit around his flagstone garden with the stream, small pond, and waterfall as points of interest. And then we were in the living room on the Wipuk level of his house again.

I thought I had dropped down onto the sofa first. But Desmond had chosen to sit beside me. A little too close.

The warmth of his body beneath the fine trousers that brushed my fishnet stockings was all too easily sensed. The crisp mountain stream scent of his filled my nose. He'd stopped talking some time ago. And now all he did was stare. My stomach did aerobics whenever I'd glance at him and note the intent gaze trained on my face.

I leaned forward, setting my elbows to my knees to ease the vertigo I was beginning to feel courtesy of the alcohol. Desmond leaned forward into an identical position. So I shifted my legs until the one near him was drawn as close to my body as possible. I pushed it beneath the other, leaning away from his fragrant body. He lifted his wine glass to his lips. And then within a minute's time he'd mirrored my pose.

"Dinner was good," I said uneasily, breaking the uncomfortable silence. "I'm not much of a wine drinker, but this wasn't disgusting." I shook the glass at him.

He nodded. "It's a good local wine. I'm glad you liked dinner. What would you like for dessert? I have the ingredients for bananas foster, strawberry shortcake, or raspberry sorbet with shortbread cookies."

Oh for Zeus's sake! Dessert? I'd assumed he'd be taking me home any minute now!

"I don't need dessert—"

"That's part of the deal, an activity, dinner, and dessert."

I shook my head while gesturing toward him with my wine glass. "That was part of the deal for *your* date. This is my date."

His lips spread in a slow smile. "And what would you have done on your date if I hadn't planned it?"

"This is how you do it, isn't it?"

He drew back, no longer mirroring my pose. The expression filling in his pretty features was cautious. "How I do what?"

My confrontational tone continued. "This is how you get your way. You make plans when no one else has plans, and then they have no choice but to do what you say."

Desmond laughed softly before taking a sip of his wine. It was all the answer I needed.

"It's still manipulation you know." I gestured at him with the glass again.

He reached out to take the glass before I could slosh the dark liquid down on his sofa. Our fingers touched on the stem of the glassware, energy zinging between us. We shared a loud gasp. But Desmond didn't release my skin.

Instead, he transferred the glass into his free hand while lightly gripping my hand. The glass was placed on the floor out of the way without his gaze leaving mine. His beautiful aqua irises mesmerized me—how they bored into mine unceasingly even while he saved his upholstery from a woozy, drunken goth girl.

Carefully he drew my fingers up, an inch at a time, so slowly I almost didn't notice he was doing it. But

I did notice it. My breath grew shallow in anticipation of what he intended to do once he got my hand wherever he wanted it. Without pulling his gaze from mine, Desmond brought my fingertips within inches of his lush lips. The warmth of his breath feathered against my skin, sending chills down my bare arm. I held my breath to keep from making a sound, knowing even as I hid the reaction that he'd see the light bumps exploding across my skin.

Easing forward at an almost imperceptible speed that gave me plenty of time to protest, he brought his lips to my fingers. A nanosecond before the silky skin touched my wrinkled knuckles, the music in the kitchen changed from Massive Attack.

To Etta James crooning "Sunday Kind of Love".

****

I swear my stomach fell out of my body at the familiar refrain. My sharp gasp and quick scramble startled Desmond into releasing my hand. As soon as I was free from his grip, I murmured an incoherent phrase that ended with "restroom". Then I ran headlong for it.

Behind the safety of the closed door, I slumped to the floor beside Desmond's stone tub surround. My heart hammered wildly in my chest as though it might disengage and pop out of my mouth any moment.

Was this a coincidence, some freak happenstance that had Desmond's music player spitting out *this* song? Or was *Trip* here—freed from his punishment? I didn't know which answer I wanted to be the truth. And that disturbed me.

Rather than contemplate those questions, I made myself stand. The mirror showed me a haunted and pale young woman. At the sink I splashed water on my face. A little warm water helped my color.

I made myself go back out into the living room. Desmond wasn't there. The wine glasses were where we'd left them on the floor. Had he decided to make dessert?

A steady vibration from the right caught my attention. A sleek mobile phone shook on the side table. I glanced toward the kitchen, carefully listening for if Desmond had heard it. He let out a soft curse from within an enclosed space, perhaps a cabinet, but there were no footsteps. So I leaned closer to the phone.

The most recent text message was displayed on the screen. It had come from the address book entry "Allison".

Have u sexed her in2 giving u the crystal yet?

Fury rose sharp and searing until I knew I would do something violent if I didn't leave. But he was my ride.

Charon take it. Why hadn't I insisted on driving?

A baying dog in the distance halted my brief pacing. I whirled around. My mother stood near the edge of the living room in overalls and pink T-shirt, mist coating her. Her mouth softened into a rueful smile.

"Sorry to interrupt," she said in the Spirit Realm where Desmond wouldn't hear her. "But I need a favor."

I gestured in the direction of Desmond's front door, hoping she'd understand I'd meet her out there. Fear he'd stop me had me tiptoeing over the flagstone. If I could get out the door, I could disappear without an explanation. But if he caught me, it would be much harder to explain how I'd vanished into thin air.

My heart pounded heavily as I quickened my pace. With my hand on the front door and it partially open, I called out to him. "An emergency came up! I have to go!"

I ran before he could catch me. My mother's cool hand grabbed me at the end of Desmond's stone stairs. And then the world went black.

Chapter Thirty-Three

Nell had inquiry written all over her face. No doubt she wanted to ask how the "date" with Desmond had gone. I didn't want to talk about it, so I shoved my head into the storage closet.

It was Wednesday. I'd completed my mother's favor in record time. The Death witch who had been trying to raise a battalion in Gettysburg had been easy to track. His Death magic had pulsed all across the cemetery so powerfully that I'd picked it up from the spot I'd been dropped, a quarter mile away. The only delays had been waiting to see if he'd truly go through with raising Civil War era corpses and then putting the dead back to rest after he'd tried. Fortunately, I'd stopped the Death witch before any of them could burst through the ground.

Once home, I'd hidden in the bedroom with the lights off and headphones shoved in my ears so I couldn't hear Desmond knocking on the front door. He'd come by on Tuesday evening as well—a surprising occurrence considering he hadn't wanted to be seen with me in public. But I supposed his obsession with the crystal balanced out his disgust.

Desmond didn't have my phone number. My phone probably would have rung until the battery died if he had. But he might come by today. He knew where I'd be until nine. Maybe he'd call instead. I could hang up the phone if he did.

"Everything is stocked," Nell said from the foot of the stairs as she gazed at me in my spot halfway between the floors. "You're just avoiding telling me what happened. Was it that bad?"

Was it that bad? I didn't know.

I was angry with myself and with Desmond. I'd almost let him kiss me.

Well, I'd almost let him kiss *my fingers*. The anger came when I acknowledged I'd *wanted* him to. In fact, a warm rush of sensation passed over my skin every time I recalled the feel of his warm digits gripping mine and the heat of his breath brushing my knuckles.

Kore's knees. I was hopeless.

"He's a dick," I told Nell as I closed the storage closet door.

"Duh. That doesn't explain what happened and why you're avoiding me. Did he try to put the moves on you?"

I took a few steps down, and then plunked my tush on the stair. It put me eye level with Nell. Her ivory arms were clasped around her tank-top's middle. She had one hip jutted out and a long crop pant covered leg extended to the right. I suspected she'd start tapping her sandal if I didn't speak up soon.

"I don't know," I said dully.

Her eyebrows drew down into a deep V. "How the shit can you not know? Either he put the moves on you or he didn't."

Should I come clean? I did trust her to keep the crystal safe but only because she'd had a chance to steal it and hadn't. Trusting her with details of my life was another story.

"I had to leave early. I think he might have tried something if I hadn't."

Allison's text message agreed.

Nell muttered a defecation-related curse under her breath. "We're never gonna find out if he's gay or not."

I had a pretty good idea he wasn't gay. Bi-sexual perhaps, but certainly not gay. But I kept my mouth shut.

"So where did he take you?"

Because I no longer felt like moping on the stairs, I joined Nell on the Sedona side of the shop. No one ever visited the Wipuk side. We'd be safe with it unmanned for a bit.

"An arboretum in Flagstaff," I said. "And then he made dinner at his place."

Nell followed me to the glass display case. "I've heard his house is super nice."

So she hadn't been in his house, and she didn't know if he was gay or not; that implied they hadn't had any sort of romantic falling out.

I nodded for her, not too quickly or too broadly. "It's nice, not my cup of tea, but definitely nice. He's got indoor waterfalls and streams. It's a Water witch's dream."

The sound she'd made in the base of her throat sounded closer to a grumble than a contemplative noise. "What did he make?"

I explained how he'd cooked steak and fed me wine. And how he'd cooked without staining his shirt. I kept mum on what had happened after dinner but admitted I'd left before he'd made dessert. Nell grilled me about the brand of wine right down to the year. She wanted to know what his kitchen looked like, what sort of plates he'd used, and if I thought he cleaned his own dishes. Was she a touch obsessed with him?

Eventually she dropped the subject. The arrival of our first customer of the day had something to do with that. And that the first customer was the tattoo enthusiast from Saturday's solstice ball was the remainder of it.

The tattoo enthusiast looked better in his black T-shirt with its ripped sleeves and notched collar than he had in his black suit. The tribal tattoo that had peeked over the collar of his dress shirt Saturday was now visible extending over his right shoulder. Thick black tribal art and Asian symbols dominated the ink all up and down his arm. The yin and yang symbol made me smile as did the earlobe full of metal.

He smiled back. The piercing on his bottom lip creased beneath his pleasant expression. "Damn, Kora. You're a hot little goth girl, ain't you?"

I couldn't stop my grin. I'd forgotten I'd been all dolled up in a sophisticated dress when he'd met me.

He nodded an amiable greeting for Nell and then returned his attention on me. The broadening smile warmed me. *He* wouldn't be embarrassed to be seen with me in public.

"Well, now," he said with a drawl of appreciation. "I'm thrilled to hell I stopped by. I'd hoped that blue hair was a sign you'd be fun."

What had he said his name was? Hades, sometimes my memory was horrible.

Tattoo guy glanced around the store quickly. His eyes came to rest on the incense display. He checked it out while we checked out his tush. It wasn't bad, a little on the nonexistent side, but that was better than being flabby. He drew a stick under his nose, taking in the scent.

"Cloves?"

"It's not about the smell," I said. "Those help focus the mind so it's easier to get into a meditative state."

He grabbed two.

"Five dollars," I said, holding back a wince. They were ridiculously expensive as far as incense went but totally worth it. "Uh, you don't have to burn them for long to get the effect."

He flashed me a grin. "I can handle five bucks." Tattoo guy winked. "If you'll give me your phone number."

Oh, a tattooed vanilla human. He would do in a pinch.

Provided Trip didn't scare him off.

I swallowed down a sigh because I still hadn't heard from my nemesis about Monday's stunt. The mystery of the Etta James song at Desmond's place had kept me awake Monday night. I'd even used the penlight to look for Trip. The only thing in the Spirit Realm had been amorphous blobs of energy.

Tattooed guy's broad smile earned him my phone number on his receipt. He took my scribble and his plastic bag of incense with a half smirk. Shaking the bag at me he said, "I'll call you and let you know how these worked out for me."

I nodded for him. "Okay. Have a good one."

A little wave was all he gave Nell before slipping out into the parking lot.

"Nice," Nell said with a small laugh. "The solstice ball earns you a date with a bad boy. The only thing I earned was a voicemail box littered with Curtis's messages."

The reminder of her fate soured my mood. Nell got busy making signs extolling the benefits of each item while I worked on updating the budget for the week. We settled into companionable silence that lasted clear until lunchtime.

****

The BMW pulled in the Sedona lot fifteen minutes after Nell had left for lunch. Did Desmond have someone spying on the shop? How else could he reliably show up when my employee was out? But his appearance at the Sedona part of my shop again irritated me. Clearly he was too embarrassed to be seen frequenting my establishment in Wipuk.

I held my body stiff as he unfolded himself from his car. A charcoal suit hung masterfully off his sinewy body. I could almost smell the scent of a mountain stream before he came inside the building. He didn't look at me until he'd pulled open the door, stepped inside, and glanced around to make sure we were alone. I made myself breathe as he closed the distance to the glass display case.

"You left your belt in my car." He set the thick leather strap on top of the glass. I hadn't seen it hanging from his arm because I'd been watching his face.

"Thanks."

Desmond stood silently, perhaps waiting for an apology. He wasn't going to get one. He still owed me an apology for accusing me of *murder*.

"You left in a hurry," he said the obvious moments later. His eyebrows pulled down over his hooded eyes. "How did you manage to disappear without a trace?"

"Someone picked me up."

"There were no cars. I would have seen or heard one."

I mumbled, still avoiding his probing gaze. "Must have been too quick."

"The security guard said no one arrived or left after us."

I didn't want to lie, so I merely sat mutely beneath his steady, irritated scrutiny.

"The only way you could have gotten out of the community was if you'd flown out." His pitch lowered. "Or if a vampire had picked you up."

What had made him jump to *that* conclusion? I'd left at seven thirty in the evening. The sun would have just begun to set. Exactly how bad was his relationship with the vampires?

Maybe an apology I didn't mean would appease him and send him on his way. I hadn't wanted to give him one, but I'd do it if it got me off the hook. I couldn't very well admit that my goddess mother had Voidwalked me to Pennsylvania.

"I'm sorry I left early," I said stiffly. "The emergency couldn't be helped. But thank you for bringing by my belt."

There was one certainty. I wasn't going to thank him for the date, not when Allison's text message had proved it to be exactly what I'd assumed—his continued obsession with Kali's Candle.

"What kind of emergency could a new age shop owner have on a day her shop is closed?"

I worked on maintaining my even pitch rather than allowing my frustration and guilt to manifest. "It was a family emergency."

He shifted his pose without really moving—a irritated motion more than anything. "You said your mother had passed and you didn't know your father."

Being caught in a situation I couldn't easily slide out of made me confrontational. I raised my eyes daringly and held his. "You're not my employer, Marino. I don't have to explain myself to you."

He pushed a noisy puff through his nose. I tried desperately not to fidget beneath the intent gaze. Though he wasn't manipulating me with his power, I still felt as if he were willing me to tell him the truth. No amount of bullying would get me to tell him that.

Desmond's voice dropped into a quiet volume. "I hadn't taken you for a coward."

I rose to the challenge without thinking. "I'm not a coward."

"You didn't even give me a chance to say goodbye. You ran like a spooked animal, conveniently calling from the door so I couldn't catch up."

What Desmond wasn't saying was *why* I'd run like a spooked animal. From his point of view he'd been millimeters from kissing my fingers and I'd freaked out. He didn't understand the song in his kitchen had done it. Someone like Desmond probably wasn't used to women freaking when he made a move. .I was damned glad Fate had interfered. I might have done something stupid only to discover he was still on the quest for the crystal.

That reminder made it easy to coolly answer. "You would have tried to stop me with a guilt trip about your fifty thousand dollars and my emergency might have become critical. That doesn't make me a coward. It makes me realistic."

His pretty lips went thin in irritation. "I would have tried to stop you. There was something—"

"God, Desmond," Nell called down from the top of the stairs, interrupting him mid-sentence.

I said a silent thanks to the gods for getting me out of this mess. Desmond immediately stiffened. He must have forgotten Nell could easily park in Wipuk and pass through the building. Her errand had been short today.

She made it to the bottom of the stairs before she finished her statement. "When are you going to get the clue we don't like you?" Pointedly ignoring his existence, Nell turned toward me. "Did you set up a date with that hottie?"

"It's only been like an hour." I blushed and shot Desmond an apologetic look because though I wasn't terribly fond of him, my employee had been rude beyond her usual anti-Desmond behavior. He looked twice as miffed as he'd been minutes ago no doubt because he'd been openly dismissed. I opened my mouth to thank him for bringing the belt. "Thank—"

Nell cut in. "That's plenty of time to go home, light it up, and meditate on what a cute goth girl you are." She tossed her leather purse down on the rolling cart with a loud thud. "You two are going to have such cute little tattooed, cerulean-haired babies."

She was trying to tick Desmond off, but it hardly seemed the way to go. Insulting him had always worked better.

He spoke in his blank, professional tone a moment later. "You're seeing someone?"

Nell lied for me in a caustic tone. "Yeah, she's seeing someone. He's not a complete douche-nozzle like someone who will rename nameless."

The accusatory glint in Desmond's eyes made my insides squeeze sympathetically. He thought I'd told her everything. And he was miffed.

But why should he be miffed? He'd only been after the crystal.

I stepped toward the stairs because I needed out of this situation, and neither of them showed signs of backing down. "I've got to check on something upstairs. Thank you for bringing that by, Mr. Marino."

Or was it Dr. Marino?

I didn't stick around to find out.

Chapter Thirty-Four

Nell was in a hurry to leave because it was taco night at the Kranz's house. I sent her off early to end her incessant sandal tapping against the bamboo floor. It helped that the shop had been slow all day.

I wasn't sure how long I was going to be able to pay her wages if I didn't get more business. Scratch that, I wasn't sure how long I was going to *have* a business if I didn't get more business. Wipuk's citizens' refusal to visit the shop really stuck in my craw. Someone had blackballed me, and I bet that someone had a killer body and the prettiest lips on any human. Damn that Marino.

He'd gone away easily today, but that couldn't last for long. Eventually he'd want to make a move with his new pawn in the quiet war with the undead. With the secrets he already knew about me, I wasn't sure I'd be able to refuse his demands. But so long as he kept his lips away from my fingers, or anything else, I could handle anything he threw at me.

I muttered under my breath at the flare of warmth the memory had brought as I locked up the Wipuk door. And then something heavy slammed into my skull. I recalled cursing the gods before I hit the black top with a brain-busting crack.

When I woke to excruciating pain, I thought part of my brain really had busted out of my skull. My hair felt damp where it rested on the hard surface of wherever I was. I couldn't see anything, be it because of darkness or a failure of my vision. The location didn't smell familiar. There was no smoky incense in a specific flavor denoting a witch. All I smelled was Sedona air.

Drawing in a ragged breath, I reached for the aether. I asked Air to give me a general idea of the size of the space, temperature variances, and if I was alone—the most important note.

However Air didn't answer.

I gasped in alarm. Never had magic failed to respond. Was I deep underground beneath something made of steel? Even then I ought to be able to access Air magic while there was oxygen left to breathe.

I called on Earth magic to give me an approximate location. Earth would at least tell me if I were still in Arizona. For all I knew I could have been transported halfway across the world while I'd been unconscious.

But like Air, Earth was silent. Now I was *really* worried. In quick succession I called on Water, Fire, and then the other schools. There wasn't so much as a twinge of my magical consciousness. As though I was completely human. Or *neutered*.

Hera help me, had I been killed? Was I in Tartarus instead of my nemesis?

"Trip?" I whispered.

"Don't bother," a scathing female voice said from what sounded like the right corner of a narrow room. "No one is going to save you, bitch."

I recognized that voice. Ascencion Boleda. I wasn't dead. But that might change if I couldn't wield magic. What in Hades had she done to me?

My mother's warning that it was easy for a half-blooded mortal to be hindered came back to haunt me. But I hadn't consumed alcohol since Monday night. I'd managed to sleep for a few hours last night. And I didn't think I suffered from a lack of Vitamin C.

Could Ascencion have drugged me?

My mother had given me the ring to fight this. All I had to do was say the invocation word "apotropaios".

But I wouldn't risk that while Ascencion was in the room until I was certain I'd die otherwise.

The vampire hauled me up by my hair before I'd heard her move. I couldn't feel my arms or legs but the same couldn't be said of my scalp. Her ripping tugs translated into instant discomfort. The drip of warm liquid down my neck proved I was definitely bleeding.

"How do I get your ring to work?"

I blinked back confusion because I didn't understand her question. Ascencion gripped my hair tighter.

"What?" I whined in pain.

"How do I get your *ring* to work?"

She was talking about my mother's gift. If she were asking, then it must mean she'd removed it. Hades's tiny nose hair! I was as good as dead.

She screamed directly into my ear at a drum-blasting volume. "Your ring! You're human. You hit me with a fireball. You used the ring to do it. How. Do. I. Get. It. To. Work?"

"It's just a ring!" I cried out in a shamefully high-pitched voice. "It doesn't do anything!"

"There's no such thing as a sorceress! You used weaves. It has to be that ring. You always wear it. How does it work?"

"I swear I didn't use the ring to call Fire. I am a sorceress."

Ascencion slammed my head against the hard surface of wherever she'd dropped me. Pain drilled my nerves as my wounded skull smashed through the wood. Splinters ruthlessly sliced through my scalp. Ascencion didn't release her grip even as my body fell through the cracked table onto a cement floor. Instead, she hauled me off the ground so she could shriek in my face.

"Tell me how it works or I'll peel your skin off inch by inch!"

My body shuddered fearfully. Tears poured down my cheeks. She really would do it. And I couldn't blame her. I *had* set her on fire in front of her lover. While it satisfied my conscience, failing to kill my enemies wasn't a strategic move.

Feeling began to return to my legs and arms. That wasn't a good thing. The pins and needles sensation made me hiss through chattering teeth. The tears flowing from my eyes doubled in volume. But in between the pain and crying, I did note she hadn't bound me.

"Maximo be damned." Ascencion snarled while digging her fingernails into my neck.

And then she bit me.

I screamed in outrage even as a delicious warm pulse filled my veins. I didn't care that it felt *sublime*. She was *biting* me! I'd told her I'd annihilate her if she did that! Charon take it! What had she done to me?

Ascencion shoved a finger between my gasping teeth a moment later. I bucked my body, but the lethargy of whatever drug she'd given me, combined with her strength and the table's debris made my attempt to knock her off pointless.

It wasn't until I recognized what she was doing that I *truly* freaked out. I hacked, choked and spit, kicking with all my might, but nothing budged her. She was trying to exchange blood! Ascencion was trying to *enthrall* me!

The vampire clamped her hand around my cheeks, holding my mouth open for the squeeze of her thumb and forefinger. I roared to the gods as the chilly drops of her lifeblood dripped down my throat. She massaged my neck until I'd choked and swallowed the small bit of liquid.

Then she released me all together.

Ascencion retreated to the other side of the room with a clicking of her heels. "Tell me how the ring works."

The bitch's words echoed in my head. Compulsion to do what she'd commanded rose up within me. Screwing my mouth shut worked until she repeated herself in a scream. The words whispering in my mind lifted in volume and doubled in speed.

The vampire grabbed hold of my face. She shrieked her demand once more as she worked my lips apart.

Words tumbled out of my mouth unbidden. "Put it on and invoke it work the word 'apotropaios'."

"Excellent."

It was the last thing I heard before she knocked me unconscious with a blow to the head.
****

A jaw-snapping smack across the left cheek brought me out of unconsciousness. The numbness in the right half of my face hinted it hadn't been the first. Three seconds passed before I recalled what had happened when I'd last been awake. And then I was smacked across the right cheek.

Ascencion's vicious voice hissed from in front of me. "Wake up, you skinny little pissant!"

I was awake. Unfortunately.

"Get up."

Her command echoed in my head. My limbs stirred. I was horribly weak and in a serious amount of pain. And though I was no stranger to pain, I generally didn't have to feel the *same* pain for long thanks to my access to the Healing school of magic. But whatever the vampire bitch had done had removed my magical ability. I flopped back against a hard, cold surface with a panting grunt because it simply hurt too much to move even though she'd demanded it.

She let out an irascible shriek. "Get up!"

Her hands slammed down atop the cold surface, sending an uncomfortable vibration into my throbbing skull. Along with the pain came the doubling of the speed and volume of the chanting command in my brain. *Get up. Get up. Get up.*

Again my body complied with her demands. Vertigo sent me sprawling onto my tender scalp. I cried out from the unintentional blow. For my failure, the leech's fingernails slashed over my mouth. The flesh split as if they'd been dry and waiting for an excuse to do so. Warmth poured over my chin.

It was the last straw.

Now I was simply angry. Calling on years of experience taking beatings from Trip, I pooled energy into my leg. And then kicked her as powerfully as I could manage.

The attack must have smarted because she yelped. "Fuck! I shit on the mother who gave birth to you! *Get. Up!*"

My legs quite literally hoisted me up off my tush upon the triple utterance of her demand. I found myself listing to the side beside the awful stone surface. Sharp-clawed fingernails dug into my left arm to keep me upright.

"I am going to fuck you up," Ascencion said as if she hadn't already done so. "I am going to destroy your beautiful face as you did mine."

I didn't think my face was terribly beautiful, but I was in no shape to argue. The pain in my skull was unreal. The agony my upright position brought cooled my anger. Against all hope I called on Healing to help myself. Healing did not respond.

I was essentially a badly wounded *vanilla human*.

"But you will not heal what I do to you," Ascencion said in a grave voice. "He will not want you when I have finished with you."

I didn't know who *he* was. I hoped she didn't mean Maximo. He didn't want me, did he?

Oh, the pain. It was unbearable. Why couldn't I be unconscious for this?

Her monologue continued, pitch lifting higher with each new statement. "You have no style. You are *poor*, living in an *apartment* on the wrong side of town with a car that was cheap when it was new! Your shop is a failure! No one wants you here! You have the body of a ten-year-old boy!"

Now that was just plain mean. I may be skinny like a ten-year-old boy, but I did have breasts.

"And yet he wants you!"

Ascencion let out a shrill sound of outrage before backhanding me across the left cheek. My nose broke long before my face landed on it atop the cement floor.

"Get up!"

My body struggled to follow the echoed commands in my head. The vampire didn't rely on the blood bond to get me into position this time. She clawed her fingers around my arm. Up I went. And down again when she threw me across the room. I slammed into a wall, crying out as my already throbbing head hit the stone surface.

She was going to kill me, and I wasn't going to be able to do a damn thing! I was the most powerful magical being on the face of the Earth, and yet a *vampire* had easily brought me down. I swore to Kore if I got out of this, I was never going to let another vampire get the better of me.

She screamed at no one in particular. "Why? Why you? Why you! So many have come! So many I have made leave! So many—You are shit!"

The vampire shot across the room. She buried her pointed pump into my ribs. The horrible cracking noise implied she'd broken something, but I was too numb to feel it … yet. That would come in time.

I would die having spectacularly failed my mother. Not only had I not completed her plan for me, but I'd also lost her ring, a ring that would make Ascencion Boleda the most powerful vampire in the world.

"You are less than shit! You are the insects that *feast* on shit!"

I wouldn't go out without a fight. I wouldn't.

Ignoring the awesome pain in every part of my body, I pulled myself onto my knees and flailed out for anything I could reach. I caught onto fabric and *hair*. With a satisfied and weary lift of my lips, I tore at both with everything I had.

Her shout hinted I'd done some damage of my own. I had only a half second to revel in my achievement before the undead bitch's foot smashed into my face, knocking me into a blissfully unaware state of unconsciousness.

****

"Pout, darling. She isn't dead."

Ascencion's voice dripping with sweetness was what roused from unconsciousness. My vision was still black, but this time I recognized it was because I'd been blindfolded. My body hurt in a thousand different places, none of them numb this time. How was I alive after the bashing I'd taken?

"I'm not pouting," Maximo de Sole said with icy enunciation. "I'm glaring. I made a claim to her,

319

Ascencion. You didn't merely touch a hair on her head, as I'd expressly forbidden. You've *enthralled* her!"

Despite his roar, she spoke in a syrupy voice that would have ordinarily been reserved for small children. "Don't be mad, darling. I did it for you. Think of this as a gift. Look. I have her ring. She is nothing without her ring."

"She doesn't need her ring."

How did he know that?

Was he correct? Nothing had happened the last time I'd called on any magic. While they continued their discussion, I silently prodded the magical portion of my body.

"It isn't much to look at," the bitch said while I worked. "But it is vastly powerful. If you're a good boy, I'll tell you how it works." There was a pause before she made a sound of mock dismay. "Oh, you don't believe me? Well, just look what I can do."

A loud whoosh preceded one of the most terrifying experiences of my life. Flame engulfed my head with instant, searing heat. I screamed, thrashing around wildly as the horrible sound of singeing hair and flesh filled my ears. Somehow I recalled what had happened to Ascencion when she'd done the same.

Despite my unwilling body, I rolled myself around in the hope of putting out the fire before it did irreversible damage. Someone slammed on top of me before I could roll more than once. Their hands swatted at my face and head repeatedly. My continued screaming and pathetic thrashing didn't upend them.

"Hold still," a male voice said impatiently. "I'm trying to put you out."

There was a sound of outrage from our right. The figure atop me quickly vanished but not before the flame was extinguished. A wall smashed in a shower of cracked wood. Someone yelped, and it wasn't me.

"I should have set *you* on fire!" Ascencion screamed hoarsely. The distinctive smack of a hand hitting flesh echoed in the room. "Don't you dare! Maximo, if you so much as touch her, I'll kill her!"

"If you touch her I'll kill *you*," he said icily.

She inhaled a sharp breath. "You can't mean that!"

Someone shoved the other up against a wall with a rapid thud and click of heels. Maximo's voice was low and furious. "I told you she was mine. I told you not to exact revenge. You deliberately ignored me. You caused enough trouble with the murder of the Water witch you pinned on her!"

"What?"

He ignored Ascencion as if he hadn't heard her question. "Too long I have let you twist me around your finger because I didn't care enough to fight you. I care now. You have gone too far."

"I haven't gone far enough!"

A second crackling whoosh slammed into my chest. I reacted far more intelligently during this attack, rolling as quickly as I could manage while simultaneously calling Water. A creaking pipe was the only source of water nearby. But my ability to sense it at all was promising. My furious draw on the pipe forced the metal to break through the drywall. A spray of liquid doused me in a heavenly shower.

Now Ascencion would have to resort to a different brand of magic.

The room had plunged into silence. I flopped onto my back in the puddle forming on the floor. Between the burns on my face and chest, the multiple blows to the skull and the lingering drug in my system, I couldn't work up the energy to move. Plus I'd have to conserve my energy for the next attack.

Arms grabbed hold of me. I thrashed and howled for release.

"Hold still."

Maximo. Was I better off?

Now that I could call magic again, I had a good chance of fighting him. I slumped so he could do whatever he'd planned to do. Only then would I know what I'd have to defend against.

He lifted me and carried me to a soft piece of furniture. Maximo set my head on a pillow. I winced at the brush against my tender flesh.

"What did she do to you?" His whisper was a hair too reverent as he lifted my head slightly so he could get a look. Carefully he set it down again, murmuring an apology as he did.

His footsteps faded from the room. Fear spiked within me because if he weren't there to protect me from Ascencion, she could easily set me on fire. I no longer had my shower of cold water to keep me safe.

"It's Max." His voice echoed through the space from the next room. "I need a favor. Can you get here as fast as possible? Thank you."

Quiet footfalls brought him back to me. "Open your eyes, Miss Walsh," he softly said while gently removing the blindfold.

I let my eyelids flutter open. Amazingly I could *see*. The look of concern creasing his features told me how bad off I was.

"Sleep," he whispered.

And I did.

Chapter Thirty-Five

The discomfort I experienced upon waking wasn't because of a bloody head, broken body, or a flaming face. It was because I was sweating beneath three heavy blankets—three of *my* heavy blankets. My eyelids flipped open to find it dark. But this was the familiar dimness of my bedroom.

Had it all been a horrible nightmare?

I drew my hands up to my face. The skin there was whole and smooth. Bolting upright—a move that didn't cause me pain—I darted toward the bathroom.

And I nearly fell on my tush. Vertigo hit me hard. Grabbing onto furniture and walls for assistance got me slowly to my destination.

I flipped on the light and got a look at myself in the mirror. I couldn't hold back my squeak. Though my face was smooth, unburned and shockingly bruise-free, my hair was singed and jagged. Several clumps had burnt dangerously close to my scalp. Holding my breath, I grabbed a compact. I checked out the back of my head in the tiny mirror. No burns had reached my skull, but the jagged pattern continued throughout.

One thing of note was the blood that should have been dried in my hair was missing. What hair I *did* still have was clean. I felt around my skull for the gashes and blows that had been there. They too were missing.

Someone had Healed me. In a massive way. And someone had cleaned me up.

With the help of furniture and walls I made my way back into the bedroom. I flipped on the light beside the bed. There was a note on the side table. I unfolded the paper and read the fine scrawl.

Miss Walsh,

You're no doubt confused how you arrived in your bed with no memory of returning. I thought it best you remain unconscious until you were free from pain. You were returned to your home after a bath and a visit from a Healer. I give you my solemn word no one placed a hand on you except when necessary.

In closing, I would like to offer my heartfelt apology for Ascencion's attack. Rest assured she will bother you no longer.

Yours cordially,
Max de Sole

I read the letter three times, eyes squinting deeper each time I did. Ascencion had enthralled me. There was a whole *lot* of bother she could do if she wanted. How exactly would Maximo stop her?

Unless … the room had been awfully quiet after she'd hit me with that second fireball. Had he…

Had Maximo de Sole killed his lover?

I shuddered at the thought.

My weight gave way beneath me. I slumped down onto the floor and stared at nothing in particular.

The LED clock read two in the morning. *Thursday* morning. I'd missed my check-in with my mother. I hoped she'd understand I'd been held up. Literally.

I inhaled a deep breath for courage. And then I called her.

She appeared in front of me in her gauzy ceremonial robes, quickly sliding down onto her tush on my floor.

"I'm sorry." A flush filled my cheeks. "I didn't make coffee."

My mother chuckled softly. "I know. You were busy."

"I really messed up," I whispered.

She didn't argue. Instead, she spoke startling revelations in a neutral tone. "He still has the ring. He doesn't know what to do with it because he killed her before she told him. But he has my ring."

Maximo had the ring she'd given me. He'd killed Ascencion. He'd really done it.

She waited a beat. "You have to get it back. And you must avoid being enthralled."

I let out a desperate laugh. "All while avoiding bankruptcy."

My mother popped to her knees. The mist fell away from her as she closed the distance to me. Her soft lips pressed to my forehead. "I have faith in you, Kora."

Her warm words drew a smile along my lips despite everything else.

She fluffed my poor, singed cerulean locks. "Don't worry too much about your hair. I think it will be cute with a little styling gel. You'll look like a punk rocker. It could be a whole new look for you."

"Great." I gave a quiet, sardonic laugh. "A whole new look for a whole shit ton of challenges."

A fond smile spread across her mouth. "There is no one better to tackle them, my precious girl."

She inclined her head in a deferential nod, and then vanished back into the Void. The baying of the dogs outside faded along with her.

I fell back against the bed, staring up at the ceiling.

The massive misstep I'd made with Ascencion had come to a violent end. Though she'd attacked *and* enthralled me, I couldn't help but think there might have been a way for us to compromise. Perhaps if I'd manipulated her with Water magic instead of burning her that first night, the centuries old vampire might not have met the final death. But she had. And it was my fault as much as it was hers.

I popped back up and pulled the cotton sheets taut. Only when they were smooth did I slide beneath them. Shadows played on the ceiling of my big girl apartment, distracting me from my musings. Maybe I *was* more like my mother than I thought.

I resolved to put my guilt and worries out of my mind at least long enough to sleep. There would be plenty of time to retrieve m y mother's ring from the city's murderous vampire ruler. And deal with my hopeless hair in between infiltrating the coalition *and* serving as Desmond's mole.

After all, I had my whole life ahead of me.

The End

www.anyabreton.com

Evernight Publishing

www.evernightpublishing.com